Born and raised at Porton Down in W
for the NHS in Salisbury, J A Higgins
crime, history and the unexplained. /
Nell Montague mystery series, which
the past are still very relevant today.

To Kate

FINDING RUBY

J A Higgins

Many thanks

JA Higgins

SilverWood

Published in 2019 by SilverWood Books

SilverWood Books Ltd
14 Small Street, Bristol, BS1 1DE, United Kingdom
www.silverwoodbooks.co.uk

ISBN 978-1-78132-876-7 (paperback)
ISBN 978-1-78132-877-4 (ebook)

British Library Cataloguing in Publication Data
A CIP catalogue record for this book is available from
the British Library

Page design and typesetting by SilverWood Books
Printed on responsibly sourced paper

This book is evidence that dreams can come true if you are prepared to work hard, find a professional team to support you, and are brave enough to take a leap of faith. Never give up.

Prologue

Last night I dreamed I fell in love. I was walking down a sandy lane – well, someone was walking; a girl my age, thirteen or perhaps older, but small like me. There were others there too. I was at the back of the group and we were laughing. Not because something was funny but because the sun was setting in splashes of pink and orange, and the summer air was soft, still and warm.

I cast my gaze on the track beneath me. My tanned legs were clad in shorts, my sandy feet in espadrilles. As I watched each foot fall, one in front of the other, I felt the smile easy on my face and heard my friends' voices gently lap around me. My skin tingled, each nerve humming, waves of hot and cold chasing each other over my bare skin, because he had slowed down and was walking by my side. He never walked at the back of our group, always up front, leading us. Now we were heading for the beach, the surf roared close by, and he had given up his position to walk at the back with me. And this was the other reason for the laughter, but it was not meant unkindly. No, these were my friends. I belonged. They merely saw what was happening and were giving their approval. Their laughter was a sunny soundtrack to a momentous scene in my life and I felt the need to bottle it somehow, to remember how I felt.

As we approached the dunes, the track narrowed. I was aware of his easy stride next to me, long limbs moving like a dancer. I sneaked a peek: long, soft brown hair draped over his face was lifted by the ocean breeze. His head hung down but he smiled, self-conscious maybe. My right arm hummed as I sensed him moving closer. Each breath I took was sharp and shallow – and then it happened. Taller than me, his hand brushed my arm, making the small hairs reach up in celebration. A jolt of electricity shot through me and I felt my face flush. Then his hand brushed again and reaching down his fingers slid over mine. Softly they locked into place. Warm, dry, gentle, but secure and purposeful.

"Is it OK?" he whispered.

I nodded, then glanced up to him. His dark eyes met mine and I felt like my feet were lifting off the ground.

"Yeah, I like it." Was that lame? But there was no time to worry. His face split into a huge grin which made his eyes nearly disappear into his face.

"Good. I like it too."

And that was the moment I knew I was in love. All the songs wrote of falling in love, and I had read countless stories which described how it felt. To me love was a warm strong hand holding mine, claiming me as his girlfriend in front of all our friends. Then later, when the sun sank into the inky, foam-topped water, and the breeze turned cold, love was being wrapped up in his hoody with his arms holding me close.

"You're beautiful." His breath was warm on my face and when he placed his lips gently on mine he tasted of salt from the surf.

I knew at that moment, blissfully unaware that I was dreaming, that this was the happiest moment of my life, and whatever else was planned for me, I would never again feel this safe or this loved.

I wake and open my eyes to darkness. The pain pauses for a moment then pounces. My lips are dry and cracked, and my mouth swollen inside. My body aches for water and food, but there is none so I close my eyes against the horror of the darkness, of the hideous stench and breath-robbing fear, and instead will myself back to my dream. As my ears begin to buzz I hear his voice again. I sink back into my dream to find him holding my face gently in his hands, kissing away my tears.

"I think I might be dying." I feel the words form on my lips.

"You've got me now. Come on, let's go."

And I am suddenly lifted and being carried back along the sandy track, his arms strong, being brought back to warmth, food and life. My cheek rests against his cotton T-shirt and I can feel his skin quiver from each heartbeat. I press my face to feel the warmth of his flesh through the soft cotton, and his arms tighten around me.

"Rest now. I've got you."

I know that I will wake again at some point, shrouded in utter sound-numbing blackness; my hands will beat against the cold door, slippery with blood. My voice will become raw with screaming, and then dropping back on the damp mattress I will let despair anaesthetise me. But for now, in my dreams, I am safe.

1

Friday, late August

Noon – and at Wiltbury crematorium a sudden hush fell on the congregation. A screech of brakes outside sent a ripple through the black, grey and navy clad assembly, causing necks to turn and the minister to hesitate.

Outside, twenty-nine-year-old Nell Montague gathered up her bag, pushed her sweating bare feet back into unyielding shoes, and hastily paid the driver. Her hand trembled as she passed over the note, damp and crumpled from where she had clutched it throughout the journey. She was late, and as she struggled to open the black cab door, her grandmother's words echoed in her aching head.

'You'd be late for your own funeral, my girl.'

As she stepped down from the cab, her bare toes crunched inside the smart black shoes, and she wished again she had worn something else. Too late now. Adjusting a chunky bangle to hide a fading bruise, she paused to let the full force of the midday sun hit her. The flush of heat that swept her body caused her skin to blush comfortingly, but then a wave of nausea chased it away and the birds fell silent. Taking a deep breath to dissolve the dark spots before her eyes, Nell realised that her frail courage could yet fail.

"For God's sake, pull yourself together, Nell," she muttered quietly, as she had done all morning, "and get a bloody move on." Painfully conscious that time was running out, she picked her way carefully over the treacherously smooth tiles and into the overzealous air conditioning of the foyer. Puddles of colour lapped at her legs from the modern stained-glass window above. Over the years it had provided a calming effect on the droves of mourners who stared at it, grateful for the brief respite from their grief and the ordeal of the funeral service. Fixed in the entrance foyer, it caught the midday sun and splashed red, blue, yellow and orange onto the pale floor, in competition with the flower memorials in the garden of remembrance outside.

'It makes your mind jump, like an adrenaline rush,' her grandmother had enthused. *'I want the mourners at my do to be hit with colour as they walk in with their boring black clothes.'*

Nell's mouth twitched into a smile as she remembered the day they had come here to 'source out a suitable venue'. But now her nose began to sting and for a moment she wondered if the tears she had blocked were breaking through. Taking another deep breath she opened the door and went in.

This was the funeral of eighty-year-old Elizabeth Montague, which she had planned meticulously with her granddaughter, Nell. It was her last project; filling the months from diagnosis until the lung cancer took total control of her body and her days became filled with medication, hospital beds and pain. She was well liked and the more mobile residents from the home, along with staff, filled the rows.

Nell winced at the loud clatter from her shoes. The congregation looked up and a few smiled in recognition as she took her place in an empty row near the front. Desperate to avoid looking at the coffin she concentrated on the rich robes of the rented minister and mouthed 'sorry'. From behind she could hear a few sniffs and snuffles. She felt silly having a whole row to herself, like she smelt bad or something. But it was reserved for family – the grieving relatives – so Nell sat alone. It was comforting to Nell that her grandmother had found friends in her last years, after so many years alone. The friendly, patient carers had always been ready with a steadying hand, or some light-hearted banter which Nell and her grandmother had both found comforting. It had been a home in the true sense of the word, and the carers and residents on her grandmother's wing had been like family. But today, Nell alone represented her blood family, as her grandmother's only son, Nell's father, had dropped off the radar years ago.

Now the temperature contrast was even more evident and she shuddered as the hard-edged wooden seat bit into the back of her legs. Rubbing her arms she scolded herself for not bringing a jacket, and for nursing the hope that her father might have made an appearance today.

Music began to play and Nell smiled as Massenet's *Meditation* swirled into the air. Finally her eyes drifted to the tasteful pale coffin in front. She must have made a noise because a hand from behind fell onto her shoulder. Pleased at the distraction, Nell heaved herself around.

"Hello, Eleanor?" The portly care home manager said in a whisper that everyone could hear.

"Nell," Nell corrected, then realised she sounded rude. She tried a smile to soften her retort. The woman leaned forward and offered her a fleshy hand poking from a tweed sleeve. There was a waft of sweat lurking beneath the heady perfume. Nell took her hand awkwardly, not sure whether to shake or squeeze.

"We have met. I'm Mrs Harrington-Brown. Such beautiful music. She arranged this all herself as you know."

The face flipped from comedy to tragedy and a flake of mascara spiralled to the ground.

"So sorry for your loss. Nell, yes now I remember," she repeated, feeling for firmer ground. "You brought those lovely roses on dear Elizabeth's birthday. And that chocolate cake." This last remark was punctuated with a wink. Had the cake provoked an orgy amongst the octogenarians, wondered Nell, as the entire congregation stared at her.

But knowing how fond Elizabeth had been of the elusive care home manager, Nell produced a more genuine smile and granted the kindly woman a nod. Satisfied, Mrs Harrington-Brown shifted back in her seat and stared at the coffin again.

The music ended and the minister began his speech. There was a slight pause each time he used the deceased's first name, as if trying to remember whose funeral it was. If it is noon then it must be Elizabeth Montague, one o'clock would be someone else. The large empty row stretched out around her. Alone and on display; like Nana in her pale coffin. Now she wished she had sat at the back; was it too late? Or creep in at the end of someone else's row? It felt like a hundred eyes were flicking from her shivering back, to Nana, and then back to her again. The front row was practically sitting on the coffin. This made her smile, despite the sombre occasion, and the fact that she had been crying and throwing up since dawn, because it was something Nana would have said. If she closed her eyes she could feel her sitting next to her, muttering about the cold and clutching her bag on her lap, like it contained a bomb. Now Nell's jaw felt stiff, like it was too tightly hinged. This was not right. How could the only person in her world who truly knew her, who would always have her back and put her first, be gone? How could she be left behind, alone again? And this was far worse than before because there was no Nana to love her. Her jagged fingernails burrowed into her soft palms in vain as she blinked back burning tears and listened to the words being said.

Despite the man's unfamiliarity he did a good job. They sang *Jerusalem* – Elizabeth's favourite hymn – and the snuffles and sobs around her kept Nell's own tears in check again. The loss felt like a full sink with a tap dripping over it. Cold, heavy and at any minute about to spill over the edge and onto the floor, but she had long ago learned to keep her feelings private and she was desperately trying to do so now.

The minister went on to document Elizabeth's childhood years, her marriage, family, and her love of art, music and cooking. Then there was a mammoth jump to the happy years in the home.

Mrs Harrington-Brown grunted as each new point in Elizabeth's life was ticked off and Nell wondered if the absence of any real mention of her father was intentional or had he just never been spoken of. It then occurred to her that she also had only been given a passing mention, which was puzzling since Nana had written this herself. Perhaps she had tried to spare Nell from such a public sharing of her love. Knowing how torturous the whole funeral would be for Nell she had made it almost sterile. Now Nell shifted on the hard wooden seat, like a child who had been left behind on a railway platform. Alone. Truly alone now. Ever since the diagnosis, Nell had tried to prepare for the moment when she would be left alone. She had expected fear, despair, misery, but nothing had prepared her for the physical loss. Sounds were too loud, movement hurt her eyes, she was incapable of carrying out an action, and on top of it was the continual quivering inside as if she were a volcano about to erupt. Plus the concrete block that was wedged in her lungs, making breathing difficult and crying painful.

For a moment Nell wondered how Ruby would have coped, and involuntarily she glanced at the back of the room as if to watch her arrive. Of course there was no one there but the door was caught in the act of closing, as if someone had just crept out. Ruby would have been on time, elegantly dressed and not with her head down the toilet all morning. She also would not have had to check her body for visible bruising before deciding what to wear.

As the second hymn started, Nell wondered if her father had had a funeral. How careless, she mused, not to know if your own father was alive or dead. Had Nana known? It was the one thing Nell had wanted to ask her but never had the nerve. Each time she had visited her grandmother and listened to the silences that grew longer and longer, as Nana's breath had become less and less, she had wondered if it was a good time to ask. Now she realised that there had been no good time to ask, only time, and even that had finally run out. Too late now.

Nell had placed an announcement in *The Daily Telegraph* in a desperate attempt to flush him out. It had been a long shot but if he was still out there somewhere she had wanted this chance to reach him. She vaguely remembered him reading the *Telegraph* at the kitchen table when she was small. Not the best way to hear that your mother had passed away, but better than never knowing. Nell would not have minded. A well worked out daydream began to surface, of him walking up to her with all the explanations that she needed, complete with overflowing, unconditional love wrapped round a secure future.

Her memories of him were thin from their constant rewind, play and pause. Nell had a few photographs of a tall man, with dark brown hair, smiling at her as a toddler or holding her as a baby. Her favourite – one when he had actually looked at the camera – had been taken at her seventh birthday party. He had been hugging her as she squealed, and the Instamatic had captured a moment of pure love. He had walked out a week later, gone to work, and never returned. Now even the photograph had faded with time so that Nell dared not look at it, in fear the colour would fade irreversibly in the harsh reality of daylight.

Suddenly, there was a loud clunk and the coffin began to jog its way along the conveyor belt. Reminiscent of the seventies show, *The Generation Game* which Nana had giggled to, it dented the velvet curtain and jolted out of sight. There were more audible tears now and Nell bit her tongue harder. A vision – complete with sound effects – came to her mind of Nana lost in a large white hospital bed, clutching at the blanket as she struggled for each breath. The gurgle of the medication, the tubes, the smell, but mostly Nana's eyes filled with panic as each breath failed to ease the pain. Minute after minute, hour upon hour. Elizabeth had waited for the one moment when Nell had gone to speak to the nurse to pass out of life. For days Nell had admonished herself for leaving her to die alone until the nurse had confided that the dying often waited to be alone before letting go. It had been a comfort to know that her absence had brought an end to the pain.

Suddenly, the doors at the back opened and a suited middle-aged man walked in. He hesitated when he met Nell's enquiring brown eyes, then took a seat opposite. His aftershave stretched towards her, hinting of autumn smoke curling around old leather, and his movements suggested a body not used to the confines of a suit. Nell glanced at him out of the corner of her eye, quelling the jitters that were fighting behind her ribs. He was the right age. Early fifties, tall, with a skin colour that suggested weekends spent outside.

Then the funeral was over and Mrs Harrington-Brown reminded everyone they were gathering for tea and cake in the conservatory back at the home, all welcome.

"Mr Austin, I think Elizabeth would have been pleased. You've met her granddaughter, of course." It was a statement rather than a question and in confusion Nell realised the suited man was staring at her.

Mr Austin? Probably the solicitor, then. Nana had always kept her legal affairs private so Nell had never met him. Hoping the disappointment was not too evident, she attempted a smile.

"My sincere condolences, Miss Montague." Nell thanked him, and pondered that although clichéd, his words still had the power to comfort. His voice was deep, and held a note which hinted at a European accent, though Nell could not be sure. Nell's own voice was pitched unnaturally high and her nose felt like it was starting to run.

"Are you free this afternoon, Miss Montague? We need to talk."

A stab of fear twisted in her stomach.

"Will it take long? I need... I have to get back to work."

He shook his head dismissively, offered his card with a tight smile, then together with the congregation, they drifted into the courtyard. The flowers of that morning's cremations were displayed alongside those of her grandmother's. The word DAD was spelled out in white carnations and a strange shape nearby, which could have been a rugby or football was made of red and white rose buds. Elizabeth's were simpler: cream roses, elegant lilies, and from Nell a bouquet of pastel shades.

Catching sight of her reflection in the glass windows Nell realised the simple black shift dress worked well. She had worried about sweating through something with sleeves but had not anticipated shivering in the air conditioning. Her wavy dark brown hair, however, was a disaster. She had been unable to coax it into a chignon, had tried plaiting it, and in the end given up and let it have its own way, which was to lie just below her shoulders; one side flicked out and the other side flicking under.

Suddenly there was a buzzing from her bag. Mr Austin moved away and drew out his own phone, while Nell dug desperately in her bag, spilling a lipstick, an inhaler and a packet of tissues onto the ground. Extracting her lipstick out from under the football flowers she glanced at her phone. Gary. She waited for the message service to pick up, knowing it would be short, and then played it back.

"Well, it's me again, and this is now the third message since we landed. I'm worried. Ring me."

Nell frowned at the tone but had no time for analysis because a young man in an ill-fitting black suit was climbing out of an equally black car and heading straight for her with the intensity of a heat-seeking missile. He might as well have had a blue flashing light above the car, thought Nell, but the stern expression diluted when he held out his hand.

"Eleanor Montague? I represent Davies and Brown, your grandmother's solicitors. May I offer my sincere condolences and apologies for my late arrival? At a time convenient to you, shall we discuss your grandmother's estate?"

In confusion Nell turned to Mr Austin, but he had gone. She glanced at his card and frowned. It was white, one side held a mobile number and on the other two words lay in a simple typeface in the middle of the card. Skeleton Key.

2

So the funeral was over and Nell had survived. Her stomach growled, mutinously empty, but a memory of kneeling in front of the toilet bowl that morning meant that food was not an option. Her head ached mercilessly and the lump that had lodged in her throat since Nana had died showed no intention of shifting. Since the initial opening of the devastating floodgates, Nell had not allowed herself to cry. Well, apart from that morning. Now her body was punishing her. But she had never been comfortable with public displays of emotion, of any type, and envied those who were able to weep and wail in front of other people. Keeping it all inside had not preserved her dignity however, it just meant that her nose had run like a melting icicle for the last hour and her bag was full of sodden tissues.

Had the funeral been what Nana wanted? The sun's power was tempered with a soft breeze which ruffled the petals and cooled the congregation, and Nell decided that yes, Nana would have approved of this. Apart from Dad. Nell looked towards the outskirts of the mourners. If Dad was still alive somewhere in the world then surely he would have come today.

Despite feeling slightly faint, and aching all over, Nell refused all offers of a lift into town. She knew it made her appear unfriendly but her mind was a cacophony of confused thoughts and unanswered questions and it was with relief that she saw the same taxi which had dropped her off earlier, lumbering over the speed humps towards her.

"Where to next, love?"

Now there was a question. Nell's eyes met her driver's in the rear view mirror.

"Never mind. Traffic is blocked going into town so you've got time before we need a decision."

"I'm supposed to go back to work; the area manager is in this afternoon and wants to see me. But the solicitor wants to see me too. I wonder if I've time for both? I wish I could just go home. I've had enough now."

"Not going to the wake then?"

The home's trio of mini buses were still loading up their precious cargo. Nell looked at the familiar faces of the staff and residents and for a moment imagined herself walking back into what had once been Nana's home, walking past Nana's empty room again. Yesterday she had painfully cleared it out of the few items she wanted to keep, and it had nearly destroyed her. She had expected the photographs to be emotional hand grenades, but when she opened a drawer and saw Nana's socks neatly balled with the name labels showing, she had felt the air literally sucked from her lungs. It had been a strange time; sewing name labels on to all Nana's clothes. She had ordered them online and Nana had chosen a design in a clear font, green, with a kitten motif. Sewing sock after sock, jumpers and nightwear, even tights and bras, Nell had felt like she was sending a child to boarding school. Then Nana had complimented her neat stitches and she was back to being a child again. Even shoes and slippers, toiletries, Nana's hairbrush, needed her initials written in permanent markers.

No, she could not sip tea and chat to the residents, and put on a strong smiling face, knowing she would never return again.

The taxi driver aimed her vehicle back over the speed humps and let her passenger chew her thumbnail in peace. They inched slowly forward, past the garden memorials and dedicated benches. Nell had been given strict instructions about what to do with Nana's ashes, and ornamental pots or dedicated roses bushes were not it. She crunched her nail in silence for a few seconds and then pulled out her mobile again. A quick qualm of guilt heaved itself over in her stomach as she thought about Gary, but she would deal with that later.

Luckily her supervisor answered the phone and Nell's worries evaporated as she took charge.

"Nell, you poor thing. Yes, he's already here." She laughed as Nell swore softly and then apologised; any other day Mr Page would roll up late with tales of traffic jams or cancelled trains, while the aroma of beer on his breath and gravy in his beard told a different story. But today he had scheduled a meeting with each of his senior administrators, turned up on time, and Nell had to be there.

"I'm on my way in now. No honestly it is fine. It will take my mind off things, and I will go home when he's done with me and collapse on the sofa. No one else but you knows where I've been today, do they?" Sympathetic comments and looks would set her off wailing again.

"Well, they didn't hear it from me Nell, but I think people have guessed." Well at least she was warned.

Decision made, Nell gave the taxi driver the directions for work.

"Oh you work there, do you? That must be fun, arranging all those glamorous holidays. I bet you are always jetting off somewhere exciting."

Nell smiled indulgently at the familiar misconception. But although the furthest the company had taken her was the next town for training, she enjoyed her job and lately there had been rumours of a promotion within the team. Unfortunately, there had also been rumbles about redundancies.

One problem solved, Nell dealt with the next one by easing her shoes from her protesting feet. A blister the size of an outer

Hebridean island had formed on her left heel, so she resorted to rummaging in her bag again. Last time she used her 'good' bag had been the engagement party of someone Gary worked with. Anticipating that the evening would be long and tedious, Nell had stashed cushioned plasters and headache tablets in the credit card sized zipped pocket. By one thirty the following morning Gary was picking fights and unable to walk unaided. The long drive home was silent except for incomprehensible mutterings, and belching. Then the power of coherent speech returned.

'Gonna chuck...'

Nell steered into a bus stop where Gary pebble-dashed the pavement, road, and car, with half-digested finger buffet swimming in a Guinness sauce. Nell had not been able to face spicy chicken or Guinness since.

Wincing at the unmistakable aroma of sweaty feet, Nell glanced at the driver, but she was busy shouting at a bus. Suddenly a gap appeared in the next lane, the driver made a dash for it and Nell's shoes skidded across the floor, crashing against the door. Adjusting her position, Nell gathered the contents of her spilt bag but decided to leave her shoes where they were. Then she noticed the card from Mr Austin lying on the plump leather seat beside her. Picking it up in her left hand she resumed exploring the rough edge of her right thumbnail with her teeth. Who was he? Mrs Harrington-Brown had known him, so he must have visited Nana. Skeleton Key: apart from a vague memory of a good film, the name meant nothing. She should ring him. Maybe later. Puzzled by the feeling of unease, she stashed this latest problem to the back of her mind where it jostled for space alongside everything else, and concentrated on the next job at hand.

Walking into work felt like breaking through an invisible membrane. She left all thoughts of Nana, the solicitor, and even Mr Austin – whoever he was – behind as she adjusted her mind into work mode.

"Oh yes...Nell." Vivien, the stereotype of a middle-aged receptionist, from the condescending rise of her pencilled eyebrows, down to the pursing of her smoker's lined lips, was peering over her glasses.

"Afternoon." Nell rarely said more in greeting. Experience had taught her that the woman had the sincerity of a politician.

"Hang on, lady. Mr Page wants to see you in his office immediately."

Nell stopped dead and rounded on the startled receptionist with a big smile.

"Yes, I know Vivien. Why else would I be here on my day off?" *You shrivelled old hag.*

Vivien's foundation creased into brown lines at Nell's unexpected parry and returned to peck at her keyboard. Once out of sight Nell felt her smile droop a little. Mr Page was seen only rarely, preferring the more expensive views from head office. Promotion would be amazing, a confirmation that at least one area of her life was progressing. But redundancy was terrifying for more reasons than one. Feeling slightly sick, Nell tucked her hair behind her ears and took a deep breath.

As she turned the corner into her working area, a wave of genuine sympathy hit her. Everyone wanted to know how she was feeling, and pass on their condolences. Even the most junior member of staff, perhaps lost for something appropriate to say, commented on how smart she looked and added, "You're the first one in. Everyone is shitting bricks."

Jane, her supervisor, appeared from her office looking flustered, her flowing red hair uncharacteristically tied back in a neat plait. Blinking rapidly to dispel mutinous tears that were welling, Nell followed her in to the office.

"Nell? Come in and take a seat."

Silently, Jane closed the door and took her own seat. She stared at Mr Page expectantly. Nell, who was trying to catch her eye, felt the nerves rise in her throat.

"I'm so sorry that this meeting has collided with such a sad day for you, but with the other cogs turning…"

He did that, thought Nell; left sentences hanging. She was never sure if he thought his meaning was so clear that further explanation was not needed or he just did not know what to say so left it open for interpretation.

"Now, I wanted to speak to you first. It is about the promotion."

Desperately, Nell tried to stop the grin breaking out over her face, but it was too late.

"We are expanding our cultural team, which means more admin who will need a team leader." The words, ripe with meaning, hung in the dusty air like sweet fruit.

"Wow." Oh, that was a great response. Try again. "I feel ready for a new challenge."

For the first time Mr Page looked her in the eye.

"You are the obvious choice, but the one thing holding you back at the moment is your sickness record." These words were also heavy with meaning, but this time the fruit was rotting. Jane was looking at her hands.

"The time has come for us to talk about this matter."

The silence was deafening and in it Nell could hear a telephone ringing in the open-plan office outside. Her face began to burn as she stared at her ragged fingernails.

"It is unfortunate that we must discuss this today, but you were absent last time I was in."

This was bad, very bad, and Nell's palms itched to be wiped on her skirt. Silence again. Black spots were forming in front of her eyes and peering through them Nell saw Jane and Mr Page observing her patiently, waiting for an explanation.

"I've been quite run down lately, because of my grandmother," was her first attempt. Her line of sight had blurry edges now as well as dark splodges like ink blots.

Mr Page sighed heavily and shook his bald head.

"Yes, but if anything you have had less time off since her illness."

He opened a file and Nell recognised her return from sickness forms.

"There is a pattern, you see." Jane continued gently. "Mondays, or the Tuesday after a bank holiday."

Silence again.

"We obviously need to see an improvement. You are not only letting Jane and your team down, you are letting yourself down too." Nell burned in her chair and felt her nose begin to sting. Determined not to cry, she tried again.

"I..."

"I know you are a very private person, Nell," pleaded Jane, "but I have wondered if everything is alright at home." The line had been crossed. Nell clutched her wrist and blinkered rapidly. This time her inventiveness was not going to help.

"Things...um...things are better now. He's," her eyes flicked to Mr Page in explanation, "my boyfriend, um, partner, has been under a lot of stress at work."

Jane was looking pained again but nodded encouragingly when she saw Nell's panic-stricken eyes on her.

"Nell, if things at home are affecting your work then they need to be addressed. You can talk to me, or to occupational health."

"I'm so sorry..."

"It's not about blame, sweetheart, but for your own sanity you need to sort things out. We can help."

"The promotion," Mr Page interrupted, "will go to one of your colleagues and this is because of your absenteeism."

Nell felt something heavy drop into the pit of her stomach. So it was over, after all her hard work. Gary was going to kill her. Ignoring her trembling lip Mr Page pushed on. "We need to make an agreement that things will improve. For instance, shall we say no more than one episode of sickness in the next three months, and we will review this again after that. But if things don't improve then unfortunately..."

He rose slowly from the heavy leather chair to indicate the meeting had ended.

"Thanks for coming in today."

Jane, who was still frowning at Nell, turned to Mr Page in irritation. "Surely we don't need to make a decision about the promotion today." Nell stared at each of them in turn, like an enthusiastic tennis fan, and felt hope flutter again from somewhere below her ribs. But sighing heavily again, Mr Page shook his head, causing his beard to scrape against the garrotte of his tight shirt collar.

"I am very sorry, but..."

Jane headed for the door and motioned for Nell to follow.

"Well, I tried. I honestly thought it would be good news or I would never have suggested you come in today. I am so sorry. Go home, Nell, you've had a horrible day." She threw a black look at her boss. "We will have a chat on Monday."

Feeling like a child dismissed from school, Nell stumbled out of the office.

Getting to the ladies toilets without making eye contact took a will of iron. Hoping her flushed face and watering eyes would be mistaken for grief, she bolted herself into the first cubicle and let the misery wash over her.

"Bloody hell."

She kicked the cubicle door, immediately regretting it as the plaster slid off and her shoe scraped across the blister. On cue her mobile began to vibrate. Wiping her eyes with her spare hand she peered at the display screen. Text message from Gary. 'Where are you? Phoned your work and they said you had day off. I'll be home by three.'

Panic stirred her blood. She had less than two hours.

Dashing out of the building she was relieved to see the now familiar taxi waiting for her.

"Hello again. Where to next?"

"Do you know Davies and Brown solicitors?"

"Park Street? Yeah, yeah." So it seemed that taxi drivers really did know everything and everywhere.

"You OK?"

"Work just told me I didn't get the promotion I've worked my arse off for."

"Shit."

"Quite."

"You really are having a bad day, aren't you?"

Her phone buzzed again. Another message from Gary. 'Traffic clear. Back soon.'

"Oh, I don't believe this. Look, scrap that plan. Can you take me home please?"

"You're the boss."

As she executed an illegal u-turn Nell thought she saw a familiar face in the car behind. He certainly looked like Mr Austin, but surely that would be too much of a coincidence. Ten minutes later they were pulling up outside the terraced house which she had shared with Gary for the last eighteen months. Passing over more damp crumpled notes, Nell met the driver's eyes.

"Thanks for today. You sure I don't owe you more?"

But the driver shook her head and smiled. "Now, you've got my card. If your car's not fixed when you want to see that posh solicitor, give me a ring and it will be my pleasure to take you. Now pour yourself a drink. I think you've earned it."

Nell gave her a friendly wave and watched her pull back into the traffic. Searching her bag for keys she felt the stress of the day beginning to surface. All she wanted now was a cool shower and a lie down but as she opened the front door the first thing she noticed was the suitcase then the cutting smell of cigarette smoke halted her.

"Where the hell have you been?"

Gary was back.

3

Nell hesitated on the doorstep.

"Nell?"

The softer tone dispersed some of the tension in the air so Nell stepped into the hallway and into role.

"It's OK."

"Is it your Nan...?"

"I didn't want to disturb you on your holiday."

"Oh shit. I should have been here."

His skin felt unpleasantly damp through his shirt as he hugged her. She waited a few seconds then carefully pulled away and headed for the kitchen.

"The funeral was at twelve."

"I'm sorry, Nell. You must be knackered, going through all that on your own. I'll get you a drink."

"No, just some juice..." The wine bottle was already being tipped. Gary topped up his own glass then threw a glance at the wine rack. Nell followed his gaze.

"I had a glass the night she died. Thought it might help me sleep."

"Well, here's to her." He raised his glass. "Out of pain at last."

He gulped it down and reached for the bottle again.

Dutifully Nell sipped her warm white and grimaced.

"You've lost weight, Nell. You're nearly the size when I first met you."

Nell flinched at the sting.

"Strangely enough I haven't had much appetite in the last week."

The sarcasm flew out before she could stop it but Gary's attention was elsewhere.

"Look, that bloody stray's back. Go on, piss off."

Jester observed Gary through the glass door then gracefully mounted the garden wall. Nell cast a furtive look at the floor but she had moved his dish that morning. Time for a subject change.

"So, the holiday was good then?"

Scratching the back of his neck, Gary smiled smugly.

"Great laugh, and got in loads of golf. Just what I needed."

He reached for his cigarette packet then stopped guiltily. "Oh, sorry. Si got me back into bad habits over the two weeks." There was an awkward silence as Gary waited for Nell to say it was alright to smoke, and Nell said nothing.

"Have a shower, then tell me all about your Nan."

Happy to abandon her wine Nell headed upstairs, retrieving her bag from the hallway as she did. While she climbed the stairs she deftly removed Mr Austin's card. As an afterthought she extracted the taxi driver's too. Slinging her bag on the dressing table she shed her clothes on the floor, then reconsidered and obediently reached for a hanger. She then stashed the cards in the messy drawer where she stowed her make-up, hair grips and anything and everything that did not have a proper home. They blended into the chaos; out of sight but not hidden. Next she grabbed a fan of magazines that littered Gary's side of the bed and threw them underneath. A last look revealed that although not tidy, the room would pass inspection.

Standing under the shower water, Nell tried to relax. The shower had a contrary nature; if the dial was turned to anything more than an insipid splatter, the temperature became unstable. When they first moved in she had been subjected to its tantrums that plunged you from pleasant, to scalding, to a violent lashing of icy, before reaching pleasant again. Gary endured it only once, which was how one of the glass panes became cracked. Since then it was on the 'to fix' list that waited for an increase in money or for the letting agency to send someone out who was competent.

The sound of Gary invaded from downstairs. The TV droned in the living room, the radio yelled in the kitchen.

"Alright, mate?" Gary was on the phone in the hallway.

He had taken the news of his exclusion from Nana's funeral well, but was bound to talk about returning to work. Then he would remember her work and the promotion meeting which had been the one good thing she had to talk about before he went on his lad's golf holiday. Images from the recent meeting shuffled in her mind and she felt humiliation and shame flash through her again. The rhythmic tattoo of water patted her softly between the shoulder blades and stung her raw heels. Safe in her glass cocoon the world disappeared and Nell let her mind take shelter.

She imagined she was Ruby. Smart and cool in a summer dress, she would have commanded attention. In the meeting Ruby would have refused to accept the situation and come up with a clever argument which would sway the decision in her favour. But then Ruby would never have been in that situation in the first place. She was strong and charming, not awkward and clumsy like Nell. For a moment Nell played several scenarios through her mind, unconsciously adopting Ruby's confident smile when she was handed the promotion.

"Engaged! She pregnant or something?" Gary's voice intruded.

Nell felt her smile dissolve. She was not Ruby; and the one person who would understand why she clenched her toes in anger, yet still tried to please Gary, was nothing but ash. She was totally alone in the world; she came first in no one's life, and had no family apart from a father that had abandoned her when she was too young to understand, who might, or might not be still breathing.

Sometimes she looked back on times in her life, when she had felt suddenly melancholy for no apparent reason and wondered if this had been the moment of her father's demise.

Suddenly images of Mr Austin rose again, along with the feeling of unease. Nell turned the dial, stepped out of the shower and allowed the breeze from an open window to cool her, before wrapping a towel around her slim frame. Ruby would not have fretted; she would ring Mr Austin, once she had Googled the name 'Skeleton Key'.

The internet! Panic swept through her like a forest fire. She had forgotten to delete the history; one idle look would show she had spent the last few days looking at the price of one-bedroom flats and bedsits to rent.

Leaving her hair to drip Nell ventured into the hallway. Gary was still on the phone. She crept into the small second bedroom which they used as a study, and where she stored her long neglected artwork. The laptop booted up agonisingly slowly as she listened to his conversation from the doorway, ready to move quickly should it sound like ending.

"No, mate. I can't tonight. The missus is upset. Yeah, the old bird finally snuffed it. How about tomorrow?"

Finally, the home page materialised and a few quick clicks cleared the history of all evidence. Re-adjusting her towel Nell sneaked back into the hallway and through to the bedroom. She dressed quickly in tan cropped trousers and a black sleeveless T-shirt. Taking a deep breath she faced the evening.

Anyone watching would have thought they were a happy couple. Nell's nerves could be explained away with the stress of the past week, which had climaxed in a truly awful day. Gary kept one arm around her shoulders as she explained what had happened since he was away. Only once when she described Nana's last hour, did Nell's eyes well. Gary hugged her then with such tenderness, kissing the top of her head and shushing her tears gently.

Nell cried for the parents who had left her, the grandmother she had cremated today, and for the love she had once had with

Gary, which slowly and painfully he had ripped out. But as she wept she took the comfort he offered and wondered desperately where she would find the strength to leave him when every last grain of energy had been spent on staying with him, and on watching Nana die. Only when he was like this, like the old Gary, did she fear that her nerve would fail her. What was worse; the fear of living with him or the pain of being alone again?

She was just fifteen when they first met properly. Some of the rough girls at school were making fun of her. Gary, a year older, had mouthed off at them, putting an arm around her shoulders. They became friends, sort of, but lost touch when he left school. Bumping in to him again a few years back had been like discovering an untainted part of her childhood.

Things had turned sour when they moved in together. But which couple didn't have problems? she argued with herself.

"That was Mart on the phone. He's got engaged to that Cindy. They've invited us over tomorrow night, if you want to go."

Dread seized Nell. "Umm, well…"

But Gary was not waiting for an answer. "I said we'd go. It will cheer you up."

Well it might, conceded Nell. Mentally exhausted she reached for the wine bottle, filled her glass, and stopped playing an active role. In this way the evening passed pleasantly enough while her subconscious played out its never-ending game of 'should she stay or should she go'. Later, when she finally slept, she found not a repetition of meaningless scenes but the re-enactment of every painful part of the day. Just before she woke herself up she smelled again the scent of old leather and autumn smoke and felt oddly comforted.

Saturday was football for Gary. Flushed with the pleasure of the night before and the anticipation of the day to come, he crashed around the kitchen early, burning toast and stewing tea, while Nell clung to the remnants of a dream. She woke with a start as the bedroom door crashed open and Gary proudly deposited the breakfast tray on the bed.

Nell, drugged from sleep, felt oddly touched by his spontaneous gesture and was suddenly very hungry. They spent a contented twenty minutes eating toast, gulping tea and chatting.

"You alright if I go to footie?" Sometimes Gary looked like the teenager she remembered, his dark blond hair was still thick and prone to curl unless kept short. His blue eyes looked at her now, framed by long eyelashes.

"We'll miss that party tonight, shall we? Do something else?"

Nell's answering smile caused Gary to hold his hands up as he laughed.

"What have I said?"

Almost like the old days. Maybe it wasn't too late to turn it all around.

"If you are still sober when you get back from football, we can talk about it then."

Feeling more positive about her relationship, Nell kissed Gary goodbye when his friends picked him up. She then fell into her usual Saturday routine of washing clothes, vacuuming, changing the bed. Then a sudden thought hit her; she had his car. What on earth was she doing indoors on such a hot day? Dressing for the weather in a loose cotton dress she grabbed a bag and was just heading out of the door when the telephone rang.

"Miss Montague?" Nell was surprised to hear the solicitor. "So sorry we didn't meet up yesterday. By happy chance I'm in the office today." He left the suggestion hanging.

Nell looked outside at the powder blue sky but realised this was the perfect opportunity with Gary out of the way. At the back of her mind she wondered if excluding him was wise, but she reasoned with herself that if Nana had left her anything then she could surprise him with the news later.

"OK. I'll see you in half an hour."

The car park sign threatened to clamp non-hotel users but there was nowhere else for miles and Nell did not fancy a long walk in the heat. Trying to look as if she could afford to stay in the prestigious

Park Hotel she locked the car and headed for the street.

A bronze plaque, glistening in the sunshine on the modern building opposite, revealed that Davies and Brown resided on the top two floors. Feeling slightly lazy she headed for the lift, her sandals slipping on the tiled floor. Had she not been so intent on her purpose she might have noticed a sleek black car pulling up outside. Mr Austin watched her for a second then drove on.

They must charge a lot, thought Nell as she sank into the expensive leather sofa the receptionist indicated. Bright abstract prints reminiscent of an Egyptian spice stall stretched out across magnolia walls. The receptionist, an elderly woman with a face like a melting candle, peered across at Nell suspiciously. The telephone did not ring, no other clients appeared and Nell wondered how they could justify opening on a Saturday. No wonder the receptionist looked pissed off.

Finally a door opened to reveal the man from the funeral.

"Miss Montague. Thank you for taking the time to come." He held his door wide in invitation. "I'm John Elliot." His hand was cold and clammy. Walking into the large room, Nell resisted the urge to wipe her hand down her dress.

"Such a warm day, perhaps we could step out to the roof terrace?"

So, this was how the other half lived and worked, thought Nell as she sipped her mineral water, seated on a comfortable chair amongst the potted palms. The sun beat down on the awning, casting dappled shadows onto the decking. Nell listened lazily to the traffic below. Mr Elliot reminded her of a nervous schoolboy. Surely no older than his mid twenties, he seemed incapable of sitting at ease for more than a few moments. Finally he stopped fussing with his paperwork and laptop, and clearing his throat indicated he was ready to start.

"Your grandmother requested I see her earlier this year, when she first understood the nature of her illness."

"You mean diagnosed with lung cancer?" Nell interrupted, impatient with the unnecessary caution.

"Yes, yes, indeed. Quite so."

Pompous arse, thought Nell, but then pondered why she was being so unkind. As he continued to prattle Nell considered why he might be so uncomfortable. Perhaps Nana had been his first client or was he about to disclose something that would upset her. She tuned back into his grating public school voice.

"At Mrs Montague's request we will forward money from the sale of these shares into an account for you. A rough calculation estimates that we should be looking at around..." and he resumed tapping at his laptop and then stroked the side of his nose, "twenty-five thousand pounds." He smiled for the first time. "I take it this is a pleasant surprise Miss Montague, but we haven't finished yet."

Twenty-five thousand pounds. Suddenly she felt a great affection for this nervous young man. But he was waiting for permission to continue.

"Then we come to the property. Number eleven Church Lane was sold two years ago to pay for your grandmother's care home fees. She wished, on her death, for any residue from this sale be split between a number of named charities including those at the care home."

So, thought Nell, you can say death but not cancer. Blinking rapidly she concentrated on his words and tried to put the image of her grandmother's face to the back of her mind.

"However, that leaves us Lark House and the apartment in Devon."

"What apartment in Devon?" This shock was too great to keep in her mind.

"Your grandmother has suggested that you sell Lark House but keep the apartment. Though naturally, this is your decision to make."

Nell nodded to show she was concentrating but in reality her mind was split between the need to run around the roof top shouting 'Holy Shit', and vague memories of sand dunes, rock pools and the roar of Devon surf.

"Your grandmother was considering splitting Lark House into apartments. She had a company in mind to carry out the renovations, but even after all the costs you should be looking at a good profit."

Nell gulped down her water too quickly, her eyes watered and she began to cough.

"Did you have any notion of this?" enquired Mr Elliot innocently.

"I thought Nana had mortgaged Lark House to pay for the nursing home. I thought Church Street went years ago and I didn't know about Devon. How could I not know about all this? Not even about the shares?"

But there was one thing worrying her. "What about my father?"

But he shook his head. "I'm afraid that is a separate matter."

"What do you mean? Has she left him something? Do you know where he is?"

But Mr Elliot just shook his head apologetically and refused to say more.

"Here are the details for the apartment in Devon, and the key. Oh and the key to Lark House with all the details of the building firm and their plans."

And suddenly a file of paperwork was handed over.

As Nell's sweating fingertips touched the cardboard the reality of what had just happened hit. She was now the owner of two properties and for the first time in her life she could look forward to a future where she had financial freedom.

"Bloody hell." Squinting at the powder blue sky she felt the smile beginning to bloom over her face.

Mr Elliot stood to indicate the meeting was over, held out his hand and, with a tight expression which was fifty years too old for him, spluttered.

"Well, yes. Quite."

The journey down in the lift was a little fuzzier than on the way up. Nell found she kept wanting to smile, but then thought of Nana and felt more like crying. Crying for her loss but also for the secret and beautiful surprise Nana had kept for her. Vaguely she remembered Nana grabbing her hand once when she had been late to visit and muttering that Nell should have her own car.

'Financial independence is one of the most precious gifts you can ever have. It can change your life.' At the time Nell had thought Nana

was hinting again that she should break up with Gary but with hindsight it now made more sense. On her advice she had taken out a loan and got a small car. The same car that was now needing repairs at the garage. Gary had been furious.

Back on the busy street the air was hot with car fumes and the scent of coffee from the café next door. Nell smiled: Gary would be many hours yet. With a spring in her step she returned to the car, which had reached an oven-like temperature. She turned the fan on full, wound the windows right down, then swung back into the busy traffic, heading for the suburbs and her childhood home.

Mrs Green's tinny piano playing still rang in Emily's ears as she waited outside the British Legion hall, scanning the road for her Mum's grey Volvo. Her denim shorts were snug over her black tights and leotard, and as the late afternoon sun gave a final blast of heat, she began to wish she had bothered to change after class. But she had been chatting with Phoebe about the party next Saturday and it was not until Mrs Green had started pumping the tatty upright for the next class to start their warm-up that she realised she was late. Mum hated to be kept waiting so she quickly unwound the black ribbons of her ballet shoes, pulled on her shorts, laced up her Rocket Dogs and dashed outside. Mum would tut at her attire but Emily secretly loved the way she looked. Like a proper dancer. She even kept her hair in its bun, even though Mum had wound it too tight and one of the pins was scraping her scalp.

"Emily, you still here? Do you want dropping off somewhere?" Phoebe and her dad had just emerged from the hall, his Nissan bleeped and flashed as he approached.

Emily settled her back against the rough brick wall and squinting into the low red sun, smiled sweetly.

"Thank you, but Mum should be here in a moment. See you tomorrow, Phoebe."

She kept smiling as they drove past, Phoebe waving enthusiastically.

But the smile slid off her face once they were out of sight. Mum was late. If Emily kept her waiting then there was hell to pay. *'Do you think I have nothing better to do, Em, than hang about waiting for you to come out of school, ballet or piano?'*

Bored, she looked back into the hall's window at the next class who were still at the barre. They were mostly older girls and shyly, Emily looked at their slender waists and gently curved hips. One of the girls was particularly lithe and Emily watched with admiration at the effortless height she reached with her long legs. At thirteen, Emily's body was still showing no hint of the elusive puberty that some of the girls in her class were already exhibiting.

Subconsciously her mind went back to today's ballet class and in time to the music she positioned her pumps into second position and executed a half-hearted plié. Sometimes in class she imagined she was dancing on stage, instead of the dusty wooden floor with the ancient fluorescent lights humming overhead. Keep your toes pointed, back straight, arms soft, neck long. Madame had complimented her today; it had just been a brief, 'that's lovely, Miss Blake' but praise from Madame was rare and her cheeks had flushed in pleasure.

But there was another side of her who hated the prissy leotard and classical music. When she had first seen street dance performed in the market square she had been captivated. The loud bass had vibrated in her chest and she had almost broken through the crowds to join the dancers who spun and flipped and stomped. In her practice mirror at home she had tried out a few moves and even made up a little routine. A daydream of her being called from the watchers to join them made her smile guiltily. Could you really love ballet and street dance? They managed it in the films. A ripple of pleasure trickled over her; as long as her body was moving to music then it did not matter what the music was or how she moved. Dance was dance, and it was her whole world.

Suddenly a car pulled up. Not Mum but a familiar face leaned across the passenger seat.

"Hello, Emily. I thought it was you."

Emily smiled politely and took a step nearer to the kerb.

"Waiting to be picked up?"

Feeling slightly embarrassed Emily smiled and nodded.

"I expect your mum got delayed by the accident on Bridge Street."

Emily started to grimace but then remembered that Mum said it looked ugly so opted for, "Oh, really?"

"Well I hope she's here soon. Have a nice evening." He glanced in his rear-view mirror, put the car back into gear, then seemed to have a change of mind.

"Look, say no if it is a stupid idea but I could drop you off if you like. You could ring your mum to let her know. Save her the trouble."

Four seconds. Maybe five. Afterwards she ran the scene back over in her head and wondered how long she had thought it through. The silence as she looked down the empty street in the hope that Mum might appear, and then back to his now open car door, had felt awkward.

"Never mind. I'm sure she will be here soon." He looked annoyed at her hesitation, impatient and perhaps hurt that she did not like his idea. She felt an itchy bead of sweat scratch down between her shoulder blades. She could be home in ten minutes if she went with him.

So Emily smiled her practiced-in-the-mirror smile that she knew made her eyes sparkle. "OK, thank you."

The door closed behind her as she fastened the seatbelt and they drove off. Five seconds was all it took for her to do something so stupid that she could never put it right.

4

Nell steered the Punto through half-remembered streets. Evidence of time's passing stood in the name change of a restaurant, the bright new bus shelters which blossomed on widened pavements, and a batch of smart balconied apartments where once a garage had stood. A new set of traffic lights caught her by surprise, as did a mini roundabout, but soon she was riding the broad quiet residential roads flanked by beech and plane trees.

She turned a corner and Lark House filled the windscreen. Five years ago Nana had given up the Victorian mansion in favour of the simplicity of the care home. Nell had supervised the move, watching antique dealers transport the better furniture into their over-decorated vans. Their scarves, tweeds and corduroy trousers, in what Nell thought of as Yuppie Pink and Yuppie Yellow, rubbed alongside the jeans of the removal men with their gloves, ropes and old blankets, who moved the items that really mattered.

Nell had promised herself to return but once Nana was gone the house seemed full of ghosts. A property firm had let it initially but it was too big and too old and finally metal casings had been clamped over the windows to secure it from squatters. Once a month someone visited to check pipe work and remove junk mail. It should have been sold years ago.

Large, Victorian, with weathered bricks and iron railings. The windows gave nothing away behind their galvanised crusts. Only the dormer windows were left without cataracts but they reflected nothing but green trees set against the cornflower blue sky. The house had seen everything: tears, terrors, but also joy and games. Picnics on the lawn and camping out in her tree house. Her sixteenth birthday when she and a friend had drunk vodka on the garden steps and told their wishes to the stars. Her first kiss, friends over for film nights, hours of sitting on a cold staircase with the chunky black telephone sweating against her ear while she gossiped with school friends and her breath created condensation in the mouthpiece. But also the loneliness of long visits after her father's disappearance when she had lived in limbo within a wall of adult anger.

Long, long ago. Nell looked down the overgrown path of memory which led back to those bewildering days when everything changed. Mum had been ill and Dad had left them. Nell had painted a picture at school of wobbly flowers in a wonky vase to give to Mum. Dad was supposed to pick her up that day but she had waited and waited. Finally Nana arrived to take her to the hospital. Nell remembered Mum and Nana hissing half conversations through their teeth when they thought she was out of earshot. Brittle smiles, overflowing eyes, and hands that trembled. Nell's card was stood proudly by Mum's bed and the nurses gave her biscuits. Nell often thought back to the last time she saw her father, dredging the grainy memories for any clues. Did he say anything that hinted he was about to leave? Did he hug her any differently? But there was nothing. He had simply walked out, never to return. Mum was ill, a reoccurring malaise that came and went and came back again. Every time she was discharged home it seemed she had changed a little more. Not just in appearance but her whole character. It was as if the illness had got bored of its host and was planning a spot of redecoration; change of outside colour from grey to white back to grey again, add an extension of paranoia, smash down a wall of humour, maybe add a tremor, just to make it feel more like home. When Nell had first seen *The Exorcist* she wondered if all families who watched the slow demise of a loved one saw the parallels in the portrayal of the demonically possessed. Even Nana had taken on the rasping of Regan's laboured breathing. Mum's death moved Nell to Lark House permanently and now Nana's had brought her back again.

She parked her car on the overgrown driveway and bounded up the worn stone steps that led to the front door, as she had many years ago. This was not the day to remember the ghosts of her past. Thanks to Nana she now had a future to look forward to.

Somehow she had expected the house to smell the same; for the scent of nostalgia to seep through the dusty hallway to make sense of her past, and bring with it a clarity to her present. But instead she was greeted by the stench of damp, even on such a hot day, curling in foggy swirls around her legs. She had intended to visit the rooms first but instead headed for the ancient conservatory and the steps that led down to the overgrown wilderness which was once her domain. Strangely it was in the garden, with its heady scent of old roses and sweet dry grass, that she found a familiar peace. Here, with the messy flower beds and fruit trees, she had once found her escape from life. Endless hours of dangling on a rope swing or hiding in her tree house; this was where she was happiest. She remembered her grandmother's deep voice bellowing her in for tea, or to take a phone call, or to tidy her room.

'Eleanor! Where are you? Nell? I'm not going to ask you twice.'

For a moment Nell's eyes strayed over the ancient garden wall and through the jungle of brambles to the deserted house next door. Butlers Yard had started life as a home for lunatic women. Nana had always said that most of the poor girls that had ended up in 'the Yard' had probably just been unmarried mothers or those suffering from post-natal depression; in the days when the Victorians thought they were breaking new ground on all scientific fronts. Sometimes Nell thought that the very bricks must be soaked with screams and rib-wracked sobbing. Then it had become an orphanage – more tears probably – then a convalescent home, and finally left to rot into the sodden ground which supported it. Nell spent many hours as a child, cross-legged in her tree house, spying over the garden wall into Butlers Yard. Nana always made her promise that she would never open the old garden gate and venture into the wilderness beyond, that she would never play near Butlers Yard. And Nell kept that promise in part. The old gate had long ago rusted shut, but Nell found that the wooden panel had rotted and that if she levered it open she could just squeeze through. She never played near Butlers Yard; she would just feel the thrill of being on the dangerous side of her own garden wall and then scoot back through her home-made cat flap. All in all it was nicer to spy from the safety of the tree house, knowing that she was well hidden from those she spied on.

Nana had moved to Lark House as a new bride. She remembered Butlers Yard being a convalescence home, and a children's home before it was boarded up and abandoned. As Lark House thrived as a home, with fresh paint work, home cooking and cut lawns, Butlers Yard sank into neglect and sad memories. But over the years it had found new friends; stray dogs, stray humans, gangs taking drugs, kids having sex, and other activities. Nell abruptly turned away from the brooding Butlers Yard and faced Lark House again. Butlers Yard was dangerous ground, filled with oubliettes of dark secrets and pockets of bad memories. She had spent over twenty years trying to forget certain events; she had enough problems in the present without digging up the past.

A flush of excitement pulsed through her as she remembered the events in Mr Elliot's office. She was rich; Nana had made sure of it. Sitting on the lichen-etched garden steps Nell raised her face to the afternoon sun flickering through the trees. Nana. The house had always smelt of good food cooking. Tea was always ready when she got home from school, greeting her as she opened the door. Jam making in the summer when every room was filled with the sweet aroma of strawberries. Cakes baked for any and every occasion, and unforgettable roasts and curries. Nana's friends calling in for a chat and Nell's friends staying over. An image of Nana raising her eyebrows at a fifteen year old Nell's experimental retro clothing rose before her.

And then it happened. First, her face began to itch and then the scalding tears fell in torrents. Bird song echoed in the tall trees, a woodpigeon and blackbird trilling a strange duet. Nell rested her head in her hands and let the emotion take hold, aware that her armour would only be strengthened by this temporary release in her childhood shelter. It was impossible to imagine a future without Nana, but the cancer had not only eaten the flesh, it had corrupted the precious moments that they had left together. Nell wanted to remember Nana as she had been, not the frail, fearful old woman that cancer turned her into. And it was for the real Nana that her tears fell.

Eventually her breathing stilled. She wiped her eyes, blew her nose, then as an afterthought took a quick puff of her inhaler.

What would she say to Gary? That they were rich now? She was rich anyway. As she pulled herself up from the hard step and headed back into the house she knew Nana's plan to develop the house was the right one. She would never live here again. There were too many triggers waiting in the shadows.

The house felt pleasantly cool after the humidity outside. She opened the living room door and half expected to see Nana's old floral three piece suite and cluttered mantle. But the furniture was gone and the photographs were newly stored in her own attic. Then she mounted the sturdy staircase and crossed the landing to what had once been her bedroom. The walls were pock-marked with Blu-Tack where the last tenants' teenage son had placed his posters. Nell waited for a second wave of emotion to hit her but there was nothing. She had once lived here, but no more.

As she crossed the landing again she glanced up the next flight of stairs. She had rarely visited the top floor of the house when she lived here. The few rooms had been cold and filled with old furniture. One room, her father's study and her grandfather's before him, was always locked. Nana said the study held too many memories for her and she preferred it was left alone. But an inquisitive Nell had long ago found the key and when Nana was out she would sometimes let herself in.

Looking through the keys on the bundle Mr Elliot had given her she realised the study key was missing. It was always easy to spot because it had been the only new key. But as she approached the study she stopped dead. The door was open.

With heavy feet she crept forward. Splinters of wood lay on the floorboards where the door had been forced. Who would do such a thing and why? The room had been cleared of everything when Nana had moved out, and there had only ever been a desk full of old photographs and papers anyway. Nothing of much interest. Perhaps it had been the last tenants? But the splinters looked too new, too raw.

As she stepped into the room a noise made her jump. A tapping was coming from the window. The windows this high in the roof had not been covered and a stray branch from the magnolia was scratching patterns through the thick dirt on the glass.

She gazed down to the quiet street for a few moments, imagining she was twelve again and looking out for Nana's return, and then returned through the empty room and headed downstairs. She would ring the developers, see what they offered her, get a second opinion and then make a decision. But what would Gary say? A strand of caution wove its way around her heart as she thought of plausible excuses of why she would not tell Gary yet. Not until she had decided whether she was really going to leave him or not.

Parked under a heavy plane tree outside, Mr Austin drew out his mobile phone. His hazel eyes flicked first to the left, then the right and finally rested on the leafy suburb through the rear-view mirror.

"It's Austin." He tapped the vintage leather of the steering wheel while he waited.

"And?" The voice that answered spoke of too many Havana cigars and too much brandy.

"And…I've been following her, as you asked. She's outside the house now."

His voice betrayed no irritation but his jaw clenched.

"And?" The tone seemed genuinely inquisitive but Austin caught the scent of danger.

A dog began to bark nearby filling the ominous silence.

"Are you making progress?" He drawled the last word into two separate syllables, each laced with razor wire.

"Yes."

"You said she would make contact yesterday."

"And she will."

"But she saw the solicitor first."

"I..." but he stopped. A face had appeared in an upstairs window.

"She will ring me. You've waited over twenty years for this, surely you can wait a little longer."

"SHUT UP!"

But Austin had had enough.

"No, you shut up. You're paying me good money to mind the bait, and that's what I'm doing."

"Let me remind you, Mr Austin." The evenly spaced clipped tones again. "No Montague equals no money. Not for anyone and especially not for you."

"He will come."

"He had better."

There. Finally Austin heard the first crack and he allowed himself a smile.

"He will come," he repeated. "He will want his share."

"Yes, he will," hissed Morgan. "But instead he will find you, and you will deliver him to me in one piece. What I want, Mr Austin—"

"Be quiet a second."

"You forget yourself..." But he was interrupted again.

"I think she is in his study." He grabbed the plan again from the front seat, a duplicate of the one Nell had seen earlier at the solicitors.

"What?"

"Yes, she's in there." Finally, a breakthrough.

"Then we were right? He did leave something behind and she knows about it?"

"That must be it. Why else go in there?"

The question lay before them as always, spinning slowly, temptingly, the answer concealed. Without the evidence they could do nothing, even if he walked straight into their trap.

Austin's right hand clenched the steering wheel as his body pulsed with adrenalin.

"Then, Mr Austin, you know what you must do."

Now the smile was genuine but his eyes shone with a malevolent luminosity.

"I will get back to you. I have a little house call to make."

Austin terminated the call, pocketed his phone and willed Nell to appear and get in her car. Or should he knock on the door? For a moment he pictured forcing her into the room and making her reveal where it was. That was what Morgan wanted but Austin had a different plan, although it was frustrating. How many times had he combed that room? Every floorboard, every dusty corner, but still he'd found nothing. For a second he pictured Nell's pale face at the funeral. A generous mouth and impish nose gave her an unusual appeal. No, he would play this game of hide and seek a little longer, and protect the girl as best he could. When she made contact, and she would make contact, he was sure of it, then he would follow the plan.

Shifting his aching back a little in the driver's seat he pictured Morgan by his pool. A glass of amber liquid would be swilling in his hand as he waited for Austin to call. Age had increased the man's evil reputation, a reputation Austin had been aware of for years, long before he had been approached by one of Morgan's associates. Once again he wondered if there might be a happy outcome to this business, but Morgan didn't do happy. He did revenge and he did death.

Finally, a figure appeared at the front door and Nell's slight figure trotted down the steps and slid into her car. She reversed out, glancing in the rear-view mirror. For a moment her eyes locked with Austin's. Again he felt an odd pang stir deep inside. Nell was in deep danger, whichever way you looked at it. Morgan had seen to that. The girl was left hanging, her scent spread to the four winds. It was just a matter of time before someone came sniffing.

"Come on, Montague. Let's finish this," Austin muttered as he closed his car door and approached the house. "You can't hide forever."

5

As Nell stepped through her own front door a chill settled over her. The familiar sounds and smells were all around; the monotonous bleep of the answerphone, the flat thud of her footsteps in the hallway, Gary's cigarette from earlier mixing with burnt toast. But it felt awkward, as if her mind was out of focus with what she was seeing. Nothing fitted properly. The scent of Lark House, her childhood home – dry sweet grass and heavy headed roses – played like a drug in her weary mind. An aching need to go back to being a child again where she was safe, and loved.

She thought of her mum then. The mum before her illness had gathered momentum and Dad left. When she was still sweet and funny, patient and calm. After Dad left she became weary and apologetic; dark smudges above prominent cheek bones, stark against her naturally pale skin. Eyes, heavy and full of fear, seeking forgiveness. Her death had in many ways marked the end of Nell's childhood.

Bloody hell. Nell smiled wryly at her trip down misery lane. "Pull yourself together girl." She listened to the answerphone messages. Two hang-ups – probably someone trying to sell something – and then Gary shouting from a pub to say could she make her own way to Mart and Cindy's for seven? And could she bring some beer? So they were going after all. It would buy her a little more time though; another excuse not to tell Gary yet about her good fortune.

The luxury of having a day to herself continued. She strolled into her own small yard, perched on a tatty garden chair and sipped iced coffee from a can. This house had never quite felt like home. It was too tidy, too Gary. She would not be sorry to leave it. Even the bedsits she had lived in before had been more homely. Perhaps she was not a natural sharer. Maybe she needed her home to resemble a single turreted castle with a deep moat and drawbridge: safe and private. Had this house been hers, and hers alone, this yard would be filled with life; a harvest of vegetables in grow bags, and pots with herbs spilling over. A small patch of sunlight hit the concrete where she sat; if it had been her house there would be colour and sweet smells, and joy. Instead there was concrete, her tatty chair and Gary's long forgotten mountain bike under its dirty protective plastic cover. She closed her eyes, shutting out the scene, and imagined she was at Lark House again with the sun dusting patterns on her eyelids as it flickered through the leaves. There was a soft plop behind her as the stray tabby dropped from the garden wall.

"Hello, Jester. You hungry? Only I'll have to feed you out here or we'll both be in trouble."

Jester's fur was hot under her fingers as he stretched out. Clearly they were both in the mood for an afternoon nap. Leaving a pile of biscuits from her secret stash, Nell strolled back indoors. She had time for a quick nap before getting ready for the evening.

Could there be anything more luxurious than cool cotton against weary hot skin, a Gary-free house and breathing that was slow, steady and promised sleep within five minutes of hitting a soft pillow? She kicked off her shoes, lay down and immediately her eyelids collapsed and she felt like she was sinking through cool water. The sound of traffic outside ebbed and fell into a soothing rhythm in time to her soft breathing.

For a moment she saw a flickering of images from the day flash before her; the mineral water at the solicitor's office bubbling in the sunshine, green leaves stirring against blue skies at Lark House. Then the menacing Butlers Yard rose before her. She quickly replaced it with an image of insects swimming like exotic fish on a coral reef of blue lavender and drooping pink rose heads.

She slept, at first the light sleep of train journeys which needed only the slightest interruption to wake her. But as the seconds passed her exhausted body sank deeper and deeper. Outside a wisp of cloud obscured the sun's burning rays and Jester paused in his washing. But the cloud moved on and stretching, he settled down again on the warm dusty concrete. Nell's eyelids flickered; she was dreaming.

Barefoot, scampering up a wooden ladder, a book clamped between her teeth like a scholarly pirate. The tree house floor was littered with chocolate wrappers and drink cans. Flopping down stomach first onto her nest of cushions she resumed her spying of next door. No frown lines marked her smooth forehead, no nervous expression in the chocolate brown eyes; it was a summer's day before Dad left, before Mum died, before everything changed forever.

Then something shimmered before her eyes. She searched the scene in front to find what had caught her eye. Nothing in front of Butlers Yard, nothing in her own garden, then looking back at Butlers again she saw it. Behind one of the grimy upstairs windows, a pale face watched her.

For a moment she thought it was a trick of the light, a complex reflection in the glass which had formed itself into a face. Then it moved. Someone, a young girl, was looking out of the upstairs window, over the wall, and straight at the tree house where Nell lay. The girl put a hand up to the window, a wave? A warning? Then with a flick of red hair she was gone and darkness filled the space she had occupied.

Lying on the cool bed the adult Nell stirred in her sleep. Aware she was dreaming she tried to wake up. The dream was old and she knew what came next. With a gasp she sat up in her own bed. So much for a nice nap; the dream reached out tentative fingers, lulling her back. She swung her legs off the bed, groaning at the effort of moving under heavy blankets. For a second she closed her eyes, dizzy and disorientated. The room was dimly illuminated by a pink lava light, and a yellow glow crept through the gap under the bedroom door. The bed's gravitational pull was strong but forcing her eyes to stay open, she placed her feet onto the soft bedside rug and stood.

Something felt wrong, very wrong as she moved forward on feet that did not seem to belong to her, and reached the door handle. Somehow she was now in the hallway. Soft thuds came from her dad's study upstairs. Then a door opened, slammed shut and heavy footsteps thundered down the stairs. Nell thrust her back against her bedroom door, frantically feeling for the handle, but though the pulsing thuds filled the stairwell, no figure appeared. Slowly the pounding of feet evened out and became the throb of a slow heartbeat. It bounced against the walls and pooled around Nell's head until she could feel the beat in her chest. Unconsciously, she began to breathe faster. The throb felt like the slow, menacing rumble of an approaching avalanche. Then just as Nell felt her hands rise to cover her ears, the sound stopped. And the hallways plunged into inky darkness. Darkness and silence filled every particle of air, every jagged breath Nell took. Then insidiously the blackness turned to spots of grey and finally a small voice broke through the silence. A faint whimper, a cry, almost a mewing sound was coming from the stairs below.

Nell felt herself glide forward and in alarm tried to take a step backwards, but slowly and surely she drifted like smoke down the stairs and towards the thing that was crying like a planted trap in a teenage horror film. She was having a nightmare, another one, Nell was very aware of the fact; but it seemed too real. Part of her could feel the smooth cotton duvet above her body and was aware that her eyes were on the point of opening and would look upon her own bedroom, not the hallway of her childhood.

A small bundle lay on the stairs and it was this that was whimpering like a stuck record. A bald doll lay face down, wrapped in a shroud of dirty white lace. Against her will, Nell's fingers reached out to it. The shroud was grave cold but soft around the hard doll as Nell picked it up and turned it over. Her gasp of disgust echoed dully as she pulled her shaking fingers to cover her face, for where an angelic face should have been etched, with cute rounded cheeks, rosebud lips and large innocent eyes, was instead a contortion of suffering. The baby face was pulled into a mask of screaming, of agonies that no infant should every have to endure. A scene of domestic hell from a war-raped village; of babes ripped from the arms of their mothers to be mercilessly smashed against walls or flung into fire pits.

Peeping from the shroud's folds was a small knitted rabbit with button eyes and embroidered whiskers. Its long ears were lined with velvet and tiny stitches to its head showed where it had been lovingly repaired. The contrast to the tortured baby doll was stark and Nell dragged her eyes away from the bundle and straight into a mirror's murky surface on the wall above her. The hard angles of the banister, stair and walls were disturbed by a flicker of movement. Nell hesitantly raised and lowered her own arm, but the thin hand which snaked around the banister then pulled itself up to reveal a skeletal arm that kept moving. The face from her dream earlier rose like a flame. Her checked school dress was torn and stained and her bare legs marbled with bruises and dried blood. Red hair and white face, her eyes were locked on Nell's as she crept closer and closer.

Time to wake up. Nell forced her eyelids up, but they slammed down again like a guillotine and the screaming doll lay in her hands like a grenade with the pin pulled. Thin white arms were reaching towards it. Nell took a ragged breath in and her eyes opened again but as she looked at her own ceiling the faint outline of the doll danced like an eye shadow, before it faded. With a stomach-churning lurch Nell sat up in bed to hear the phone downstairs. Then silence as the answerphone activated. Breathing hard, Nell tried to control her need to vomit. Instead she reached for her inhaler and took a deep breath which turned into coughing.

A nightmare, bloody hell. Was she not a little old for nightmares? Creepy dolls and murky mirrors. And the ever-present red-haired girl who had filled her dreams since she could remember. The adult in Nell tried to rationalise what had just happened, but as she swung her legs off the bed her hands clenched in fear that she might not be properly awake yet. But this time there was no lava lamp, no heavy blankets and no rug.

The stairwell was soft and warm, safe, after her nightmare. Still feeling shaky Nell sat on the top stair and listened to the voice still recording downstairs.

"...Yeah, and I'll have a lamb madras, no...a lamb vindaloo. Cheers, Nells. We'll see you at seven."

Nells. Gary only called her that when he was pissed and the message was clearly the usual request that she pick up the Indian takeaway on her way over. Nells; how she hated that name. Better than Nelly, preferable to Eleanor but why couldn't he just call her Nell?

The nightmare still hung around her like a boa constrictor, so in an effort to shake it off she lay on the sofa and reached for the television remote. The worried face of a news reader appeared, a school photo of a young girl behind her. Nell recognised the story which had dominated the news for the last week. A thirteen-year-old girl in Devon had disappeared.

"Police are again appealing to the public for any information they may have relating to the disappearance of Emily Blake. Thirteen-year-old Emily was last seen..."

For a moment the red-haired girl from Nell's nightmare swam before her but Nell shook the image firmly off. Maybe a shower would do the trick.

Later, wrapped in a towel, Nell stood before her wardrobe. What to wear to a drunken after-football party to celebrate the engagement of two of the most annoying people Nell knew? Cindy thought she was stuck-up, so if she went smart she would be overdressed, if she went casual she would be accused of not thinking they were worth dressing up for. Flicking through her wardrobe Nell went for plain black linen trousers and a sleeveless white cotton shirt. Now she looked like a waitress. Stuff them, she thought as she thrust her feet in the funky sandals Gary thought were ugly; she felt comfortable in this outfit and she would dress to please herself.

And I don't want a bloody curry, she thought as she struggled to find the menu from the pile on the hallway table. I don't want to bloody go to the bloody party.

Then at the back of her mind she remembered that she was the owner of two properties and had a large amount of money coming to her. For the millionth time that day she sent a love-filled thank you to Nana for giving her this chance. She would leave Gary, so this might be the last time she had to do something like this. The thought gave her confidence and disappearing back upstairs she pinned her hair up delicately in a chignon which flattered her heart-shaped face but would annoy Gary who liked her hair down. She then applied make-up, just a little; she didn't want it sliding off her face during what looked like it would be a muggy evening.

Just before seven she parked outside their block of flats, knowing she looked overdressed and not caring. Laden with a plastic bag full of beer cans, and a brown paper bag from the Indian, she stomped up the concrete stairs. Actually, it was a nice block of flats. Not good enough for Mart and Cindy, who were always moaning about it, but Nell wouldn't have minded living there, on her own, without Gary, maybe just with Jester.

On the third round of increasingly irritated knocking, the door fell open and a flustered Cindy stood there.

"Good, it's you. I'm sober and they're driving me fucking mad." The warmth of the welcome took Nell by surprise.

Maybe it was going to be a good evening after all.

After the curry was devoured it soon became clear there were two sides to the party. Gary, Mart and a sweaty man with flustered wispy hair were spread out in the lounge, smoking. Nell and Cindy occupied the kitchen, gulping diet cola and chasing melting ice cubes round glasses wet with condensation, with pink bendy straws.

Nell felt out of place, but better here with Cindy than out there in the smog.

"So, let's see the ring."

A slim hand with bulging red false nails was offered for inspection.

"Wow." And Nell meant it. Cindy might be an airhead Barbie whose idea of marriage began and ended with the wedding reception, but it was a nice diamond on her finger.

"It's going to be a lush wedding," and keeping count on her fingers, she recited her wedding plans, finally describing the honeymoon with a clap of hands and a rapid beating of heavy black lashes.

"But there is one problem. Gran can't stand my stepmum, and Mum says she won't come and I should wait until after the baby because no one wants to see a fat bride waddling up the aisle."

"Pregnant? I didn't realise."

Cindy looked slyly through the open kitchen door, but the men were making too much noise to hear.

"That's the only reason he wants to get married. I'm not stupid."

Several protests formed in Nell's mind – concerning Cindy's intelligence as well as Mart's intentions – but she decided on a different angle.

"Do you want to get married?"

Arguing came from the living room as more people arrived and the serious business of the after-match post-mortem began.

"Yeah, I do, and I suppose I want a baby, but not yet. Maybe when I'm thirty."

Thirty. The dirty word had been released into a hostile world. Nell would be thirty soon and wasn't thinking about it. Wasn't thinking about what she had hoped to have achieved by now and clearly wasn't going to. Good husband, great job, maybe a child, lovely home with her own art room. A qualm of guilt heaved over in her stomach; she hadn't drawn anything in years. Once she had seen everything through eyes that could separate shapes and colours and angles. Intricate designs growing on virgin white paper, time lost in a world of delicate lines, sharp and exact.

"What about you and Gaz?"

Nell blinked stupidly as she was brought back to reality. For a moment she gazed at Cindy's thick Cleopatra-like make-up and couldn't think of an answer.

"Um…God no," then realising that sounded harsh, "well not for a long while yet."

For a moment understanding lit Cindy's pale eyes.

"Yeah, sorry about your Granny."

"Nana." Instantly Nell regretted the correction. Placing her hand on Cindy's thin arm she smiled. "Thank you. It's weird – even though I'm glad she's out of pain I miss her so much."

In irritation she realised her eyes were stinging. Cindy put down her drink and gave her a quick hug and that was all it took for Nell to start howling again.

"God, sorry. No, really I'm fine. So silly," but the tears were splashing down.

"I'll get Gaz."

"No!" Nell quickly got her breathing back under control, and wiping her eyes, gave a wobbling smile.

"No, thanks. I'm just being stupid."

"I've been blubbing. Hormones. You're not—?"

"No. Definitely not pregnant."

And at the worse possible moment Gary appeared at the open door. He had obviously caught the last of their conversation and swaying slightly he looked at Nell, then Cindy, and back to Nell again.

"Pregnant? You're not are you?"

Cindy erupted into ear-piercing shrieks of laughter.

"No," said Nell firmly. "Just Cindy."

Unfortunately, it seemed the men had run out of conversation and were looking for a diversion. The two parties merged. Looking in from the outside Nell realised that Cindy did not really fit in either, but unlike her was making an effort. Maybe she was just making life difficult for herself. Everyone was friendly, so why did she always feel like an outsider? Looking at Cindy, now deposited on Mart's lap, she realised that this could be her life. Gary would settle down eventually, with her money she could give up work if she wanted to. The thought of going back to the office and telling Mr Page where he could stick his job made her smile.

Gary had seen the half smile and was lumbering towards her. She cringed inside at his hot breath as he began smearing wet kisses on her neck.

"Ah. Sweet," muttered Mart who had obviously not seen the face she was pulling.

"Don't be miserable." Gary protested as she began pushing him off.

"You know I love you, Nells." Amidst the whistling Nell realised just how drunk he was. Then he collapsed onto his knees and grabbing her hands looked up to her horrified face.

"Nells…Shut the fuck up you rabble." There was a hiss of shushing as he began again. "Nells…will you marry me?"

A shard of ice shot through her veins and she realised her mouth had literally fallen open. Closing it shut, she looked at Gary's face as he tried to smooth his grin into an attempt at sincerity. Mart was cheering, Cindy shrieking, and Nell realised her mouth had fallen open again.

The seconds passed. What the bloody hell should she say? Yes to keep the peace? No, she needed more time? Too late, Gary's face was a mask of fury. Struggling back to his feet, he turned to the shocked audience.

"I take it the answer is no. Mart, pass the Jack Daniels."

"Gary, wait. You just took me by surprise."

He shook her hand off. "No, fuck off. You had your chance."

The awkward silence was metallic to the taste.

"Gary. Of course I want to marry you, I just want to wait a bit." Unfortunately, the last few words were lost as there was general cheering again. But Gary was sulking and Nell withered inside knowing that she was in serious trouble.

Oblivious to the growing storm of emotions, Cindy and Mart waved them off later with suggestions of a double marriage. Gary's social smile slid off his face the moment they were out of sight. Despite Nell's attempts, he did not want to talk to her, let alone talk about the proposal. The drive home was painful and Nell felt her face set like wax as the all-familiar black spots began to cloud her vision.

The front door closed behind them. The silence hung like a poisonous gas. Nell kicked off her shoes in the lounge and headed for the kitchen. A series of sharp smacks from the lounge, as each shoe was flung into the wall, brought her to an abrupt halt.

"You fucking whore."

Gary arrived in the kitchen.

"Look, I didn't say I wouldn't marry you." But he was beyond listening. Grabbing her hair tightly in his fist he dragged her back into the lounge and away from the open blinds of the kitchen.

"Gary...stop. Let me explain." But as she spoke Nell knew it was futile. He threw her onto the sofa.

"Now, let's have a little talk about how the sluttish whore thinks she's too good to marry me."

6

"Be honest."

Nell struggled to sit up.

"Answer me." The punch to her shoulder sent her sprawling across the sofa again. Her face sank into the soft furnishing and bizarrely she was aware of the happy scent of suntan lotion. The arm which Gary had punched burned fiercely.

"I know you don't, but I want to hear you say it."

Slowly Nell sat up, wiped her hair away from her tear-wet face and looked him firmly in the eye.

"That's right, Gary. I don't want to marry you. We're over."

"Oh, here we go again." He laughed. "We're over."

"I mean it this time, and I don't speak like that."

"Yes you do, you snobby tart. We're not over, you just love winding me up. I think you like a bit of rough treatment."

"Fuck off, Gary." She attempted to get out of his range.

"Oh, you're not going anywhere. We're having a little chat. Did your daddy give you a bit of rough before he ran away? Maybe good old 'Nana' used to slap your arse."

And the truth finally dawned on Nell that this was more than the usual bullying. Their relationship was punctuated by his bad temper. The slaps, the name-calling, usually, but not always when he had been drinking, but never before had he dared mention Nana. She struck out before she realised what she was doing; her small fist hitting just below his ribcage.

"I'm leaving you. Tonight."

Gary's laughter stung as he clapped his hands slowly in mocking applause.

"What a drama queen. Quite a performance." Then he grabbed her jaw, his blunt fingers digging into her damp cheeks, and dragged her face within inches of his own.

"So, that's it then. You've dumped me? Who've you been shagging? Some nice male nurse you met at the hospital when the poor old bird was croaking her last?"

"How dare you!"

"Oh, quite easily. There's poor old Nana calling out, but you were too busy flirting to hear her. Did you fuck in the room where your Nana was dying? Did she have to watch you with your knickers round your ankles, while some male nurse was ramming his dick into your rotten cunt?"

Nell doubled up with pain as his fist struck between her legs and half digested tikka masala filled her mouth.

"Don't you dare puke on me."

Nell wiped her mouth and took a shuddering breath.

"I'm not the one who gets pissed and pukes." Another blow to the side of her head made the black spots dance again.

"You whore…just like your whoring mother."

He was now jabbing his finger into her temple while his other hand prevented her escape with an iron grip on her shoulder. Nell closed her eyes tight while something inside her turned to water. Then her mum's face rose in her memory and the water turned to ice. Whatever she had suffered in Gary's hands before, this was going to be much worse. Lines had been crossed. It was all about survival now.

"You see, Nell? I've heard it all before from you. You'll never leave me because you've no one else, and nowhere to go. No family, no friends, no home, NOTHING. You leave me and you will spend the rest of your boring, miserable life alone. You are too screwed up by your past for anyone else to ever want you."

A rattling wheeze dragged itself from Nell's chest. Gary's eyes brightened.

"Oh dear…sounds like you need your inhaler."

Nell tried to shake off Gary's grip.

"How long have you got I wonder?"

"Please, you wanted to talk. Let me get it and we can," she ventured, trying to sound casual, trying to hide the panic that was stirring.

"Oh, I don't think so."

Nell's chest tightened; an iron band across her ribs.

"Tell me you're not shagging behind my back and I will let you get it."

So, he'd gone off the subject of marriage and her family, thought Nell ruefully.

"You know I'm not. But Gary, it just isn't working between us anymore."

"I don't hear you promising."

Bright points of light were dancing now in front of Nell. This was not going to be just a rattle, if she did not get to her inhaler soon it would be a full attack, probably brought on by the stressful fight after an evening of passive smoke inhalation. Despite the rage burning inside her, she needed to survive.

"I promise you I'm not shagging behind your back."

Gary nodded several times, then tilted his head to one side. "Say it again but add in that you haven't in the past either. And you haven't flirted with anyone."

Nell was beginning to shake. Dark spots gathered now, like flies, in front of the mask his face had become.

"I promise that I am not shagging behind your back and I never have. And I am not flirting with anyone and I never have. Please, Gary." Had she said it right, not left anything out? Gary could carry on like this for hours until he was satisfied with every word. If she stuttered or spluttered or breathed in the wrong place he would make her repeat it again and again until her throat was hoarse and nerves shredded.

But he nodded dismissively, and looking hurt sank into the armchair, one leg slung over the arm. Calmly Nell walked over to her bag, found the inhaler and took a deep breath of it. The silence scalded her ears. Her keys and purse were in her bag. Should she make a run for it? How far would she get in bare feet?

"Maybe it is too soon to talk about getting married," muttered Gary petulantly, "what with your Nana dying."

Nell took another deep breath of her inhaler, the medicine hit her teeth where she had taken it too quickly and her ribs ached. Absently rubbing her bruised arm, she watched him, ready to spring out of range if necessary.

"I'm sorry, Nell. It's just that I love you so much and seeing Mart and Cindy tonight made me wish it was us."

Holding out his arms he smiled sheepishly. The mood had shifted but Nell knew it was just a scene change; the drama was far from over yet.

"Love you, Nells. I don't mean to hurt you but you wind me up."

"I can't go on like this, Gary."

He held up both hands as if to halt her, or protect himself. "OK, I hear you. But can you stand there and tell me you don't love me?"

"Oh I love you, Gary, but I don't want to and I'm not in love with you. I was, but you beat that out of me."

This had all been said before; he knew it and so did Nell. But this time she knew it would be the last time. She was going off script. For a second she felt dizzy, standing at a crossroads and wanting to bolt for the familiar path. A path where she forgave him after he had apologised and promised it would never happen again. He had brought up her family tonight, had hurt her in the most brutal way. If she forgave him he would not hit her again tonight and part of her ached for peace. But his outbursts were getting worse and instinct told her that this may be her last opportunity to finish it. Nana's money gave her a burst of courage.

63

"So, that's it, Nell. We're over?"

"Yep. I'm going upstairs to pack a bag. I'll come back in the morning for the rest of my things."

In the back of her mind she contemplated where to stay. He'd guess at Lark House, but there was the apartment in Devon. The money would not be through yet but her credit card would put her up somewhere until she could phone the property management agency in Devon. For the first time in her life she had options. Desperately she swallowed down the smile that was rising from somewhere deep below.

"OK. I'll help you pack."

"No, wait." But it was too late. Gary bounded upstairs and his heavy footsteps could be heard in the bedroom. There was a sound of clattering and slamming and her clothes began to parachute down the stairs.

"Gary, stop."

"I'm helping you pack. Here's your underwear, because we can't say knickers, can we? No, that's far too common for Eleanor."

There was a heavy thud as her Samsonite case slid down the stairs and landed by the front door.

"Oh, and you'll want your Nana's stuff. I'll help you pack those precious photo albums."

In desperation Nell ran up the stairs, slipping once on a silk dress and landing painfully on her knee.

"Gary, stop. For fuck's sake."

"Ha ha, thought that would get the slut up the stairs." Gary's face was a mask of glee that she had fallen for his plan. Cackling insanely he looked like an evil clown as Nell tugged at his arm in a feeble attempt to stop him opening the study cupboard where she had stored the albums. Nana had given them to her when she was first diagnosed. Gary had held her as slowly she turned the musty pages one by one to reveal photos she had never seen before. He had even wiped her eyes as she cried. The pain slit a fresh gash through her chest as Nell realised he would rip up every last photo if she did not stop him.

He slapped her hard and she fell against the skirting board.

"For chrissakes, Nell, stop screaming. Next door have just got back," he whispered. "Do you want the police round here?"

"YES!"

"Shush."

"Just leave me alone."

Gary shook his head slowly.

"Always a fucking drama with you, isn't there? Get up, I only tapped you."

But Nell was beyond following instructions. From her position in the spare room doorway – rammed against the cupboard door – she drew her knees up to her chin and hid her face in her hands.

"Just go away."

"I'm having a coffee. Do you want one?"

"NO!"

So it was over for now. He had hit her a few times, called her names, and scattered the contents of her drawers all over the hall and stairwell. Now the mood had switched and he was moving on. If she sat and drank coffee meekly it would be over. At Christmas he had lost his temper and the tree along with decorations and lights had been slung at Nell from across the room. Seconds later he had thought the whole thing hilarious, but had hit Nell when she refused to 'see the funny side' of the fused lights and smashed baubles. It was more than just a ruined tree, she had tried to explain, it was Christmas Eve and he had poisoned the magic.

"Come on, have a coffee. Then I'll help you clean up all this mess you've made." He was grinning at her now, trying to coax a smile with his feeble joke. Within five minutes he would be sobbing his apologies and promising to take her away or buy her something to 'make it up'. But she wasn't going with his script and that meant anything could happen.

"I'll come back tomorrow for the rest of my stuff."

"Nell, look I'm sorry. But you humiliated me in front of everyone. I love you so much I just want us to get married, have a kid."

He helped her to her feet.

"Shit, you've ripped your trousers and your knee is bleeding. I didn't do that."

He looked like a small boy.

"No, but you did this." Nell jabbed at her cheek bone which felt hot and twice the size.

"Nells, I said I was sorry. Let me make you a coffee, you're beginning to wheeze again and you always say that coffee helps. I'll start tidying the mess in the hallway." And then astonishingly he began to smile. "Your underwear is hanging over the banisters."

"Oh, Gary. It's not funny. We've not been having some sort of laugh here."

His smile collapsed again.

"Oh, get over yourself. I just tapped you. It's me who should be upset."

He was building up again, his face already twisting into a sulk.

"We can't go on like this."

"I'll get antiseptic for your knee."

Obscenely he began to whistle as he bumped around in the bedroom. He opened her drawer and the whistling stopped. Nell realised that this could be her only opportunity to get out of the house and on shaky legs began to head downstairs.

"What the fuck is this?"

Halfway down the stairs Nell felt herself turn round in answer and hated herself for it. At the top of the stairs Gary stood with a small business card in his hand. The card Mr Austin had given her at the funeral.

"Who is this?"

At the back of her mind Nell knew the stairs was a dangerous place for this sort of encounter but she needed the card.

"Give it to me."

"If you want it, you come and get it."

But she shook her head and went back downstairs. She was not playing his game anymore. And he did not like it. He followed her downstairs and the real interrogation started. She tried; she hit back, but this was unchartered territory. As if aware a line had been crossed Gary did not let up. He wanted to know who the card was from and although aware that defying him in this way was suicide, Nell's last pulse of rebellion was stirred into action and she refused. A push sent her across the room; she knocked into a table and sent her bag tumbling onto the floor. She grabbed it and made a desperate run for the door but never got there. Gary grabbed at her arm, making her swing round. He lost grip and Nell went flying. She fell to her knees, skidded along the laminate flooring and with a sickening thud her head caught the edge of the suitcase. There was a blinding white light and then the world went on mute. The hallway floor became as soft as new fallen snow as she sank into it. Then darkness closed over her.

7

The sultry summer evening had gorged itself until only a thunder-storm would relieve the head-splitting tension. From where she lay in the hallway Nell could hear the last few nightclub stragglers heading for home. The sharp clip of stilettos beat in time with their drunken voices and a car speeding by hooted.

"Piss off." A girl retorted and her friend giggled.

Nell saw a splash of red through the glass front door as they tottered by. The doormat was sharp against her cheek and arm. The first sky splitting crack of thunder rumbled above. Shivering, Nell mentally checked her body for pain. Her forehead was bleeding; the pain felt like a crab trying to claw its way into her head. She felt sick and light-headed. Her left hand and arm were stinging from the scrape across the doormat, and the rest of her body felt dead. Strangely, it was the mucus which had dried uncomfortably on her top lip that bothered her most.

Slowly she raised herself into a sitting position with her back against the wall. Great Saturday night! The sound of laughter in the street mocked her.

"The ambulance won't be long now." Gary appeared from the

living room, his face clouded with distress.

Crouching at her side he raised his fingers tentatively to the cut above her eyebrow. "I'd take you myself but I've been drinking."

The following silence stung her ears, but as the tension crystallised they began to ring shrilly.

Gary tried again. "Can I get you anything?"

Her voice broke the oppressive atmosphere.

"I need tissues and my inhaler."

Thankful to have something to do Gary dashed off with the enthusiasm of a gundog.

"You haven't really called an ambulance, have you?"

The fearful, uncertain expression had returned to his face.

"Well, yeah Nell, love, I did. You knocked yourself out. You can't be too careful about head injuries."

"No, Gary. I didn't do anything. This is your work."

As if on cue the glass panel in the front door filled with the insistent pulse of blue neon lights.

"Oh, Jesus Christ, Gary. I'm not going."

There was a sound of slamming doors as the ambulance crew approached.

"Please, Nell, just say you fell downstairs. I'm so sorry."

He helped her to her feet, a necessity if they were going to open the door. The hallway tilted like a rough channel crossing and Nell's stomach tightened into a fist; a fist with sharp fingernails which made her knees shake. She just wanted to crawl away and hide.

"OK, Gary, I'll go to hospital and tell your lies, but tomorrow you'll let me leave without any more of this shit."

"Yes, OK."

"I mean it."

"Yes, I said OK."

The ambulance crew had started their shift four hours ago. So far they had picked up a snack from Tesco and then helped a frail and frightened old lady back into bed, saving her from spending the remainder of the night shivering on a urine soaked carpet. Another half an hour and they would have been in the middle of the street fight that was building up outside the Spire nightclub. Their colleagues would end up with a fatal stabbing, but for them it was just Nell and her tumble downstairs.

Gary kept close by, but as Nell was securely strapped onto the stretcher and taken out into the humid night air, he dashed back to fetch her bag. The skies opened and the night was filled with sweet fragrant rain. The blanket felt soft and safe and finally Nell let herself relax. It was humiliating, frightening, but as least he could not touch her any more tonight.

"It's alright, love, I'm here."

Nell stiffened as Gary reached to stroke her cheek. Catching the threat in her eyes he put his hand down again.

The hospital smell brought back bad memories of Nana. Being wheeled flat on her back was disorientating; all she could see were off-white ceiling tiles, punctuated by large square lights. The bottle green of the ambulance crew's uniform framed her vision, and she was aware of people passing, large signs, and faces smiling down at her. Was this how a baby felt, being wheeled in its pram? Then Gary's face appeared, a kaleidoscope of social interaction and worry. Only the eyes showed the true fear, not of her condition but that she might tell the truth behind the lie.

The kind, no-nonsense approach of the nurses tempted her to confide in them, but Gary's presence stopped her. She should tell them, get the police involved, but all she wanted to do was leave it all behind her. But not without her possessions. Perhaps Gary guessed that this might really be the end for their relationship, because he played the loving boyfriend, never leaving her side, even turning on the charm and making little jokes with the nurses. Anyone watching would probably think she was lucky to have him, that he was a 'keeper'. And he was when he wanted to be, but they did not see the flip side of the joker: the clown's smile twisting into a cruel sneer, or the twinkling eyes which turned black with malice.

The nurse put temporary gauze on her eyebrow. The gentle probing on the raw site brought tears to Nell's eyes and for a moment she felt light-headed again. As the stinging increased, she tried to concentrate on something else; the sharp screaming of a child penetrating from the waiting room, or the way Gary was fidgeting with a thread on his jeans, even the stench of cigarettes rising from the nurse's uniform.

"Try to keep still please, love." Nell was getting tired. The efficient nursing team were going through every test. She had been asked her address and what day it was until she had wondered if they thought she was mad, and every fifteen minutes they shone a light in her eyes. Her finger was pricked to check her blood sugar levels, her arm cuffed for blood pressure, and it was at this point that with a dull ache of dread she realised what the next test might be.

Gary's mobile began to vibrate with an incoming call.

"Take that outside please, and switch it off before returning. No mobiles in here, read the signs." Not so friendly now, thought Nell smugly as Gary was ushered out. As if waiting for him to go the nurse disappeared, then reappeared with something covered with a paper towel.

"I'm going to need a urine test, to check your glucose, and have I your permission to do a pregnancy test?"

So there it was, the final humiliation, thought Nell as she tried to get her bladder to co-operate while perched precariously on the pan.

"How you doing?" The nurse's professional smile betrayed her exhaustion, but she grinned when Nell grimaced apologetically.

"I know it's hard to pee behind a curtain, when all hell is breaking loose out here. But don't worry, we have seen it all, pee all over the bed or on the floor, but not a dribble in the pan. I'll get your bloke to stay in the waiting room, shall I, so you can have some privacy?"

Did she guess? thought Nell, but the grey eyes just sparkled with sympathy and amusement. Then the hot flush of humiliation solidified into hatred of Gary for putting her through this. "You utter bastard," she muttered as she lifted herself over the pan and then finally managed a trickle. It was whisked away, there were a few anxious moments, then thankfully the result came back negative. Next she was wheeled off to X-ray. She was wasting their time: Gary had got angry and she had headbutted her suitcase. Gary had panicked and she now found herself flat on her back on a hospital trolley. Maybe she had just fainted with exhaustion and not even been knocked out. She felt fairly close to it again.

It was nearly four in the morning and Nell ventured the question of when she could leave. It was a question charged with contrasting emotions; part of her wanted the softness of her own bed, but the pain of her newly stitched eyebrow and scraped skin reminded her that it was her bed no longer. The pilot light of hope was fed by her anger and misery, and it was this flame that would later erupt to power her escape.

Surprisingly the only night Nell had ever stayed in hospital had been at Nana's bedside. The various bumps and bruises that Gary caused were normally treated at home with a few days off work and an excuse of being clumsy. Or she covered them with polo necks and long sleeves and telephoned in sick with a pretend stomach bug. But this time it was more serious – she had lost consciousness, had a trip in an ambulance, and was now data on the hospital information system. It had to be the last time. Now she was to spend what was left of the night in the short stay emergency unit just off the main emergency department, where the nursing staff could keep an eye on her. All because she had lost consciousness, fainted, whatever. The last time Nell had shared a room with anyone other than Gary had been as a teenager during a slumber party. As she was led into the small bay, she wondered if she had mistakenly been put in a geriatric psychiatric ward. Then a young woman with a blackened eye and her arm in a sling met her eye. No words were shared between them; but as Nell returned the weak smile she felt the sharp pain in her chest flicker once then snuff out.

Gary dashed home in a taxi and returned with pyjamas and washbag. Proudly, he crept to where Nell lay and whispered that he had packed foam ear plugs for the noise, her book in case she could not sleep, and lip balm for the suffocating dry heat of the hospital.

"Don't worry, Nell, I'll look after you." Then looking furtively at the nurse's turned back, he mouthed, "Sorry...never again..." His eyes filled with tears and against her wishes Nell felt hers fill too. Gary took this to be forgiveness but Nell knew it was humiliation, exhaustion and pain.

"Gary, nothing has changed. I want you out when I pack my stuff."

But he just smiled, and Nell knew her words were as weak as a whimper against an advancing warrior horde.

"Get some sleep and we'll talk when you come home. Don't make any decisions tonight."

And finally he was gone.

What was left of the night passed slowly, hindered by the peaks and flows of activity from the main treatment area: shouting, whimpering, snoring, phones that rang and rang, and call bells that never stopped. Nell squeezed her ear plugs in, then pulled them out, read her book, then put it down. The clock hands inched slowly round in their sterile white plastic circles. The bed seemed to shrink around her and the walls disappear into dark shadows. Vulnerable and exposed, Nell felt her muscles charge with panic and her breathing quickened.

"Shall we close your curtains now?" A strange woman stood by her bed wearing yet another colour uniform. Nell had no idea if she was a sister, nurse or a doctor, but she agreed to the closing of her curtains and sank into her discomfort again. Flashes of the fight and Gary's torment played in front of her like a trailer from a horror movie.

"Nurse? I need to go," came a pleading voice nearby. Nell rammed in the ear plugs again, closed her eyes and tried to imagine herself in Ruby's apartment. An urban loft, with exposed brickwork and open-plan living. Huge abstracts hung on the walls, in thick swirls of cobalt blue and burnt sienna, luxuriously thick with blunt palette knife edges. Ruby was gazing out of the window, wondering whether to go out. Her answering machine holds three listened to messages and she smiles as she contemplates her choices. Her reflection in the dark window reveals cropped dark hair framing Disney princess eyes. She takes a deep breath, taking in the scent of her shampoo and body lotion. The excitement of a pleasure yet to come, makes her eyes dance. Can life really be this good? For Ruby it can.

Escaping into the imagined life of her alter ego was something Nell seemed to be doing more and more.

When she was unhappy or panicky; when she was stressed or afraid. Then it dawned on her that the reason she was doing it more and more was because there was rarely a time at the moment when she did not feel one of those trigger emotions to some degree. The last member of her family had just died and now she was alone with Gary.

The gently expanding sponge plugs in her ears amplified her own breathing and managed to muffle some of the hospital noises, but they did nothing to block out the wet sound that came from the man in the bed next to her.

"Nurse?" He whimpered, then, "Nanny? I need you, Nanny." The stench which dented her garish curtain suggested to Nell that it was probably too late. She gazed at the curtain, watching the shadows of the nurses flicker across as they cleaned him up, reassured him, and made him comfortable again. One shadow seemed darker, closer. Was someone standing right by her cubicle, looking through the gap?

She tried to relax but every time her body began to sink into the hard bed it hurt in a different place. Her breath caught behind her bruised ribs like a rusty cog. The nurses were chatting now, in soft voices and Nell could smell coffee and salt and vinegar crisps. Must keep her face relaxed; it hurt too much otherwise. One of the nurses was five months pregnant. She was marvelling at how millions of sperm had battled to be the one to penetrate the egg's surface.

"If you think about it we are all bloody marvels; we have already beaten the odds to be here at all. We were winners the moment we first came into being. Our determination to succeed – our survival instinct – must have been far superior to all the thousands of others. Makes you think."

It certainly did, mused Nell. She managed to survive all that, had survived even the trauma of birth. And for what? To be adrift like a toy boat in someone else's bathwater at the mercy of every flick of their foot, or a sudden surfacing knee. In a futile attempt to escape Gary's wrath she had become as docile as a cow.

Finally sleep came because Nell became aware that she was sinking lower and lower, as if she was falling from a great height in slow motion. Her back stung, then felt icy cold as she hit the bottom. In shock she opened her eyes and found she was lying on the floor looking up at her hospital bed. Like floating in deep water she tried to turn over, to struggle to her feet. It was happening again, just like yesterday afternoon. The other patients had gone, the nurse's desk was empty, and the empty iron beds looked like they belonged in a museum. It was dark but a faint light shone through the dirty circular window in the door. Too late; once she had looked at the light she was hurtling towards it. Nell shuddered as she passed through the door and came to a halt outside. Moonlight seeped through the misted windows of a covered walkway where painted brickwork peeled like parched skin, and a twisted strand of ivy snaked through a hole in the roof.

Pitted concrete under foot was damp against her naked feet. Then a cloud crossed the moon and darkness descended like a dropping elevator. The sky shifted from cold blue to darkest black and the walls seemed to creep closer as she continued down the sloping path toward double doors in the distance.

Each footstep echoed dully, a slapping noise as her feet hit the wet concrete. As in dreams the corridor seemed endless, the double doors never closer. Hesitantly she stole a glance over her shoulder and saw the porthole of light from her room. It was as distant as the sun to an underwater diver who stares through impossible depths to the surface. The expanse of window either side made her feel exposed, vulnerable. Was someone on the other side observing her? Remembering the nightmare from earlier Nell made a promise not to look at any mirrors; or go near any white lacy bundles, however much they cried.

Then she heard it; something grating against her footsteps, a slight echo in a place that offered up none. A foot fell and then fell again a second later. She walked a little faster but the echo remained. She hesitated but the echo continued its pace just a few feet away. The darkness around her thickened and her breath billowed out in white clouds. Swallowing hard she acknowledged the unhappy truth that she was now not alone, that another person was right behind her. Fear flowed icy cold over her shoulders and she shivered in her thin nightshirt. Somewhere in the distance came a sudden clattering as something unseen moved fast, like an old cage elevator that was out of control. Nell tried to move again but her feet seemed to be sinking into the flooring. Frantically, she pushed forward, aware that the noise behind was keeping pace. The spectral footsteps were now joined by a ragged breath – which could have been her own, she reasoned – and a creaking, like an old leather coat on the back of someone creeping.

A gear shifted in her mind, the sinking feeling fled and the chase was on. She dashed through a doorway which appeared on her left and mounted the staircase. Out of a door and along another dark corridor. Branching off to the right she heard a door slam behind. She had to lose him. A lift appeared, the door slid open and Nell flew inside. She heard footsteps not far away as she frantically stabbed buttons, but the doors closed in time and she was creeping upwards. There was a smell of books left too long on a sunny shelf, dusty and cloying. An image of her face being pressed into the wrappings of an Egyptian mummy flashed in her mind, but she shook it off hastily: this dream was bad enough without being buried alive in an already occupied sarcophagus.

The lift groaned and clanked but it was nothing like the sound Nell had heard before. The lights flicked off and then on again as the lift stopped. The doors opened a slither and in horror Nell saw a small huddle of children march by. Thin to the point of starvation, they stared ahead as if walking to certain death. Their eyes had all hope and life sucked out, empty husks of skin and bone where once chubby arms had flung round the necks of parents; ashen lips which once had laughed and blown kisses and sung songs. One little girl trailed behind, trying to keep up with the group, on legs that seemed misshapen as if they had been sewn onto a rag doll the wrong way. Her arms worked in a parody of marching as she struggled. One hand gripped a knitted pink rabbit with floppy ears and a bright bow at its neck. Innocent button eyes watched Nell as it bounced against the child's ragged leg.

With a clank the lift doors began to close and the little girl turned to face her. Nell's breath was sucked from her as she looked straight into the face of the crying doll again, a waxen mask left too close to the flame until it warped and morphed into a glimpse of hell. The monstrous child dropped the rabbit, fell to her knees, and fixing her blinded doll eyes on Nell, began to creep closer like a spider in its web. Wake up, Nell. A twisted hand reached towards Nell's ankle as she frantically stabbed buttons. Then with a shudder the doors closed and the lift clanked upwards again.

The old nightmare of being chased was one that she had had before. Always an old building, where she tried to lose her assailant by changing direction and floors. It usually ended up with her on the roof when she would finally wake up. But this was different; too vivid. The lift door opened and she erupted like a cork, her ponytailed hair whipping from side to side as she ran. A clatter from behind revealed that another lift door had just opened and before she could stop herself she had turned round. It was him, the other figure from her childhood, but this nightmare character had not invaded her dreams since she was very small. His head hung down as he shuffled forward. Then he saw her and like a pointer his body stiffened. The long leather coat flapped around his skinny legs as he broke into a run. Long greasy hair trailed behind like a tattered banner. The bells from his jester's hat clanging like an alarm. Nell turned to run and then she was flying, the dark walls streaked as she went faster and faster. She was heading for the same double doors again and as she came closer they swung open. Beyond was the garden at Lark House. If only she could make it to her tree house she would be safe, invisible. But already she was slowing and then her feet hit the concrete again.

"I see you, little spy." He was right behind her, but she was nearly at the doors which had changed to resemble the garden gate. As she took a step forward they slyly shut with a groan of rusty iron. The sunny garden with her tree house was gone and so was her only escape.

"What did you do?" came the taunting voice just behind. Just dreaming, Nell reminded herself. This is nothing but a bloody nightmare and you have had enough now. Nell, wake up.

"Wake up, Nell!" she shouted defiantly as he took a step closer.

He cackled, revealing brown stained teeth through the Mr Punch mask. "Won't make it go away though, will it, Eleanor? Or me."

She felt the scream rip her new stitches, and smash her bruised ribs as she woke back in her hospital bed. Trying to halt her gasping, she listened for the nurses' feet. Had the scream been real or just in her nightmare? But all was quiet apart from the hushed voices around her. Safe then. She tried to relax her bunched muscles and in the end attempted to sit up. A soft rosy dawn was blooming through the window so there was no point trying to sleep again, and anyway sleep was no longer the sanctuary it had been. Diablo; she had not dreamed of him since she had been tiny. Now her nights as well as her days were filled with fear. A movement outside her curtain made her turn. One pointed end of a jester's hat poked through the gap, its bell jingling. Then a sharp chin and hooked nose. This time her scream was real and the hideous image dissolved as a nurse thrust aside the curtains and rushed to her bedside. A soft cackle came from under the bed and ignoring the pain, Nell threw her face into her hands and sobbed.

8

I only realise I am awake again when something moves in the corner. I open my eyes, not that it matters, for in this impenetrable blackness I can only see the specks of colour that my mind amuses itself with. Sometimes I pretend I can see the grey outline of the door, but what use is a door if it is locked? I read once in a history book about a dungeon called an oubliette. They were usually bottle shaped and the prisoner would be dropped inside, the entrance covered up, and there they would lie in total darkness until they starved to death, or died of having their legs and arms broken when they were dropped in. I had read the words at the time and written my homework for class, while listening to my music and munching on a biscuit. Homework finished I thought no more of it. I forgot about the oubliette.

I am remembering now.

9

Sunday

"Yeah, cheers, mate." Gary waved off the taxi driver then fumbled for his key. Was he still pissed or was this a hangover already? Either way he felt like piss. The scene that greeted him in the hallway did nothing to improve his mood. He had hastily grabbed Nell's clothes which he had previously chucked down the stairs, and shoved them into the open suitcase, to create an illusion that Nell had been carrying the case when she fell downstairs. What a car crash. He lit a fag and flicked the switch on the kettle. Taking slow drags he felt the nicotine infuse his aching muscles and head, calming and soothing him. Shaking his head he thought back over the night.

Why did she do it? There was no need for a drama. Why did women do so much crying and shouting? He was the one who should be feeling angry. They had all been having such a good night then she had arrived with her prissy ways and humiliated him in front of everyone. Why did she purposely annoy him? She knew he would lose it, and then she played the victim for days afterwards. The girl should have been happy he proposed. He thought it would cheer her up, especially after all the shit she'd gone through with her Nana.

A worm of relief wriggled somewhere deep and he immediately felt guilty. Nell's Nana had never liked him. Oh, she had been polite and tried to take an interest but it was obvious she thought her granddaughter could do better. But he wished he could have been there for Nell. She was always so strong, she had had to be with all the crap about her parents, so it was nice when she collapsed in his arms so he could protect her, when she was vulnerable. For all his faults he did love her, he supposed he always had.

At the back of his mind he remembered the call he had received in the hospital and felt his anger rise again. Mel – or was it Michelle – had just been a bit of fun while he was away, and how she got his number was a mystery. Had she looked at his phone while he was asleep? Bitch. He had told her the score, and now she was ringing him, trying to cause trouble.

Fag finished, he contemplated lighting another but a coffee was more appealing. Stretching, he heard the muscles in his shoulders and back pop, and then changed his mind. Sleep was top of his agenda. It had been a long day and tomorrow would probably be even longer. He dragged himself upstairs, stripped off his clothes and threw himself into bed. Nell's perfume rose to meet him as he sprawled across her side of the bed. As he closed his eyes he saw Nell's face, red and blotchy, eyes swollen and brimming with tears. He felt a moment of shame then wrapped himself back in his mantle of self pity and fell asleep.

Gary rarely dreamed, but in the early hours of Sunday morning he did. He was a teenager again and getting ready for school. Stuffing his football boots into his school bag, he prayed the zip would not break. He then threw his empty PE bag behind the bins and made his way to the bus stop. He was late; Mrs Rogers' car was already pulling out of their plastic corrugated car port, oblivious to the fact that for the kids of Yew Tree Estate, she was a more accurate measure of time than their five pound watches from the market. Gary broke into a trot and arrived just as the school bus breached the hill. It was packed; kids were already standing. That meant he had to push himself to the front of the queue so he could get one of the last few standing places on the lower deck, or he would be forced to go upstairs. Last time that had happened Gary's football kit had gone out of the window, which was why he stuffed it in his school bag now. PE bags were smaller and always easy targets. Not that Gary was a wimp. At fourteen he was already showing promise of height and was popular in his class; his skill on the football field ensured that. But the stop after his was the infamous Hawthorn estate and the kids from there were universally feared. Elbowing his way onto the bus, he showed his pass, soft like felt from too much folding and where he used the once firm cardboard to pick out dirt from his finger nails. From under his heavy fringe he surveyed the back of the lower deck and spied a spare seat next to his mate, Andy. Andy had stashed his bag there to save it for Gary and was pushing away anyone who tried to sit there.

'Piss off, pizza face.' Gary felt a moment's regret as a small boy with bad acne made way reluctantly so Gary could sit down. But he got his own back because all the way to school he was forced to stand next to Gary and when he farted, Gary got most of it in his face. Pizza face was shouted at and amazingly a space appeared in the crowded aisle, while the scarlet-faced boy pretended that his mum's fried breakfast had not given him eggy farts and that no one knew it was him. The bus came to a jolting halt at the next stop and the long line of Hawthorn kids looked through the windows to suss out the space situation.

She had got her hair cut. The ponytail was gone and a wave of rippling curls the colour of vanilla ice cream bounced down her shoulders. The grey nylon skirt was beginning to be too tight for her newly budding hips and it stretched across small high buttocks. She was laughing as she stepped onto the bus, looking back to her friend as she flashed her bus pass. The driver received a polite smile. Reassured that her attention was elsewhere, Gary allowed himself the luxury of a three second full on gaze at the object of his crush. Melanie Dickson. A flush of warm bubbles smoothed its way over his skin and he was incapable of preventing the soppy smile on his face. At that second Melanie Dickson walked by and seeing the big smile on the boy from maths class she tentatively smiled back.

Her blue eyes made contact with his and a shock of adrenalin shocked his system. The blush was hideous and purple, staining his whole body. Agonising embarrassment sent spasms through his body but she had moved on and disappeared up the stairs. Melanie Dickson was not afraid of the top deck. Over the bus's engine he could hear her feet clip up the stairs and find a seat. Right above him.

For the rest of the day he looked out for her. He knew her timetable and felt where she was in the school. He made an excuse to dash back to his locker because he knew she would pass that way to her next class. Then he rounded a corner and she was in front of him. She hesitated, smiled shyly and then walked on. Gary's face burned, but she had smiled at him. Second time that day. Finally, just after lunch he scored a hat trick, well sort of. Watching from a window, he spied her sitting on a wall in the playground. She was alone and he wondered what she was thinking. He remembered the smiles from earlier but she wasn't smiling now. As if aware she was being watched she frowned up at his window. Did she feel his eyes on her? Did she see him? The frown faltered and she looked older. But then that nerdy friend of hers, Eleanor, called her name and she was all smiles again as she made room on the wall.

Gary stirred in his sleep, then aware he needed a piss, rolled out of bed and lumbered to the bathroom. As he stood for what seemed an eternity, he thought back to the dream. How Melanie Dickson had befriended Nell was always a puzzle to him. As they got older their differences were even more marked; Nell was into art and books while for Melanie it was make-up and boys. But perhaps their shared miserable family lives had proved an invisible bond. He would never know and Nell never talked about her past.

Melanie Dickson, he shook off and bumbled back to bed with a smile on his face. They had never gone out but finally when he was fifteen he got to snog her. Lying alone in bed he indulged himself in the memory. His mates and him had gatecrashed her party. Her mum was away and she had thrown herself an early birthday party. Everyone had brought some booze, stolen from home or the local Co-op, or they had got older friends or siblings to buy or nick it.

Melanie had brought out a dusty bottle of her uncle's home-made wine which had been lethal. Had Nell been there? Gary could not remember clearly, because all that remained was when he had got Melanie alone in her mum's bedroom. They had both been drunk, and Gary had been sick shortly afterwards. She had been coming from the loo and he had grabbed her hand and dragged her into the room. The curtains were open and the amber glare from the street light outside had shone on the double bed.

'No, Gary, get off me,' but he had pushed her on to the candlewick bedspread. Her skirt had ridden up and knowing he had only a few seconds before she clouted him he had shoved his hand between her legs. He had wanted it to be romantic, but there was no time. He climbed on top of her and pushed her shirt up. At the sight of her bra he nearly hesitated but she was squirming like a worm and shouting at the top of her voice. He slammed his mouth over hers while furiously groping bare skin. A luckily aimed knee brought the moment to a close and she had never spoken to him again. But as a first sexual encounter it had not been too bad, and he added bits when he told his mates who had been suitably impressed.

The adult Gary smiled; no point wasting a good memory and some rare privacy.

Sunday morning
"Nell, how you feeling?"

Gary's strained voice hinted at a sleepless night, and went as far as trying out for a sleepless night full of worry and regret. But Nell wasn't buying it.

"Yeah, slept about an hour. Black and blue from the beating and feeling like shit." Nell was not in the mood for making Gary feel better.

"Yeah, OK, I'm sorry. Look when do I collect you?"

Nell took a deep breath. It seemed strange holding her mobile up to her right ear; she normally used her left, but the newly glued up eyebrow wanted its space.

"About an hour, or I can call a cab?"

"Don't be daft. Do I go to A & E or are you somewhere else?"

Nell had thought about this and decided that the difficulty non-emergencies had parking would play into her hands perfectly. Gary would end up having to find one of the barrier controlled car parks at the back of the hospital and this would give her more valuable minutes.

"A & E, but could you pick up some painkillers and antiseptic at the Co-op on the way?" At least another 10 minutes.

"Yeah, yeah. I'll get it now and come on up to see you. You've forgiven me then?"

Nell's fingernails pin-cushioned her soft palms for a second as a whip of anger lashed through.

"We can talk about that later."

The call ended; she had done it. Leaning back on the cosy cab seating she noticed Celeste regarding her quizzically.

"So?"

"What?"

"Did he fall for it?" said Celeste patiently.

Nell allowed herself a small smile, then winced as her scabs pulled.

"Yep. He should be leaving the house any second and then I've got about an hour, max."

Celeste repositioned her ample body in the taxi seat and smiled happily.

"An hour will be plenty."

Nell had lied. She had not managed an hour's sleep it had been more like ten minutes. But that had been long enough to have a terrifying nightmare about her own childhood phantom, Diablo; the man in the leather coat and Mr Punch mask. She had finally managed to wake herself up and for the rest of the time she sweated in the hard bed and listening to the noise around her and wondered why she had let things get so bad. Why did she not get the police involved like a normal person? Was she really so feeble? But then Nell had been pushed around all her life and she readily admitted it. Maybe losing both parents when she was so young had flawed her as Gary said. The bottom line of it was that as much as she hated to admit it, she was always trying to please people. If she did as she was told and did not make waves she would be liked. If people liked her then they would not leave her. Then she would not be alone. Calling the police and involving them meant she would have had to admit to the shame that she had been living in. Yes, she let the man she loved beat her because he was the only link to her past. Yes, she was too afraid and too pathetic to stand up to him. At the back of her mind was always the possibility that he might go too far and kill her. It was her fault. The shame was too much. They would ask questions, questions that she did not want to answer.

But the sight of herself in the mirror at the hospital had convinced her that this was her only chance of escape. If she stayed then Gary would find out about the money and she would never get rid of him.

"Is that him?"

She had found Celeste's card in her purse: the friendly taxi driver from the funeral. Somehow she had told her the sketchy plan and Celeste had seemed overjoyed to get involved. Now from their parking space four doors down they watched Gary leave the house and get in the car. He was wearing the shirt she got him for his birthday and for one moment her resolve wobbled. Then she raised her fingers to her glued eyebrow and winced. Feeling sick her resolve steadied itself again.

Gary started the engine, did an expert three-point turn, then drove right past the taxi where Nell had hastily flattened herself on the seat.

"Right," she whispered once he was out of sight, "here we go."

Nell had not expected Celeste to help carry things but she had looked at Nell's battered appearance and heavy eyes and insisted. She had even rung the garage where Nell's car was languishing and got them to agree she could pick it up later.

"How do you do that?" Nell had asked in astonishment. "They told me Monday morning."

But Celeste had just batted away the question. "Your car's ready it's just that the service team don't work weekends. One of the sales people said they'd have the keys ready."

And again Nell was grateful for ringing Celeste, knowing she would have got a different answer.

What do you pack when you have so little time? She was not going on holiday. She started by emptying drawers into her suitcase but then stopped. She would not have room. And what did she want with so many socks and pieces of underwear? In the end she packed some favourite clothes that she, rather than Gary, had bought; her beloved Doc Martens that Gary hated and had banished to the spare wardrobe, her watered silk dress in rich plum that Gary said made her look fat. Jeans and trousers, T-shirts and skirts. A few ancient but classic items that she could also wear to work. Work! Now there was a problem for another day and time. Toiletries and medication, personal documents including her passport, which thankfully lived in a concertina file in the study. Nana's precious albums, her artwork and finally she was facing the bookshelf. The CDs and DVDs faced her silently. Which could she take? Celeste returned from a decanting trip to the cab.

"Anything from the kitchen?"

Nell felt weary, time was running out.

"I don't think so."

"There's an iPod."

"Oh God, yes."

"You got a camera? Any jewellery? Come on girl, think."

Fifteen minutes later Nell was back in the cab which was now filled with her suitcase, two holdalls, her large portfolio of art work, and the two collapsible crates she normally used for the laundry stacked with toiletries, shoes, books and other items she could not leave. Without Celeste this would have been impossible.

What had she left? Like a demented bag woman she touched each bag, case and crate and recited the contents. Some of Nana's stuff was in the loft but she did not have time for that.

Her mobile began to trill. Gary. It went to message and immediately rang again.

87

"Time to go." Celeste muttered ruefully and heaved the cab into the road.

"I suggest we get your car and then go somewhere quiet where you can load up. But to be honest, love, you look like shit and I don't think you should be driving too far."

Gary finally left a message, if you could call an inhumane roar of 'I'll kill you, you fucking whore' a message.

Nell switched her attention back to Celeste.

"Good idea. A hotel out of town somewhere where my car can't be seen from the road."

The thought of an anonymous bed made her feel faint.

"Better get your car now. He'll come back to the house first, see you've packed, then head straight for the garage."

Nell was just collapsing back onto the slippery seat when Celeste jumped on the brake and the boot sale assortment of belongings clattered together.

"Damn tabby cat. Look at him, stood in the road."

Nell peered through the glass.

"Oh God, it's Jester."

"He yours? We can pick him up but I'm telling you now, the moment I smell hot cat shit I'm gonna vomit."

But Jester regarded the cab for a moment and the black woman driver scowling down at him, and elegantly bounced out of the road and disappeared over a wall.

"I can't take him anyway," said Nell quietly. "I don't really know where I'm going."

With a roar they butted into the heavy Sunday traffic. Shoppers heading for the supermarkets, retired couples on the way to Homebase and B&Q. Everyone looked relaxed and in no hurry to let a black taxi change lane.

"Shit, we're never going to make it." Nell's phone rang again and angrily she buried it in her bag.

"If we're stuck in traffic then so is he. Thank you, mate." Celeste raised a large arm, bingo wings wobbling, to salute a young kid who had let her out. His fiesta was packed with similar baseball capped spotty kids, heavy bass booming out. For a moment Nell thought he had let them out by accident but he saluted back graciously as Celeste moved in front and stepped up the speed.

Sunday browsers drifted through the polished cars gleaming in the sun. Blue and white helium balloons bobbed dreamily in the sunlight. A family group scattered in alarm as Celeste hurled into the garage. She screeched to a halt and Nell flew out.

The heavily hair gelled sales lad took one look at Nell's beaten face, his fake smile slid from his face, and he fled out the back to find her keys.

As she waited – and they all waited – for the card machine to chug into action, Nell caught sight of her reflection in the polished glass display cabinet. Some of her rich brown hair was still scraped back in a ponytail while the rest had escaped and fell in soft waves on her bare shoulders. Her face was swollen and already blossoming in the rainbow of bruise colours that would be visible long after the swelling went down. A quintet of red bruises on her upper arm would, she knew, match Gary's fingers perfectly. But it would be the last time, she thought feverishly. Once the bruises faded there would be no more.

"Finally. Sorry about the delay, Miss Montague." As he handed back her card his eyes drifted to her eye. His mouth opened to say something but he hesitated.

"Thank you. I really appreciate you putting yourself out like this, but I couldn't wait until tomorrow."

"Will you be alright?"

For a moment Nell's facade threatened to crash around her ankles, but she managed a half smile and bravely met the boy's eyes.

"Now I've got my car I will. I mean what I say, I really appreciate it."

And there it was; her little red Ford KA. For a moment she wondered how she would get all her possessions into it but that was a problem for tomorrow.

She and Celeste had suggested and discarded a number of different guest houses and small hotels. But then Nell had been struck with genius; Gary didn't know about the money, he would be looking for her at either Lark House or in a cheap Travelodge. Ten miles out of town stood the Abbey Park Hotel. Expensive, hidden by tall walls and thick woodlands, it was also on the Devon road. Perfect.

Nell followed Celeste in her big cab as she meandered along the tiny road which would eventually take them to Abbey Park. The cattle grid at the beginning of the park meant that sheep could graze happily in the grounds and Nell couldn't resist peeping out at the scruffy woolly bundles which regarded her passing. As they went further into the parkland one thought kept crossing her mind; Gary would never think to find her here.

Everything hurt; her skin stung, her muscles ached, the light was too bright. Each movement brought a protest from some part of her body and the roar of blood in her ears told her she was physically exhausted. There was one final cattle grid that stopped the sheep getting to the hotel, and as Nell drove over it she felt that her head was going to split apart and all her scabs scrape off. Grabbing her inhaler she took as deep a breath as she could manage through her bruised ribs and went to face the receptionist.

Once again she was grateful for Celeste's presence as she hastily completed the hotel's paperwork. Part of her had thought about using a false name but what was the point? Gary would never dream of looking for her here.

"I will just dump my stuff, Celeste, then can I treat you to a late breakfast?"

The smile that spread across Celeste's face was all the answer she needed.

Her room was on the second floor and feeling she had earned it after her near sleepless night, she stepped into the plush lift. For a second she had a flashback from the weird dream of that morning, but this lift was carpeted and snug. In fact, once Nell and her suitcase was in, there really was not much room for anything, or anyone else.

As the doors closed she was enveloped by silence. The back wall was mirrored and in the harsh light she could inspect her battered face in stark detail. No wonder people were staring. The doors opened with a swish and Nell wheeled her case out onto more thick carpet. A sign indicated that room 218 was to her right, so praying she would not meet anyone she headed in that direction. Slotting her key card in, she waited for the green light and loud click. She was in.

The heavy door closed behind her like a dropping portcullis, and in its wake silence fell. Leaving her case by the door she walked slowly into the room. Wallpaper of wide cream and lemon vertical stripes, light blue carpet with a cream speck, two large windows looking out to the hotel's front, a suitcase stand, large built-in wardrobe and desk, and a double bed. There was a small tray with a miniature kettle and assorted sachets of tea, coffee, chocolate and milk. And back by the front door was another door which led to the bathroom.

Nell caught her gentle smile in the large mirror and sighed. She was safe, no one could get in. She could heal here. The wave of dizziness blindsided her and she grabbed the door frame while it lapped at her head. The double bed with its cream and blue flowered cover looked inviting but she could not collapse yet. She was being brave, taking action but at some point exhaustion would claim her and then, she knew, the terror of her situation would hit, and when it did it would floor her more successfully than Gary's punches ever had.

The room was a little stale so she opened one of the large windows. The incessant bleat of the sheep mixed with bird song and the slam of a car door. Peering down Nell could see that Celeste was decanting crates into her Ford KA, and from her body language was finding it a tight squeeze. Nell checked her wallet, thankful that she always kept ample cash on her. That was another habit she had got from Nana who always preferred cash to plastic. For a moment she worried how much all this would cost her, then remembered, money would no longer be the constant headache it once had. But this then reminded her of all the calls and decisions she still had to make. Solicitors, letting agent for the apartment in Devon, bank changes, driving licence, mobile, change of address, solicitor, Mr Austin, work. She tidied her hair, washed her hands, changed into trousers that didn't have a rip in the knee, and then headed back downstairs before the worry could take over. Breakfast first and then she could have a total nervous breakdown this afternoon.

The message came through after breakfast, as she stepped out of the lift on the second floor and walked along the lush carpets to room 218. Breakfast had been in the elegant conservatory which looked out over the formal rose garden. An ornate fountain punctuated the symmetry and Nell was just commenting on it – while buttering a flaky croissant with the heavy knife – when her phone vibrated. She faltered, met Celeste's calm eyes, and determinedly finished her sustenance. They had enjoyed a lovely meal; the coffee was strong, the table linen heavy and spotless, and Nell enjoyed watching Celeste tuck into her bacon baguette. Nell's facial trauma made itself felt as she chewed on her croissant. That and the glances from other guests were a constant reminder that this was not a normal Sunday; she was having breakfast with a total stranger, her life was in boxes in her car, and her body was as wrecked as her relationship.

The message was from Gary of course, and as she watched Celeste's black cab trundle over the cattle grid from her open window, she felt abandoned. She had only ever thought about the escape; how she would get away from him? But that was old news now. Ruby would have been brave, she reminded herself. Steeling herself, she opened the message.

'Come back so we can talk or your scrapbook goes onto the road.'

Bloody hell. That was what she had forgotten. A scrapbook of her childhood days, safely up in the attic. That meant Gary had remembered what else was up there. The reality hit somewhere below her ribs and she reached the spotless toilet bowl just in time before her breakfast made a dramatic reappearance. Her bruised ribs screamed as her stomach lurched again. Dabbing her mouth she was aware of a shrill ring in her ears. Nell staggered to the double bed as dark spots swarmed on the pale wallpaper. She shed her clothes and lay down carefully on the cool bed cover. Time to face reality, but first she had to sleep.

10

Sunday afternoon

Nell slept a sleep so heavy that not even a dream could penetrate. But the loud beep of a car horn outside managed to find her mind lying trapped deep under its mountain of emotional trauma and physical exhaustion, and slowly she surfaced. The afternoon sun had moved; it now flooded through the tall open windows to splash golden on the thick carpet, and lap at the double bed where she lay. At some point she had kicked off the covers because her naked skin was pocked in goose pimples from the fresh breeze which stirred the curtains.

She had no intention of moving. Dragging the cover over the lower part of her body, she slumped back on the bed, closed her eyes and waited to sink back into sleep. But now people were talking outside. The high pitched laughter sounded like a machine gun; relentless and irritating. So in an effort to bring on sleep she resorted to her usual trick of mind stories. It was something she had done since a teenager when sleep had been difficult, and still used when her mind refused to relax. There were several different scenarios; imagining she was in a warm sleeping bag with a storm howling outside her tent, or on a tropical moonlit beach with a cool wind blowing through the palms. But as she tried to hear the rattle of palm trees she realised that nothing was going to work today.

Unbidden, a faint memory of her dad surfaced, of him perched on her bed telling her a made-up story about Nell and her imaginary friend Ruby who would get into scrapes and adventures. Unconsciously, Nell smiled at the memory. She had forgotten where her alter ego had come from until now. Her fresh pyjamas had smelled of sunshine and soap. Tucked into warm flannelette sheets in winter or cool cotton sheets in summer, both her parents had made bedtime fun, a time for painting pictures in her mind which she could enjoy when the light went out.

Sleep came upon her like a rogue wave and hidden treacherously within was the old nightmare. This time she was transported straight to the house where the red-haired girl waited on the stairs. Her eyes were smudged with dark eyeliner which tracked down her pale cheeks marking the path of tears. One second Nell was looking at her, the next she was looking at herself through the girl's eyes. She viewed her seven-year-old self; the grass-stained jeans, the untidy ponytail, eyes too big for her heart shaped face. Then the background faded and she was in an alien bedroom flicking through a teenage magazine.

Rising from a narrow bed to increase the volume on her radio she stumbled slightly on a leg that had gone to sleep. Her small foot sported a braided ankle band and her toenails were painted bubblegum pink. The room was littered with clothes in pastel shades, magazines, and cuddly toys. The girl approached a cluttered white dressing table and Nell was able to see her reflection in the dusty mirror. Dark red hair was combed back from her pixie face and held in place by a black velvet Alice band. Nell felt frustration rage through the small frame as she looked at herself in the mirror; turning first one way and then the other. For a moment Nell wondered what she was so cross about, then the girl ripped off the Alice band and shook her russet tresses free. Grabbing a black eyeliner she peered at the mirror and drew a shaky line around her hazel eyes.

"Ruby. We are leaving in five minutes." The woman's voice, which shot from an unseen source made both Nell and the girl jump.

"OK. Don't keep nagging." The girl's voice was surprisingly high, the slight lisp making her sound younger than she was.

Ruby. Why was her subconscious giving this little girl from her nightmares the name Ruby? A teenage girl with russet hair and a raging temper to match. She was now applying frosted pink lipstick to her cupid's bow. Then with a quick glance to the bedroom door she opened a drawer and brought out a notebook dotted with glittered stickers. The page fell open and inside was a paper tissue. For a moment she brought the tissue to her nose and closing her eyes breathed deeply. It was from him.

The scene shifted again. Ruby – this time in a plaid skirt which Nell recognised as the uniform of St Agatha, the Roman Catholic school – sat on a wall outside the school grounds. Her initial anger at having been kept waiting was dissolving into worry. Where was Mum? A car came by and stopped; it was him. She felt Ruby's face flush as she sprang up and approached the car.

"Sorry, Red. She's held up again. Asked me to come and fetch you home." He smiled and she felt herself how Ruby's face burned.

Ruby grabbed her bag and crossed to the passenger side. The car smelled of aftershave and the leather seat was soft.

"Here, let me help you." He leaned across to help with the seat belt, his hand brushing her arm. Lost for words and drowning in adoration, she smiled her thanks.

"Right, let's get you home."

Peering through the tinted windows she prayed one of her friends would see her. He drove the long way home; chatting about nothing, putting her at ease. His stereo played R and B and Ruby imagined they were tearing down an American highway with the top down and the sun hot on her bare arms.

"Things any better at home?" They had last spoke three weeks ago at a friend of her parents' party. There had been a blazing row and she had stormed off into the garden where he had found her crying. The tissue he gave her was one of her most treasured possessions.

How old was he? she wondered. Older than her anyway. They drew up outside her house and for a moment they just sat there.

"You can always ring me, Red, if things get too much at home."

She nodded, eyes glued to the dashboard.

"It's hard for them. They still see you as a kid – they haven't noticed you're all grown up now."

She turned but before she could speak he brushed her cheek with his lips.

"Off you go now."

She scampered out, cheeks on fire.

"Hey, Red, see you soon."

"Yes," was all she managed before she fled up the driveway. Hugging herself with joy she leaned against her front door, listening for the roar of his car to fade before going inside. He had kissed her. It was not her imagination. He really did like her. Red. It was his nickname for her. In fact she did not think he had ever called her Ruby. She had known him for four months; he worked at one of her dad's clubs but had started doing odd jobs for both her parents. She supposed it was love at first sight; he had been introduced to her and he had winked and smiled.

"Hello, Red." She had been smitten. It could work between them; she reassured herself. She would be sixteen in three years. A girl in her class had left to have a baby. He was right; she wasn't a kid anymore.

Nell stirred and her eyes opened. The full thrill of a first crush still fluttered inside her while her mind recoiled in horror. Dirty deviant. Is that how they did it; perved after young girls eager to be seen as adults? She shook her head. Where the hell had that dream come from? It had felt so real. She was sure Freud would have had something to say. Whoever this Ruby was, she certainly was not Nell's alter ego. That Ruby was everything Nell wasn't, but wished she was. No one would want to be that poor girl being groomed by a paedo. An image flickered in her mind as she remembered her in her usual setting, Butlers Yard. Why her imagination had given her the name Ruby she could not fathom. Too many Rubys collided like dodgems in her trauma-stained mind.

The sun was setting and the sweet air growing cold. It held a hint that summer was nearly over and autumn waiting in the wings. Her mobile revealed that Gary had tried again. But the sleep had done her good and already his power over her was fading. She wanted her scrapbook back but not enough to risk an encounter with Gary. Time to let the past go. Then she thought of a plan. He would be waiting for her, confident that she would turn up. The bins were usually emptied around seven. Gary would drink himself unconscious tonight so if she arrived early she could fish through the bin and retrieve anything of hers.

The bathroom still smelled faintly of vomit and for a moment it halted her hunger. But it soon returned. She needed to eat. The idea of ordering room service was tempting but first she wanted to walk in the cool air outside to clear her head of the ache that was setting in again. The thrill of her new-found independence rose in her again. She could do what she liked without answering to anyone.

She dressed quickly in jeans and a white T-shirt, slightly crum-pled from the speedy packing that morning. Twisting her hair, she fastened it out of the way with a clip, then realising that this accen-tuated her bruises she let if fall again and reached for her brush. An image of Ruby's rich tresses blinded her for a moment. Maybe she had hit her head harder last night than she thought. Was she having hallucinations now, or was this merely the product of emotional stress and an afternoon nap?

The hotel hallway was quiet and steeling herself for the unwanted attention her face would attract, she headed downstairs.

In his room on the floor above, Austin sat at the window reading his emails. Nothing from his contact in Amsterdam, but his pet plod had delivered. Austin smiled and opened the attachment. It might or might not be Montague; it was twenty years and he'd changed his name. Peering at the photo on his screen he searched for similarities between the face before him and the snapshot he had stolen from Lark House. He smiled his lopsided smile. Snap. He had seen eyes like that before and recently. There could be no doubt; the man charged with assault in Devon last year was Nell's father.

11

Monday morning

The birds had been singing for hours and a humid night meant that the inhabitants of Victoria Road had slept with their windows wide open. For those still hoping for a few more minutes in bed the arrival of the refuse lorry was an unwelcome reality. Slowly, the team clattered and slammed their way up the road. Jester viewed them from his wall with contemptuous amber eyes.

Hearing their thundering approach, Gary went to the lounge window. The scrapbook was still inside; he'd checked the bin a few moments ago. She would come, he knew she would, and he would be waiting. He had managed to buy a fairly decent bunch of roses yesterday, and had picked up a holiday brochure. When Nell appeared he would first give her the brochure and then while she picked her apology holiday he would give her the roses. He smiled. That was his Nell; flowers wouldn't do it alone but a holiday would always bring her round. He remembered their first break together. Venice in spring. It had rained non-stop and St Mark's square had been accessible only on duck boards. A haughty woman had slipped on the slimy wood and been forced to step into the flooded square.

Furiously, she had cursed everyone in frantic Italian as she struggled on her stiletto heels to regain the boarding. Nell's laughter was something he most loved about her. She laughed like a little girl, behind her hand; a really infectious belly laugh that could make anyone nearby smile.

He rubbed his chin and the stubble that had surfaced like rows of cut corn, crackled against his palm. He needed to get ready for work or he would be late. Hell. Where was she? Anger had been quickly dissolved last night in half a bottle of Jack Daniels. Quick to follow was a wave of guilt and horror at what he had done, but this was soon replaced by self pity. He loved Nell; he would do anything for her. Would kill for her. All he asked for was that she was faithful and would stay with him forever. Love him as much as he loved her. Not like his mum had been; always criticising and controlling, asking him a hundred times a day if he loved her. They had both worshipped his dad but he was never around much. When he was home his mother worried the house was not clean enough, that she did not have his favourite tea ready. Gary would be in the way then and she would nag him as if to prove what a good mother she was being. Gary had spent as much time away from home as he could; sports, or hanging around on bikes with his mates, their houses, the industrial estate where they smoked in the evening away from prying eyes.

Then there had been girls. Lots of girls. He had even gone out with Cindy once. With Nell it was different. But she was so secretive, so quiet. Even to this day he did not know much about her childhood. She made him so angry with her mousy ways but then at other times she was so independent and strong that he was frightened she was going to leave him, that she did not need him. And that stunt yesterday, when all he wanted to do was pick her up from hospital and look after her, well that just made him mad. It hurt him too. He had been stupid, but then he had been drinking. She just took it all too seriously. He had planned to pick her up from hospital and take her for breakfast. He had even put fresh clothes in the car for her to change into. Well she had left him now, but she would be back.

The refuse team were nearly at the house. He scanned the road for any signs of her. Then the phone rang.

"Fuck it!"

It would be someone from work wanting a lift. He would ignore it. But the sudden hope that it might be Nell made him dash to the hall and grab the receiver.

"Hello?" The answering machine had activated. Swearing, he stabbed the button to shut off his own voice inviting a message to be left.

"I said, hello?"

There was a clatter then a car door slammed. Too late, he realised he had been had. He threw open the front door in time to see Nell's pale face and red car tear down the street.

Grabbing his mobile he stabbed buttons but he was greeted by her message.

"Nell, for fuck's sake. I just want to talk. I've got you flowers and I was going to surprise you with a holiday." He looked down at the brochure. "Anywhere you like. My treat. Please, I'm sorry." His voice broke then and unashamedly he wept down the phone. "Please, Nell. I love you. Give me a second chance."

What the hell was he going to do without her? God, he'd really screwed up this time.

The scrapbook had been left wrapped in a plastic bag but still a faint acidic tang of bin drifted into the car. Smiling until her stitches pulled, Nell congratulated herself. She had done it.

Nell had woken with the birds at five. A tsunami of pure terror had collided with her shortly after and for an hour she had shook and wept as she curled up in her no man's land. She couldn't go back and wasn't sure how to go forward. The apartment in Devon now took on a phantom form of a dark, damp, rundown basement in an isolated Victorian mansion, straight out of a gothic horror. She pictured herself spending a lonely, dark winter with no friends, no hope, and no purpose. Perhaps she could get a job, but what reference would Mr Page give her now? And she liked her job. Gary had once threatened to storm into work and tell everyone about her family secrets.

'Let's see if they still respect you when they know about the slut's precious mummy and daddy.' It was not an idle threat; Gary was capable of anything when he was angry.

She had money, but where would she go? Perhaps abroad, but would that not be even more isolating? Finally, she had made a coffee, showered and decided that if she could not bear to think about her future, she would try just one hour at a time. By now it was six fifteen and she knew Gary would be watching the bin, having probably only put the scrapbook in that morning. So she dressed hastily, grabbed her keys and headed for the car park. As she drove over the cattle grid, her belongings creaking and groaning in the back, she lowered her window and inhaled the fresh morning air. It had rained in the night and the ground was releasing its sweet fragrance to the morning sun. Six thirty; just one hour at a time, and the only task she had to think about was rescuing her childhood memories.

Seven thirty; now back in her room and with her scrapbook safe, she felt flushed with success. Also on her list of things to do were changing her address at the bank, credit cards, getting a new mobile number, and letting her solicitor have the number, ringing work, and ringing Mr Austin. Sitting at the table by her window, she slowly turned the pages of her scrapbook. Birthday cards from her parents, postcards from family holidays, a key with a parcel tag attached with her writing on. Finally the photos; the three of them at her seventh birthday party, sitting on a beach with Nana and Dad, and her first day at school, aged four and proud in her new uniform. For a moment she looked at her own smiling face and innocent eyes and mourned for the loss of her parents and her childhood. Why did it have to be such a mess? She had gone from being happy with two parents, to having just one parent, then none, so quickly that she sometimes wondered if she had missed something vital? It was all so foggy, and just when she thought she could remember something clearly it dissolved again. Now even Nana had left her. But she had things to do and people to ring and the time for indulgent memory lane strolling would have to wait.

9.45am. Wrapping a length of hair around her middle finger, Nell waited for an answer. Sitting in the hotel lounge made her feel like a business woman. She was about to break into her old habit of imagining she was Ruby, but then a memory of the disturbing dream of Ruby the teenager stopped her. This unwelcome appearance of the other Ruby made daydreaming uncomfortable now and it was high time she stopped relying on the childhood fantasies of her dad's stories. Ruby did not exist; she was made up to sooth a small child and stupidly she had carried her all these years as a link to her dad. Always imagining how Ruby would cope with events that Nell was clearly making a hash of. Childish and stupid; always running back to her daydreams and her pretend life so that she could avoid facing up to her shambolic reality. Even Nana's funeral; pretending she was Ruby had got her in Celeste's cab. She had always wondered if she had been a little more like Ruby then perhaps her dad would not have left; but she was lying to herself. Her dad had not just left; he had run away. Not from her but from the police. Her mum had never said what he had done, but she remembered men in suits and knocks on the door which had left her mum shaken and needing to lie down.

"Austin." For a moment she was flustered, not having expected him to answer.

"Umm, hello?"

"Yes?"

"It's Nell Montague, we…err. You asked me to ring."

The tone changed.

"Miss Montague. Thank you for ringing."

In the background she heard the shattering of high pitched laughter; or was it coming from outside?

"You said we should meet. I'm free this morning," she suggested hesitantly.

"Excellent. Might I suggest The Fourways Inn at eleven? It lies just out of town. Or would you like to name somewhere more convenient…?"

The Fourways was one of the big Gastro pubs not a mile from where she was staying. Its children's play area and attractive lakeside location made it popular with the business community, with mummies who didn't have to work, and with ladies who brunched, lunched or had cream teas. It would be busy with people and therefore safe.

It was after she had ended the call that she remembered Mrs Harrington-Brown from the nursing home. She had seemed familiar with Mr Austin. It would have been sensible to get some background information first. Feeling stupid she rang the number which still came up as 'Nana's manager' only to be told that Mrs Harrington-Brown was in a meeting but would call her back. That would have to do for now; it was ten o'clock and she had to get ready. But what for? Was he a solicitor of some sort? Then surely his card would have said so.

At ten to eleven she scrunched to a standstill in the gravel car park of The Fourways Inn. There were already a number of cars including a couple of multi-people carriers with child booster seats. Dressed simply in a tan linen skirt and her old favourite white sleeveless linen shirt she looked what she hoped was smart-casual. She had no iron and her hasty packing showed in the creases, but then linen always looked creased didn't it? The swelling on her face had begun to reduce as the bruises came out. But after a day in the hotel she was used to second looks. It was part of her past and no longer her problem or her shame.

She was purposely early to gain the advantage. Now perched awkwardly on the edge of an oversized leather sofa, peering ostensibly at the lake, she kept an eye on the main door and allowed her cappuccino to go cold. She was nervous, unsettled; the last forty-eight hours had turned her life about and now nothing seemed familiar or real. Just then there was a roar of engines as a convoy of sports cars arrived outside; the same model of soft tops in a selection of different colours. They parked up in a flock of grey hair, headscarves and tweed jackets. They entered the pub with all the excitement of a school outing, calling to each other and loudly recounting their journey. Apparently Daffers and Lionel had taken a wrong turning so mobiles were extracted and finally a loud conversation managed to locate them and offer directions. Nell was so intent on watching their antics that she nearly missed the tall, tanned, middle-aged gentleman who approached her table with an open hand.

"Miss Montague." The hand she clasped was dry and firm, it spoke of holding reins or steering yachts. She recognised his cologne from the funeral but not his face. An image of a Sardinian marina or a Paris hotel appeared as she inhaled.

He ordered espresso from the bar. Nell noticed how the barmaid extracted herself from the car club to take his order. How long would she have waited, thought Nell, if she had not got in before them? Yet Mr Austin seeped importance. He must have money, she thought; but it was not just wealth, it was power.

"How can I help you, Mr Austin?"

"Before I go any further, and please just call me Austin. May I ask a personal question? It is important otherwise I would not be so rude."

Immediately on the defensive, Nell nodded, but added, "No promises I'll answer though."

He accepted this. "Who did this to you?" He indicated her bruises with a wave of his manicured hand.

Nell's face flushed painfully and she put a hand to her face.

"I am so sorry to ask but what I am about to tell you makes it necessary."

No more shame, thought Nell. Her bruises were not her fault and she had covered up for Gary long enough.

"My boyfriend did this on Saturday night. I left him on Sunday morning. I won't be back."

He seemed relieved.

"I thought perhaps, but no matter, I need to tell you something. About your father."

Is this what she had expected? Nell couldn't be sure, yet somehow had she not thought of her father the first time she had laid eyes on Austin.

She nodded, giving permission for him to continue.

"How much do you remember about him leaving?"

"Not much. He was there, then suddenly he wasn't and my mum and grandmother whispered in corners. They were angry; I was sent to stay with Nana." That was not quite true, she remembered more, but that was her business.

"This may come as a shock. Well, unfortunately there is some evidence that he may have been involved with unlawful activity. He was a teacher, was he not? We believe he may have taught in France for some time after he left, but then his trail goes cold. In fact, until recently it was strongly believed he had been killed. But you don't believe that do you? I saw your advertisement. I have been asked to investigate his current whereabouts, alive or dead."

Nell hoped her face gave nothing away. Perhaps she knew more than he did. Strongly believed he had been killed, not died, she noticed. But he was not finished yet.

"Nell you need to be aware that other people may also be looking for your father. They may contact you."

He had dropped the formal 'Miss Montague' she noticed. Once this trivial piece of information had been filed then her mind accepted what she had always guessed. If her dad was alive he was keeping away from her because of his past. As a child she had not been above listening at doors, or at walls with a glass to her ear.

"So why do you and these other people think I know where he is?"

"There is now a strong belief that your grandmother may have kept in touch with him all these years. With her passing it is possible he will be remembered in her will."

The sunny roof terrace and her solicitor, Mr Elliot, floated into her mind. Had he not said that her father was a 'separate matter'?

"I don't understand. Why do you all want him?"

"Unfortunately, some property belonging to another disappeared at the same time as your father. They would like it returned."

"What?" The careful use of words – no doubt used to avoid her unnecessary embarrassment – was beginning to get on her nerves.

"What are we actually talking about here? Drugs, money?" That could not be right, Nell thought. Her dad may have been involved with something which made him vulnerable to blackmail, but she was confident it was no more than that. But Austin shrugged his elegant shoulders.

"I am so sorry. I know no more."

Bullshit.

"Bullshit. Let me summarise. You and these 'other people'," she air quoted in an unconscious imitation of Mr Page at his most irritating, "think that twenty-three years ago my dad stole something and you all want it back. But you don't know what it is."

"Please, Nell, you are best not knowing."

"This is my dad you're talking about. He wasn't some sort of international crook."

"No he was not, but he may have been out of his depth with something. Made a mistake. He paid the ultimate price to escape; he lost his family."

"No. How dare you?"

"Sit down, Nell. I am trying to help you."

"That's bull."

"Nell, people are looking for him. They might try to find him through you. You need my help."

"And, sorry, who do you work for again?" Her raised voice was attracting unwelcome attention. "And why has no one ever approached me or my grandmother before? He's been missing all these years and no one has been bothered. Then my grandmother dies, I stick an ad in a paper on the off-chance that he might be alive and see it, and suddenly the Mafia are hunting me down. Do you honestly expect me to believe this?"

"If he gets in touch with you please tell me, or ask him to ring me. But, Nell, please be careful."

"Who are you?"

"You are in danger."

"Yes, right. Funnily enough I know a little about that." She indicated her face.

She stood to leave and was surprised he did not attempt to stop her. The car club watched on in interest.

"Oh, and don't worry about my dad getting in touch with me. He's not bothered for over twenty years so I'm sure as hell he isn't going to bother now. And if he does try, he won't be able to bloody find me because I'm taking a leaf out of his book; I'm going to disappear."

"Devon?"

She stopped dead, her hand frozen on the door handle.

"Keep away from me." Furiously, she blinked away tears.

Then for the second time that day she rushed to her car and sped off.

Seven miles away the scene of a crime team were fingerprinting the penthouse offices of Davies & Brown solicitors. A shaken Mr Elliot had finished being questioned and was preparing to ring his clients. At the top of his list was Eleanor Montague.

Tuesday morning

Just how many items could you stuff into a Ford KA? More than you would suppose, thought Nell ruefully. The reception staff at the hotel had risen a few eyebrows as she carried her possessions from the narrow lift, across the carpeted foyer and out of the revolving doors. Thankfully, most of it had been decanted from Celeste's chunky black cab on Sunday straight into Nell's car. Now she poked the last possessions into the front seat well and prayed that she would not have to brake suddenly. Satisfied that another job was complete she ventured back into the hotel and headed for the dining hall and breakfast.

Gary did not do breakfast, and so Nell had got out of the habit. A gulp of black coffee then a cigarette in the car was about as far as he got, claiming that breakfast was a waste of time and you might as well wait for lunch. That was why Gary making her breakfast on Saturday had been such a treat. The familiar wave of pain rose at the thought, like one of those trick party candles that relit however many times you blew it out. Nell's pain flared up again and again, only to be blown out by her anger.

Curious glances and double looks greeted her as she grabbed a plate and took her place in the queue. Being careful not to drop anything she placed sausage, bacon and egg on her plate and headed for an empty table by the window. She smiled her thanks as a pot of coffee arrived, and settled down to satisfy her growling stomach. Not easy to sit alone, but looking at the reflection of the dining room in the window opposite she noticed other singletons; some on business with laptops and mobile devices in action, but others without such crutches. She wondered about the other people having breakfast, pondered what their stories were. An elderly woman in designer gear twenty years too young for her, kept checking her mobile, then her make-up and hair in a tiny mirror. There was something odd about her lips and Nell realised that she was probably looking at the results of too much Botox. She did not look happy. Nearby a portly man sweated in his shirt and tie, he glanced at his watch then noticed the egg he had dropped on his tie earlier. He saw Nell watching and good naturedly smiled and raised his eyes upwards as he furiously rubbed it with a napkin. Nell felt the smile on her face as she returned his smile and strangely it gave her confidence. The forty-eight hours in the hotel had been the chrysalis she had wanted, but quite what she was emerging as was yet to be defined. Should she stay longer? The thought was tempting but the longer she stayed the greater the chance that her nerve might leave her and she might go crawling back to Gary, or that he might find her. So she paid her bill at the reception, left her door card, and headed for the car park.

Route planner on the front seat beside her, handbag on top, sunglasses on her head and a tissue up her sleeve, she turned the key in the ignition and took a deep breath. This was it then; in a few miles she would hit the roundabout where she either turned back into Wiltbury and faced the music, or onto Devon and her new life. She eased the car into first gear, took off the handbrake and slowly crunched over the gravel. As she drove along the narrow road, past the grazing cattle and grubby sheep, she turned the radio on. Elton John declared he was still standing, and smiling, Nell turned up the volume.

12

My dear boy,

*I hope my letter finds you well. I hope my letter finds you. Your girls
have settled in. All is well. Please do not worry. I wonder if you
will reply. Perhaps it will be reminiscent of when you were away
at school. How I longed for your one-sided scribbled missives which
said so much yet told me so little. What did I care for history and
English lessons? I wanted to know how you were feeling.*

*Perhaps I should start this letter again. Your girls will be
fine eventually but at the moment the younger creeps around the
house fearfully, jumping at any sudden noise. Breakfast is a tense
affair, just E and I. She gazes at me mutely, but when she thinks
I am not looking her eyes dart to the window or the doorway. The
moment the postman's bicycle is heard clanking against the railings
outside she jumps from her seat as if electrocuted and hovers by
the kitchen door. I have now learned that she is waiting for my
permission to go to the front door and collect the post. How long will
she wait for your letter before she realises that this horrible time does
not have a limit. This is how our lives will be for now. She does not*

understand, poor lamb, and there is nothing I can tell her, is there? So she drifts from room to room, looking for something, someone.

Your eldest girl has disappeared into herself. She sleeps and cries. Something is thrown in her room, something slammed into the door. Then she is angry and her shouting makes me shudder. I fear the old problem is back, though I can hardly blame her. But I do blame her. And I blame you. What good did telling her do you? You have lost everything.

But we must move on. So, my boy, write if you can. I use Davies and Brown solicitors; perhaps they would agree to be our go-between. So take care and never forget that you are in my thoughts and prayers. Please keep safe. I feel sure that things will blow over and then we can all be together. In the meantime I will keep your family together as best I can, and wait for word.

Tuesday morning

Austin was locking his case when his mobile rang. Morgan. He smiled and answered.

"Good morning, Morgan."

There was a laugh from the other end. "It is now I've had your email."

Austin allowed himself a smile.

"So," Morgan concluded, "you think you've managed to track him down."

"I believe so, but we have a long way to go yet."

"But we are finally getting somewhere. Tell me we are getting somewhere?"

"We still have to convince him to return your property."

"If he didn't sell it already."

"The transaction would have left a trace. He still has it somewhere."

"I need to know, Austin. I don't care so much for my property, but I need to know what happened. Where she is. Get it sorted for me."

"No problem. Now I need to finish packing because a certain young lady has just checked out."

110

Austin grabbed his jacket, then paused. He looked at his phone display. His conversation with Morgan had been one minute and four seconds. However many conversations he had they were never one minute eleven. One minute eleven was just enough time to say 'I worry...'

'Well don't. I am honestly fine.'

'Are you having a nice time?'

'It's alright. Anyway I've got to go.'

'I love you—' But she was already speaking to someone else, giving them her full attention.

'Lily?'

'Love you too. Bye.'

Then that night.

'Don't worry, Dad. See you soon.'

If only he had kept the text, recorded the call. But how are you to know that a one minute eleven second conversation with your eighteen-year-old daughter would be the last you ever heard from her. Sometimes when he put his mobile down, ended a call, he checked how long it had taken like he just had with Morgan; but one minute eleven seconds was reserved for that one last call. But there was no time for his demons; Nell had just left, but he already had a good idea where she was headed. Morgan wanted answers.

13

Tuesday afternoon

"Arsehole," hissed Nell through clenched teeth, then she held her breath and closed her eyes. It was hot in the little red car although both front windows were down. Grass aggravated her elbow resting on the window frame, from the high bank she was huddled against. The four-by-four eased itself past and sped off down the narrow lane.

"Thank you, too!" bellowed Nell as its shiny black back disappeared from her rear-view mirror. "Anyone else want to run me off the bloody road?" But the narrow Devon lane was empty. For the third time in ten minutes she threw the car back into first gear and edged out of the bank. Surely she was nearly there? The route planner she had printed off earlier that morning had slid to the floor and she did not dare take her eyes off the road long enough to extract it. Then she rounded a corner, the air changed, and through a frame of yellow gorse she saw the sea. For a moment she forgot everything – the early start from the hotel, the disturbing meeting with Austin yesterday, even that she had not eaten since breakfast – as she looked across the mass of water shimmering and rippling in the afternoon sun.

A lay-by appeared and gratefully Nell parked up. Her leg muscles ached as she heaved herself out of the car. The crash of the sea below was split open by the cry of a seagull, soon joined by another, who wailed their duet across the cliffs and down to the rocks below. Drifting up spasmodically was the sound of an outboard motor. A harbour lay below, with its huddle of small houses and ancient wall. Amazingly there was an assortment of smart yachts amongst the battered rusty fishing boats. One was heading out to sea now, riding the waves, its sails gleaming in the sun. It was overtaken by a red speedboat which zigzagged gaily, leaving a plume of white water behind it. Nell lifted her battered face to the sky and breathed in the sunshine.

The feeling of being cleansed and renewed had started the moment she hit the dual carriageway that morning. It had increased as every signpost counted down the miles. Now she was within miles of her new home. The wind tugged at her long hair, whipping it playfully into her eyes and catching painfully on her scabs. Grabbing it, she split it deftly into three and wove it into a quick side plait.

An orange VW campervan chugged around the corner, long surfboards riding its roof. It hooted and Nell found her hand rising in greeting. Then it was gone. Nell looked at her hand as if it was alien to her. What had made her do that? Surely she did not think they were hooting at her? But then who else? Probably just being friendly and she had been friendly back. It was a significant moment, she realised. The Nell who had gone out with Gary would never dared do that. Not even when he was not with her. She would have shrivelled into her shell and hoped to God that it was not one of Gary's friends who would then tell Gary, who would be propelled into a jealous rage. She remembered once how the office junior had seen her in town and said hello. Gary had caused a scene by asking Nell loudly if she fancied him, announcing to the scarlet faced youth that he ought to watch out; she liked them young. And so it had gone on for months. Every lunchtime and evening Gary asked if the junior had spoken to her; what he had said and how she had answered. The interrogations had exhausted her and made her even more withdrawn at work.

Apparently, she was not allowed to speak to anyone of the opposite sex, not even at work. So Nell had learned to ignore anyone she knew when shopping in town, especially if they were male. She had had to apologise to the poor lad on Monday by saying that Gary was drunk, but then been hit when Gary had made her confess talking to him later. That was the hardest thing about being in a relationship with someone like Gary, thought Nell. You learned the rules and tried to live by them, but every now and then you slipped back to normal behaviour. Sometimes Gary had accused her of being quiet, but he had not been aware of how she had to rehearse everything she said in her head first, before she dared let it loose into the air.

But that was before; the rest of her life lay before her like a gift ready to be unwrapped. A cloud shuttered the sun for a moment and cast a shadow on the sea. It skipped along like a vast school of fish, then it was gone and the sea shimmered once more. On the horizon lay the outline of an island, low and grey, it looked like the hump of a mammoth whale.

Then two thoughts broke into the tranquillity; first that she needed to eat and second that she was desperate for a pee. Opening the passenger door with care so it did not scrape along the stone wall, she extracted the printout. Memorising the name of the road she needed she looked once more at the sea then got back in the car. This was not a holiday she reminded herself; there was no clock ticking off three more days, two more, last day. She was here as long as she wanted, if she wanted.

Slowly she drove down the main road into the surfing village. Bed and breakfast signs swung in the ceaseless breeze, and hotels declared they had no vacancies. Within days it would be September and the bloom of summer would be over. Passing guest houses painted in 1970s colours, Nell wondered what her apartment would look like. The letting agent who had rented it out to holidaymakers over the last few years had assured her when she rang that morning that on her grandmother's orders there had been no bookings that season. The last person to stay was at Easter. It stung Nell to think that Nana had had the foresight to ensure that on her death the apartment would be vacant for her granddaughter. The agent had sounded truly sorry to hear that Nana had died, and sorrier to hear that Nell wanted it off their books for the time being.

The road through the village uncovered a couple of pubs, bedecked with hanging baskets and blackboards announcing their specials. There was a cluster of gift shops with postcard carousels outside, and everywhere people. Lazily moving groups licking ice creams, or manoeuvring pushchairs or bicycles, sulking teenagers on mobiles, boisterous groups in matching T-shirts playing to a wary crowd, and wailing kids whose howls rose and fell like sirens.

Nell's progress was reduced to a snail's pace with pedestrians on either side moving faster than she was. Through the crowds Nell noticed a couple of large clothing shops designed for the surfing crowd: Animal, O'Neil, Roxxy, Rip Curl. Surfboards and wetsuits were everywhere, to buy or to rent. Outside a surf shack a tall bronzed man with shoulder length blonde curls was cleaning wetsuits. Reggae boomed out from a pub and smiling Nell gave into the mood; hard not to when the sun was shining and the air rippled with music and the scent of the sea. Behind her a white van hooted. Nell glanced in her mirror and raised her hands up in a 'what can I do?' gesture as she continued to inch forward. There was more hooting.

"Hey mate, chill out," suggested the bronze god causing the van driver to suggest an alternative place for his curly blonde head, which was physically impossible. Shrugging, the god caught Nell's smiling face and winked in reply. Finally, she came to a fork in the road where her map told her to turn left, while thankfully, the sweating van driver turned right.

Slowly the road began to rise again. Although wider there were still people everywhere; holiday makers walking back to their guest houses or down to the village. Nell drove past a campsite, a caravan park, then just as the road began to narrow again she saw the sign she had been looking for. Turning left down a steep lane she realised she was heading straight for the sea. For a moment the old nightmare of a damp, rundown, Victorian monstrosity rose before her but she shooed it away. To her right was an elegant architect's dream of glass, chrome and pale wood. She glanced at it once and carried on down the road past more bed and breakfast signs and a few private houses. Now, all that was left before her was a gravel car park with an assortment of campervans and cars.

Surfers stripped off jeans and T-shirts and shrugged into wetsuits. Barefooted, they trotted through the grass with their surfboards under their arms and disappeared out of sight. Somewhere below must be an easy access to the surf that only the locals knew, thought Nell. But she had run out of road and not found the apartment. Parking up, she looked at the map again, and then realisation hit. She gazed back at the elegant building behind her, the late afternoon sun reflected in its vast glass windows.

"Oh my God."

Nell was so busy gazing at the building in front she nearly shut her fingers in the car door. The pencil sketch in her mind of a salt weathered old house sulking out to sea from its crouched spot on a cliff vanished in the fresh warm breeze. Before her stood a medley of sharp angles, white walls, huge glass windows, circular balconies and wood the colour of café latte. But rather than look out of place, the modern, architecturally designed apartments looked as at home against the cliff as did the expensive vessels she had seen bobbing in the ancient harbour.

Nell marched excitedly through the car park, her pumps scrunching on the chippings. There were six apartments and she deduced from the lack of cars most were weekend retreats for the mentally fatigued in the big cities. Fumbling slightly she unlocked the vast walnut door and stepped into the calm of the foyer. Apartment six was the top floor, as she hoped it would be. She had a choice of lift or stairs, but all memory of aching leg muscles had gone and she skipped up the shallow steps which spiralled upwards, past apartment four and five and on up until she came upon a sunny landing and her new front door.

The honey coloured door opened onto cream flooring, that led to a stainless steel kitchen which flowed onto the living area dominated by one whole wall of glass. There was a terrace outside with potted plants but it was the view beyond that demanded all her attention. The Bristol Channel lay before her; an artist's palette where swirls of crimson combined with sienna yellow and cobalt blue. The tide was in and as she strolled outside the deafening roar of surf, beating on the broken rocks and golden sands below, was clearly audible. The hot sun blending with the fresh wind stirred the hairs on her arms and lifted her wispy fringe. She could smell the rich freshness of the compost in the plant pots and the salt from the sea. A solitary seagull wailed high above, its white wings a single sail on a tranquil sea-blue sky.

Goose pimples erupted and shivering slightly she withdrew into the apartment. There was a smell of polish and floral disinfectant which betrayed the fact that it had been given a good clean recently. The letting company had been taking good care of it evidently and Nell made a mental note to make sure she went in to see them the next day. Then she checked out the bathroom and marvelled at the gleaming chrome, the vast walk in shower, deep bath and elegant green tiles. As she washed her hands she caught sight of her face in the mirror. Brown eyes gleamed through the mottled face, but already the swelling was down and the bruises had begun to work through their paint chart of colours. Soon they would fade and she would be herself again.

In the silence her body's needs made themselves clear by rumbling loudly. It was hours since she had eaten and the thought of food made her light-headed. A memory of childhood holidays drifted by; of fish and chips with vinegar, sharp and clean against the delicate freshness of the fish. Of salt awakening the senses in preparation for soft fat chips, crispy golden batter, comforting and warming after a long day in the surf and sunshine. Skin glowing warm against soft cotton; the reminder of sunburn now calming in the cool evening wind. Hunting for the last bit of batter, the remaining soggy chip stuck to the paper.

Her stomach growled again at her over-imaginative memory and she resigned herself to re-negotiating the hamster tube roads back to the village. She had not seen a grocery shop but the larger town with the harbour had everything including a petrol station, the letting agent and a hairdresser. She had plenty to do tomorrow.

Hours later, Nell sat contentedly on her balcony. Her belly felt comfortably full and the apartment smelt indulgently of the fish and chips she had just devoured. A tumbler of red wine balanced on the rim of a plant holder. The roar of the surf was soothing as she imagined it endlessly beating the grey rocks below. The wind was cold so she snuggled deeper into her purple and white spotty dressing gown. Finally, she extracted herself from the sun lounger and padded back indoors. Heaving the heavy glass door shut she heard the sudden silence around her.

She had unpacked earlier and her odd assortment of possessions looked alien against the furniture. Her books stood alongside the holiday let assortment of local interest books, maps and leaflets. Clothes hung forlornly in the vast double wardrobe. Only the bathroom felt like home. But she loved it here. Truly loved it. Who would not want to live in this modern, fresh apartment with its stainless steel kitchen and wooden floors? It was only the furniture that she did not like. There seemed no personality to it, which was what you wanted from a holiday let, she concluded. And somehow she could not bring herself to use the bed or the bedding. It was perfectly clean but she wanted her own linen, her own pillow. Well, she had the money to replace everything, she thought happily. Thanks to Nana, she could visit the big city ten miles away and buy duvets, pillows, towels, a mat for the lounge, a new sofa, damn it a new bed if she wanted. All to her own taste, not a compromise with what Gary wanted. For a moment she wondered what would have happened if Nana had not left her the money. It was a sobering thought and one she knew the answer to. It was Tuesday night; Gary would be in front of the television with a beer while she washed up in the kitchen watching a drama series on the portable. Dishwasher tablets and washing powder; she added to her shopping list. This was her home now; she was safe.

She had made herself a makeshift nest on the lounge floor, with cushions from the sofa and her sleeping bag, which had been in the car's boot. It was like camping, which was silly as there was a perfectly good bed with pillows and a duvet in the bedroom. But she wanted it to be fresh. Like a caterpillar in its chrysalis, she wanted new things, her own things, with no history or bad memories. The sleeping bag had been a promotional gift from work when they were starting their range of adventure holidays. It had never been used and was therefore suitable. Nell arranged herself facing the windows so that she would be able to see the first tint of dawn in the sky. Listening to the faint sound of surf just audible through the double glazing and the distant thuds and clatters from the other apartments, Nell felt her eyes grow heavy and finally she slept.

Hours later she was suddenly wide awake. She listened for the sound that had woken her and gazed around the lounge in the faint green standby light from the TV and DVD player. Nothing. But still the adrenalin coursed through her veins. Her ears rang with the silence and then in the dark she heard breathing. Shallow and quick. Nell rolled slowly off the cushions, wincing at the creak of the floor, then still in her sleeping bag heaved herself in agonizingly slow caterpillar movements against the wall.

The breathing was quicker now and she heard a muffled sob. Was it coming from the hallway? Or perhaps from the apartment below drifting up through a vent? Then she smelt it; cheap and sweet, the sort of perfume spray she wore as a teenager. Maybe it was just a fabric cleaner used on the sofa which had resurfaced with the warmth of her body. She was desperately trying to rationalise what was happening but there could be no mistake. Someone or something was with her in the apartment. Just out of sight, in the hallway. It began again, a shuffling sound; then another, and a yelp of pain.

Nell was breathing just as fast and for a moment she wondered if she was just hearing herself. With a gulp she held her breath and listened, eyes glued to the dark of the hallway, chest burning. For one beautiful, sane moment the apartment was silent except for the ringing in her ears and the faint buzz of the fridge. Then the shuffling started again. Whatever it was, it was inching forward, along the hallway and into the lounge. Within seconds it would be visible. In the gloom she could just make out the edge of the wall and in terror she took a gulp of air.

Then a car turned into the car park below, its tyres scrunching on the gravel. The sound of its door opening, then slamming shut cut into the night air and Nell tore her eyes away from the hallway. A woman's laughter rose from below and it broke the tension in the apartment. There was no more shuffling or sounds of rapid breathing but it still took Nell fifteen minutes to pluck up the courage to put on the light, and ten more minutes to venture into the hallway. Nothing there, but still the faint aroma of body spray lingered. In her mind she played back what she had heard and then remembered the muffled yelp.

Oh Fuck. She had heard that voice before.

14

Wednesday

Wednesday morning arrived grey and depressing. Clouds shrouded the sun casting a gloomy shadow over the sea. A strong wind had whipped the surf up to monstrous heights and the beach was empty but for a few dedicated surfers.

On the terrace outside Nell's French windows a trio of seagulls squabbled over one of last night's chips. Their screams of rage woke Nell in her sleeping bag.

"Shut up!" Squinting at her watch she groaned. Eight o'clock. She had had the sum total of about four hours sleep. Nell unzipped, crawled onto the floor and slowly brought her aching limbs to standing. She peered into the hallway and sniffed cautiously then staggered into the bathroom and turned the lock.

Had it been the wine, mixed with all those greasy chips? Nell lowered herself carefully onto the toilet seat while keeping a close eye on the door handle opposite. Maybe she had some sort of hallucination? No chance; the sweet musky scent of body spray still lurked in the hallway. But the teenage girl from Butlers Yard, or Ruby as she now thought of her, was just a nightmare, and last night she had been very much awake. Great way to spend the first night of her new life, she thought sadly.

"I'm going mad," she whispered to the green tiles. "Shit."

Maybe the blow to her head was causing a delayed reaction? Damn Gary. The reality of how alone she was hit her with the force of a speeding truck and she felt her courage begin to flicker.

One hour at a time. That was all she had to deal with, she reminded herself fiercely, just one hour at a time. Ten past eight. She would make herself a cup of tea, have a hot bath and then take her sleeping bag into the bedroom and away from the seagulls.

Eight thirty; Nell wallowed in the hot water, the familiar scent of her bubble bath padding the space around her. She had found the small bottle in her toiletry bag, left over from a weekend away that spring. Gary had raged at her in a restaurant and everyone had stared. The memory made her feel better; she would never have to suffer that humiliation again.

The hot water and even hotter tea worked their soft magic; soothing, calming. Wrapped in her robe she dried her hair with a towel and then plaited it for ease. A watery sun was seeping through the clouds and a little warmth penetrated. Nell made a second cup and ventured on to the terrace. From where she stood she could see the car park below, the cliff edge and the beach beyond, but most of her view was sea. The island was just visible in the gloom and Nell remembered its lighthouse from last night. The six flashes had kept her company in the long hours after she had heard Ruby in the hallway.

Eight forty-five and a door slammed below. Peering over the balcony Nell saw a tall man jog across the car park towards a smart four-by-four. It unlocked with a chirp and blink. As if aware he was being observed he glanced back up to the building and Nell recognised the tanned face of the surf shack owner who had shouted at the van driver and then smiled at her. She withdrew instinctively, spilling scalding tea over her hand.

The clouds finally dissolved and the sun took centre stage again. Nell unplaited her hair and let it dry in the warm breeze. All thoughts of sleep had now gone and as nine o'clock approached she planned her next hour.

The small town of Launton was bustling with holiday makers who had turned their attention to shopping. There were a number of bistros, good restaurants and snack bars along with more domestic necessities. Nell wandered about the narrow streets for a while, strolling in and out of the bright surf shops, when she spotted the estate agents who had rented the apartment, and next to them a hair salon. Combing her tousled hair with her fingers in an attempt to tame it, she crossed the road.

"Help you?" An emaciated boy with an inch of union jack boxer showing above his skinny jeans, looked in disgust through his blonde fringe at her thick rippling hair. She could just imagine his thumbs itching to attack it with the scissors.

"Hello. Any chance of a restyle today?"

When she spoke Nell realised that apart from a few murmurs to herself that morning, it was the first time she had spoken to another person since the chip shop last night and her voice crackled like an old engine turning over.

"It's alright, Tim, I'm here now."

A small woman with a round smiling face and an asymmetric black and blonde bob padded towards her.

"I'm Erin, the manager, and you've got perfect timing. My next client just cancelled."

Nell allowed herself to be led to a comfortable chair in front of a mirror, where a coffee was placed in her hand and her lap piled with hair magazines. There were three other chairs and they were all filled. The air was filled with the strong smell of hairspray and the roar of hairdryers. Nell took a sip of coffee, looked at the page in her lap and then her face in the mirror. She felt awkward, dowdy, and old fashioned.

"Any ideas yet, or would you like me to suggest something?" Erin gave her a friendly smile through the mirror.

"I just want it to have some style, but not too short," responded Nell feebly. "It's just so flyaway."

"How about I take off two inches and give you a long bob. Maybe some layers around your face and tidy up the fringe?"

"Perfect."

"You in Launton on holiday?"

"Yes, well no not really. I came yesterday. My grandmother has an apartment here. I might stay a while."

"That sounds exciting."

"Yes, it is."

"This style will really work for you. You'll be able to straighten it for a sleek look, or just dry it rough to let your waves come through."

"Excellent. I just want to look different."

"It's amazing what a haircut can do."

The door opened and a tall blonde strode in.

"Could you excuse me just a moment?"

Erin disappeared to speak to the woman.

"I'm full, but Lisa could fit you in at four?"

"Oh, you star. I look like a frigging sheep and I wanted to gatecrash that gig tomorrow night."

Nell peered at the woman through her mirror, envious of the long tanned legs. A faded Celtic tattoo cupped a broad, well-developed shoulder contrasting with an otherwise slim frame. She could be a model, thought Nell, looking at the fine cheekbones and wide smile, set in a square jaw. Or an Olympic swimmer. Yet as she stood in a classic Henry VIII stance, with hands on her hips, throwing her head back to laugh at something Erin said, Nell felt unsettled. There was a strength about her which was unnerving. Cat green eyes considered Nell for a moment, then with a rise of fine eyebrows and a smile for Erin she was gone.

"Sorry about that. Maxine never thinks to book in advance, she just arrives in a panic and hopes someone can see her."

"Is she in a band, she said something about a gig?"

"Oh God no, I've heard her sing and it's not something I'd like to experience again. No, she's a psychic. Just informally, you know. She doesn't charge for it. I don't really believe in all that stuff but plenty around here do."

Erin wrapped a gown around Nell's shoulders and led her to the sinks. As warm water bubbled over her scalp Nell felt her shoulders relax. Erin washed her hair – taking care around the wounds without mentioning them – chatting happily.

"Now, the gig she was talking about is tomorrow night, in the Smugglers Arms. Devon's answer to Derek Acorah is doing a ghost tour. I think it is mostly for tourists but you should go along. Max thinks he's fake but I went last year and I found it was really interesting. Place is supposed to be haunted you see and people come from miles around to stay in the haunted bedroom."

A soft thick towel was wrapped round Nell's head, and smelling pleasantly of tropical fruits she was led back to her chair.

"Why is Maxine going if she thinks he's a fake?" she ventured.

Erin shrugged her shoulders. "Maybe she's checking out the competition. Now, how much shall we take off? I was thinking this."

Nell nodded absently at the length of hair Erin showed her in the mirror. She took a quick sip of coffee before the serious business of snipping started.

"You talking about the thing tomorrow?" The nose-studded hairdresser at the next chair interrupted.

"Yeah, I was just saying to Nell, she should go."

"You should. It's like Most Haunted, 'cept he doesn't go into a trance or any of that stuff."

Nell bathed in the chatter as wet hair fell into her lap. Within minutes her hair was being dried and further conversation was halted. The soothing sound of snipping continued around her as Erin held up the mirror for her to see the back. She looked great. Her brown hair gleamed like a newly shelled conker and large eyes smouldered in her pale skin. She looked younger somehow. No one would believe she would be thirty next week.

New hair cut: done. Feeling deliciously light she thanked Erin, paid, then stepped into the street. Estate agents next.

Hours later Nell arrived back at the apartment. It took two trips to take her purchases upstairs. A few bags of essential food shopping to see her through the next few days, some toiletries, a few bottles of white wine, and an entire set of new bedding in pure white; totally impractical and thoroughly indulgent. Feeling more tired by the moment she made the bed, contentedly inhaling the newness it gave the room. Then she sat on the balcony and observed the distant milling of the inhabitants on the beach until she was suitably sleepy.

The wind lifted Nell's new hair, stirring the fruity aroma of the hair product in it. It smelled exotic. Sipping her spring water she thought about her solicitor. She should ring him, and the bank. Later; maybe tomorrow. The sun and roar of the surf drugged her with every breath. With heavy limbs she crawled into her new bed, marvelling at the crispness of the duvet cover and softness of the new pillows. This time when she slept there were no dreams.

15

He sniffed his hands, first one then the other. Slowly, with eyes closed and mouth open. The sweetness warmed him again, and masked the other odours. Some cellars always smelled stale, he thought. His resembled a sterile cell with white-washed walls and a concrete floor; yet still an underlying odour lurked like undetected evil. Sitting on the steep steps that led from the hatch above, he shed his everyday persona like a worn skin. His facial muscles relaxed and his mind played back elements of his day, but this time uncensored.

He felt safe in his white cellar. With the hatch down the only noise that penetrated was the soft mumbling of the TV above and the rumble of the dryer. No one knew about the cellar, or what it housed, and that was exciting.

The peace was shattered by the doorbell. It sent a shock through the Victorian terrace that made the whole house shudder. He slammed his hands over his ears. The demonic Morse code of the doorbell rang out again and he moaned softly. Something else moaned too. But he was safe here, he comforted himself. No one could get in, no one knew. One Christmas his six-year-old cousin had been given a doll that stood as tall as she did. When she was outside playing he held it and stroked the cold waxy face and limbs. Its eyes had fascinated him as they clicked open and shut.

The cellar was his haven from life and the character he played out every day. And now he was not alone. Everyone should have a pet, he mused. The doorbell rang once more and clicking his tongue in irritation he climbed the stairs back to real life.

16

Wednesday afternoon

When she finally woke the day was still warm, so, dressed in shorts, a khaki vest, and tying a white cotton shirt around her waist she headed for the beach.

The track from the cliff top car park took her past the rocks and onto the beach via a cluster of rock pools. Families were still camped on the beach and small children played in the warm shallow waters that the larger rock pools offered. Nell slipped off her pumps and headed for the sea. The tide was out and the ripples it had left in the sand were hard under foot. As she got closer the sand gave way to occasional softness and her toes sank gratefully into the warm water.

On she walked, past surfers returning from the water and people like her who were just walking. Further on and there were kite flyers; bright material straining against the wind, curling their tails in tight ribbons against the blue sky. Nell remembered the joyful tug of a kite string, of the connection to something so impossibly high in the sky. As a child she had imagined herself as a kite, wondering what she would see from her lofty position and urged her kite higher and higher until the string had run out. She had been frightened then, thinking the knot which held it onto the cardboard tube was too fragile for such a powerful thing, and frantically she had wound it in a few feet again.

Nell walked until she reached the other side of the beach then headed back. As she turned she noticed the tall antennae with what looked like a webcam angled towards the beach. There was a backpackers hostel nearby, with campervans in assorted colours parked outside. She smiled to the webcam and waved, before she could stop herself. Stupid idiot. Who was she waving at? Would it even be possible to spot individuals from that distance? Now the ugly grey post looked threatening; big brother spying on the beach and all its innocent inhabitants. She turned and headed for home.

The sun was finally losing its strength and the families packed up their belongings to make the slow, calf aching, journey back across soft sand to their cars, or one of the tents which mushroomed in the nearby fields. Hungry again, Nell struggled up the track back to the apartment. She saw a flash of wetsuit and standing aside so he could pass she saw it was the bronze god from the surf shack.

"Cheers," he smiled as he trotted by, and despite herself Nell felt her own face smile back. She was still smiling when she closed her apartment door.

Silence fell like night. She could hear distant music, probably from one of the apartments below, and the muted rumble of a car outside. She dropped her bag on the sofa and felt the wall vibrate with the sound. Alone, completely alone, with no one to care if she lived or died. The floor beneath her dropped. A silent scream forced tears from her eyes and made her throat ache. The misery swept through her and looking to distract it, Nell turned on her laptop. If she could find the webcam then she would know if by any bizarre chance Gary happened to look through it, whether he would know it was her walking along the beach and not some other gangly dark haired, nearly thirty year old woman with a beat-up face and a tattoo of visible bruising on her arms.

It took a while but finally she had the backpackers' site up and their live webcam view in front of her. Waves: it was aimed at

130

the rolling sets of breakers. Of course, what else would a surfer be interested in. Just to the left you could make out where surf met sand and a few minute figures paddling. She watched the grainy waves beat themselves out in silence. A wetsuited figure appeared with a board under its arm. Launching himself into the foam he paddled out to sea. It could be the bronze god, or a woman, or anyone, mused Nell.

There were also archive stills on the site. Some from the week before, most over the summer. Now Nell could see what really made this beach a surfer's paradise. The waves today had been strong and fierce but nothing compared to a week ago when they had reached toppling heights reminiscent of a tsunami. What made people get in the way of such monsters, and call it fun? However long she lived here – and Nell was only living one day at a time, or even one hour – she knew without a doubt she would never have the guts to be at the mercy of the sea in that way.

She could smell toast. Wrinkling up her nose she ventured into the hallway from where it was coming. It was stronger by the moment and making her hungrier than ever. Hot buttered toast, golden and crisp. She could almost taste it. But then it was gone as quick as it came. So now she was hallucinating food. That was some knock to your head, girl.

She turned back at the computer screen. It was back on the live camera. A figure was walking along the beach. Something about the figure made Nell look closer. It raised an arm and waved to the camera, then stopped and dropped its hand. As it turned and strolled back up the beach a small figure appeared behind it. In the greyscale, the red hair of the little girl stood out like a blood spot on a white sheet. The breath died in Nell's throat. The girl turned round to the camera, waved as Nell had done, then followed her up the beach, just a few steps behind. As Nell walked out of the camera's view the red head faded.

Tears crashed down Nell's face as she dashed to the bathroom and locked the door. If she was truly being haunted then she was in real trouble because she had nowhere left to run.

That night predictably, she dreamed of Ruby, but this time it was the old dream of Butlers Yard. Sitting in her tree house she saw the pale face appear in the upstairs window and resigned herself to what would happen next. But as she climbed down the wooden ladder she smelt cigarette smoke. Stopping, she looked for its source and noticed a half stubbed out butt not three feet away from her ladder.

Thursday dawned bright and warm. There were things she should do, people to call, but the fragile shell of unreality which surrounded her could be easily broken and beneath it she could feel the healing beginning to take place. A cold shadow still lurked from yesterday, and she had not turned on her laptop since, but she had taken a beating and some dizziness was only to be expected. If it got worse she could visit a doctor, but Nell was struggling to convince herself that her imaginary ghosts were just an overactive mind recovering from the stress and strain of the past few weeks. She had always been a daydreamer, and a vivid dreamer at night. Napping in the afternoon often brought impossibly real dreams and the Ruby nightmare came at any time when she was particularly stressed. But the hallucinations of Ruby were something else entirely. But then she had had a knock to the head, was emotionally and physically exhausted from escaping Gary, and still grieving for Nana. Her rationalising was almost working but then she had always been good at deluding herself.

From her veranda she could see cars beginning to arrive in the small car park, and the beach beyond become spotted with windbreaks and beach tents. Suddenly she wanted to feel the sun on her aching sore body, so dressing quickly she headed for the beach. Settling her small day sack more comfortably on her shoulders she picked her way down the narrow pathway onto the rocks. The tide was just going out and pools of glistening water filled the gaps and indents between the sharp lines of rocks. For a moment she hesitated, looking for a way down to the sand because the route she had taken yesterday was now under dark water. A couple walking in front were having the same dilemma. Burdened with a picnic basket and beach chairs they were contemplating clambering over the razor-edged rocks. Nell suddenly felt light and reckless. Dressed in shorts and vest top, with her towel, bottle of water, and a snack in her bag, she felt like a teenager again and the way seemed foolishly clear. Without a second thought she sank her right foot into the pool of water. It was icy cold, the sun not having had sufficient time to warm it yet, and as her left foot joined it and water rose over her knees she let out an involuntary squeal.

"How deep does it get?" The couple had noticed her attempt and the girl had taken a step towards her.

"No, its fine. Just over the knees." The water caught in her flip flops and Nell wondered if she could take them off, but then the water shallowed and she reached the warm hard sand.

"Mark, this way. We can wade across," the woman shouted, already rolling up her trouser legs. She gave Nell a smile and then grimaced in the cold water. But it seemed Mark was bent on clambering over the rocks, he dropped one of the chairs and made a rather undignified jump to the sand which could have been to disguise a stumble. The woman raised her eyes upwards. "Typical male, too proud to go back."

Nell smiled as Mark finally reached them. With a shout he picked the woman up and as she laughed, threatened to dunk her back in the rock pool.

Why could Gary not have been like that? pondered Nell. The water on her legs prickled as the sun warmed it; she knew just how Gary would have responded to a comment of him being too proud. And then it hit her; neither of them had even flinched at her bruises. Either that or they had just covered it up too well, but no, they really had taken no notice, it was not what was important. They were more interested in her leading them safely across the rocks.

It felt strange to be all alone on a beach full of families and couples. But if she looked carefully there were a few isolated singles; an elderly man with an equally old West Highland Terrier, who battled with a broadsheet in the strong wind, and a woman of roughly Nell's age who rooted through a bag for her book. It was OK, thought Nell, to come to a beach on her own. It was not just for couples and families. Once when she was in her late teens she had taken a city break to Paris alone. With her sketchbook and pencils she had had a romantic idea of being a wandering artist. The truth was that she had been too young to be alone, to cope with the territorial glares from the women at the hotel, who seemed to think she would try to steal their men, or the disgusted stares from elderly couples who seemed insulted by the sight of a lone female. But she was older now – much, much older – and perhaps wiser. Maybe the nineteen-year-old Nell had not quite settled into her mould. At nearly thirty, battered, bruised and an escapee, she had broken that mould. And she was rich now, Nell reminded herself with a smile, and being rich meant she had choices.

She lay out on her towel, toasting her factor twenty soaked skin, and pondered over the evening to come. A ghost tour: sounded pretty silly really, but it might be fun and it would be something to fill her time. Maxine did not seem the theatrical sort; in fact she seemed very down to earth. How could she be a psychic, and if she was, what would she make of Nell's nightmares? The sun beat down, tempered by a cool sea breeze. Slowly she felt each muscle loosen and sink and her bones adjust as her body relaxed into the sand. The Ruby nightmares bobbed to the surface for a moment, before she firmly dunked them again. Then a thought flickered, and she finally acknowledged that asking for Maxine's help had perhaps been at the back of her mind the whole time.

The sun inched its way slowly across the broad sky. A stray cloud sometimes blotted its power, and at that time it was not too difficult to remember that September was creeping ever closer. Later she braved the surf, loving the crash of the pure water as it pummelled her skin. Wave after wave, glistening in the sunshine, beating out the anguish and scouring the sadness. The spray made her eyes and nose run and she prayed these would be the only tears she knew from now on. Her scrapes stung in the salty water but as she walked back to her towel and they began to dry she felt a strange tingling. Inspecting her forearm she was amazed to see that already there was new pink skin amongst the scabs. She was renewed; a child of the sea and sun again, healing slowly both in mind and body. But she had spent the day alone and was looking forward to the evening and a chance to mix with the living again.

Just before seven thirty Nell pushed open the heavy pub door of the Smugglers Arms and stepped into a sudden chill. A group of weather-beaten men turned to stare as she approached the bar which smelled like it had soaked up a century of spilt beer.

"You looking for the ghost tour, love?" The barman smiled.

"Yes please," managed Nell, feeling like an idiot.

"Through that door and then through the restaurant. They'll be in the yard at the far end."

"Thank you." Nell fled past the staring bar proppers, trying not to stumble on the uneven flagstones. The restaurant was packed and had a more cheerful, welcoming atmosphere. An aroma of carvery rose in a happy cloud above the diners as Nell made her way through. Just then the far door opened and a nervous looking man of about fifty peered at her over his wire-rimmed glasses.

"Ah, do I spot another brave seeker of other world phenomena?"

He reminded her of a hamster, blinking and twitching, and suddenly Nell began to enjoy herself. Smiling, she allowed herself to be ushered towards a small group where, like a swan amongst tattered ducklings, stood Maxine. She was amazed to see Maxine smile in recognition.

"Erin said you might come. I'm Max."

"Nell," said Nell hesitatingly.

And after being alone all day Nell became part of the small group of ghost hunters, some looking excited and nervous, some obviously there to keep their other-halves happy. A reflection in the restaurant window caught her eye. A teenage girl in shorts and T-shirt approached the back of the group, and stopped just behind Nell. Smiling, Nell moved aside to make space, but confusion flicked across the girl's face and turning she headed through an archway to the street beyond.

Nell shrugged and turned back to the front only to lock eyes with Maxine. Maxine's smile faltered for a moment, then shaking her head as if to clear it, the smile returned.

"Right, is everyone ready?" The ghost hunter introduced himself as Rory and mentioned how nice it was to see some new faces.

"And some familiar ones." This was said to Maxine and Nell realised that perhaps he was nervous. Did he think she was going to expose him as a fraud, or was it just uncomfortable for him having another psychic in the room? Perhaps their energy was clashing. She allowed herself a small smile at the thought.

"Right, well I don't think anyone else from the living is going to join us, so let us begin."

He glanced once more at each member of the group then raised his arms in the air.

"Follow me and we will not only step into the oldest part of the Inn, but the most spiritually active. Now, keep your eyes, ears and mind open."

Over the next hour the group drifted through the old building. Rory proved to be an excellent historian, bringing the tale of murdering smugglers to life. They trooped down to the ancient cellar and heard of barrels which had mysteriously moved, and the door which although locked at night was found wide open in the morning. They then trudged back upstairs and through the bar where they were shown the supposedly haunted painting which had jumped off the wall in the previous century. Finally, up to the vacant room 4 where most of the recent activity seemed to have happened.

"Now, no promises, but let us see if we can get a reaction tonight." A silence so heavy it almost hurt fell on the excited ghost hunters. Nell felt her eyes widen in anticipation.

"Is there anybody with us who would like to make contact?"

The man next to Nell attempted to stifle a laugh then grunt as his wife dug him in the ribs.

"Henry Chesterton? Are you with us?"

Nell felt her own mouth twitch into a smile which she quickly adjusted.

"Henry? If you are here give us a sign. Make a noise, move something."

There was a sudden cold draught and the pungent aroma of tobacco. Nell looked at the windows to see if they were open, thinking someone was smoking a cigar outside. Then a sharp creak broke the silence as someone stepped on a floorboard, making the group jump.

It turned out to be the most ghostly thing that happened on the tour but the group seemed happy. Nell secretly thought the history of the smugglers who had met there before their murderous business of wrecking ships had been the most interesting. Afterwards they were invited to a complementary soft drink in the bar.

"What about you, Miss?" Rory asked Nell. Maxine's unnerving eyes were fixed on her.

"Absolutely," decided Nell and feeling awkward she accepted her complementary juice.

"Now, Henry is a most contrary spirit. I remember once..." but the barman was trying to get his attention, so with an apology he scuttled off.

"Bit disappointing I suppose, but you can't always get the ghosts to turn up. That creak was just a floorboard." Nell turned to find Maxine at her side.

"But you believe in all this, don't you? I mean Erin said..."

Maxine's deep laugh bubbled out.

"Most ghostly phenomena have a rational explanation." Then her eyes sparkled. "But not all, and it's those that excite me."

Nell sipped her drink.

"But you know that, Nell, don't you?"

"Pardon?"

Maxine shook her head slowly.

"What did you experience in room 4?"

"Nothing, I mean, I heard that bump."

"You were looking at the windows."

"I wondered where the tobacco smoke was coming from," and the moment the words were out she realised what she had said.

"Henry liked his pipe, apparently."

"You don't mean..."

"People experience ghosts in different ways. I smelt it when I did the tour last year, and someone else did too. I smelt it down in the cellar too. I reckon he was there – the temperature dropped suddenly – maybe it's not so disappointing after all."

"Wow."

Maxine smiled again but this time the flawless skin was marked with a frown. "But I have another question for you. Have you been watching the local news lately? I'd guess not because if you had you'd have recognised the young girl who was with us briefly at the beginning. She appeared just after you arrived, then bolted."

Nell suddenly felt something sharp stir in her belly and her arms erupted in goose pimples.

"Sorry, you've totally lost me."

Maxine nodded slowly.

"It's a bit weird actually. I see shadows of the dead – always have – but the spirit you attracted was, I believe, a doppelganger, and definitely still living. For now."

17

For a moment Nell was distracted by an eruption of laughter at the bar. Frowning she leaned forward so she could be sure she heard properly.

"Sorry...a doppel-what?"

"Ganger. Fetch, wraith, whatever you want to call it. When a living person is seen simultaneously in more than one location at exactly the same time."

"Right." Nell had the feeling she was floating, then crashed back to earth. "The teenage girl in the yard?"

Maxine smiled her joker's smile again.

"There you go. I knew we would get there eventually." Then she sobered. "Her name is Emily Blake. She went missing last week and the police think someone took her."

"Are you sure it was her?"

"Her face has been all over the paper and TV for the past week. Gave me quite a shock seeing her. Only ever seen one doppelganger before and that was my mum just before she died. I like to think she came to say goodbye."

"Yes, but maybe it really was her. I mean the teenage girl and I'm sorry about your mum. You should ring the police."

"She appeared from thin air and disappeared before she reached the street."

Nell let Maxine's words sink in. Then a thought struck her.

"But you said you see ghosts. Maybe she's dead."

Maxine considered this for a moment.

"No, the energy was different and anyway I don't in the strictest sense see ghosts. It's like I see them in my mind. Yeah, yeah, I know that sounds wacky, and it's no good protesting now, I saw the disbelief in your eyes. But consider this; it was you she was looking at."

"Christ, what is it with me and bloody teenage girls." Suddenly Nell stifled a yawn. "Sorry, it's not you, and I'm not a disbeliever."

"Not sleeping?"

"Bad dreams."

Maxine's green eyes seemed to glint for a second. Nell felt herself drawn to them in a way that reminded her of Jester, the stray cat.

"Just a dream or something else? I'm asking from a purely professional point of view, you understand. And what did you mean by 'bloody teenage girls'?"

Despite herself Nell smiled. Should she confide, or would she sound silly? Suddenly the thought of making a friend seemed very appealing and Maxine was the sort of friend who might be able to help. After all, had that not been the whole purpose of coming tonight?

"Made up your mind yet?"

"Shit. Can you read minds as well?"

Maxine laughed, and Nell felt her own mouth twitch in response.

"No more than most people can. A great deal of communication is non verbal you know."

"OK, well this is going to sound strange."

Leaning forward Maxine grinned. "Oh, I just love a story that starts like that. Actually, hold that thought, I'm getting another drink. Do you want something stronger?"

Nell shook her head and Maxine bounded up to the bar, her long, lean limbs and cropped blonde hair reminding Nell of a Weimaraner. Left alone, Nell fussed with her drink and sneaked a peep at herself reflected in the dark window opposite. The long bob and sweeping side fringe suited her heart shaped face and made her cheekbones stand out. Did she still look like Gary's Nell? Not so much, she concluded.

Maxine was making her way back to the table, a pint of Guinness in her hand. She was taller than Nell had thought, at least five-ten at a guess, and although not skinny she filled her clothes neatly without bulges and overhang. Size twelve, thought Nell, but well stretched over a tall frame. Dressed in skinny black jeans and a cotton top there was something powerful about the way she moved. Confidence, thought Nell enviously, and more rock chick than medium.

Elegantly she took her place opposite Nell again.

"Right, now where were we?"

And then Nell was telling her all about Ruby. "It started like a reoccurring dream, but it's so old now I don't know if it's based on something real or not. And lately it's got worse." After that there was no going back. The whole story of the dream, which had recently taken on a life of its own, was out.

"So, you don't know who this Ruby is – or was?"

"Nope."

"Or why she was in the house next door."

"Double nope."

"Did you have some sort of trauma lately, a shock or an unusual amount of stress?"

"Umm, several."

Maxine waited expectantly and then smiling at the silence tried an open question.

"OK, and they are...?"

For one moment Nell considered a lie, something small and white so she would not have to admit to this confident stranger opposite her what she had put up with. Her hand trembled on the glass, nearly knocking it over. Maxine bit her lip and gently wrapped her hand around Nell's. For a moment Nell felt a shock of warmth which contrasted with the ice cold glass, then Maxine pulled away.

"Sorry. I didn't mean to pry."

"No, it's not that, I just…my nana was cremated last Friday—"

"I'm so sorry—"

"—and on Saturday my girlfriend-beater boyfriend proposed, then put me in hospital when I said no, so I ran away on Sunday after they discharged me."

Maxine's eyes flicked up to Nell's battered face before she politely adjusted them. Nell observed the green eyes and felt a warmth spread through her again. Then annoyingly her nose began to sting and her eyes itch.

"I am so sorry, Nell. I wondered about the bruises but you don't look like the type—"

"To be a battered wife?"

"Well, no." Maxine squirmed.

"Trust me, I'm not. I always looked down on women who let themselves be bullied. I thought they were weak and deep down must enjoy it or else why would they put up with it. But it happens really slowly. It creeps up on you. It starts with trying to keep the peace, you know, all those little compromises and adjustments you make to please your moody other half. Then there is a big row and you get hit, but you are told it's your fault for driving them to it and that's where you make the fatal mistake. You see, you should tell them to go to hell, but you don't. Because you love them so much and you honestly believe that it won't happen again. Especially when they are so sweet and sorry afterwards. You think that things will go back to normal again and it will bring you even closer. Because you love them, you forgive them, and after all it is better than being alone."

Nell locked with Maxine's eyes again, defying her to show anything but understanding, but she had no cause for concern. Maxine sat quietly, judging nothing.

"But you find you are a little more careful around them after that. You don't want to risk making them angry again. But somehow you do and you get hit again and although you know you should leave, it's just not as simple as that when you love someone. Then finally the love has gone but you're just too scared to go, for lots of reasons. You don't want to be alone and you've lost your confidence. You are frightened about what he will do to you or your family. You read it in the papers every day, women are killed by their partners or ex-partners – beaten to death, drowned, torched. And you see, he doesn't like your friends so gradually you've stopped seeing them – to keep the peace. So you've no one. Well, I had Nana, but she was so ill and I didn't want to worry her. I didn't want her to know how bad things were or to put her in danger."

"But you did leave—"

Nell nodded defiantly. "And I've got my mail forwarded to here, I've a new mobile number, and only work and my solicitor know where I am so he shouldn't be able to find me."

"Just Ruby then."

"Yes, she always finds me."

The silence wrapped itself around them. Nell's secrets had been released into the air and she felt like a heavy coat had slid from her shoulders. Despite everything she felt comforted.

"Poor Emily." She said finally. "But you know these latest nightmares might just be because I had a bump to the head. I might have hallucinated seeing Emily."

"Unlikely, and I saw her too."

Maxine seemed lost in thought for a moment but then brightened.

"I wonder why they come to you. If I thought for one moment the police would take me seriously I would ring their incident line and offer to help. I've done it before, though last time they were rather churlish about the whole thing. I think I dented their pride."

"But say what? 'this battered woman on a ghost tour is haunted by teenage girls and we saw Emily, only it wasn't really Emily and she wasn't a ghost'?"

Maxine exploded with laughter which turned the heads of the

bar proppers. Rory was chatting to a middle-aged couple from the tour and smiled over to them.

"Oh God, it's almost too tempting. I can just see DI Carter's smug piggy face. But why you, Nell, what is it about you that attracts them?"

"Who is DI Carter?"

Maxine's gleeful features wavered for a moment. "Oh, she's just someone I used to...know."

Nell looked up, puzzled by the hesitancy of her words.

"Nell, I've got it," and she clapped her fine-boned hands together like a crashing cymbal.

"I feel a little private séance might be in order."

"Oh no..."

"Oh yes, just you and me and Ruby makes three. Or perhaps Emily makes four. Oh I don't know. Anyway, we can find out what she wants and if there is any correlation between her and Emily."

"But..."

"Maybe my place would be best – if you don't mind? Can I have your beer mat, mine's soggy," and she riffled through her black leather jacket for a pen.

"This is my address, you can't miss it. I'm above Ricky's Surf Shop. Only don't park near the florist, they get really anal. The Indian has a car park and they let me use it. What's wrong, you want to find out, don't you? I don't charge, think of it as public duty. You can take me out for a drink sometime if we find out anything." And with one more wide smile, she sealed the deal. Exasperated at the speed everything had happened, Nell took the beer mat and agreed a time and date.

"Tomorrow then at seven. Don't have nightmares."

Five hours later when Nell woke drenched in sweat with the agonised screams of a young girl still ringing in her head, she was to remember Maxine's words and to wish it could have been as easy as that. She was also tempted to ring her but the friendship was too new, too special, and she did not want anything to ruin it. She needed it too much.

Happy from the enjoyable evening and nervously looking forward to the séance at Maxine's flat the following night, she had practically bounced out of the pub earlier.

"I've made a friend." She told the night air as she drove along the cliff road with her windows down. Then a doubt appeared like a wonky floorboard underfoot and she had felt unsettled. She did not actually know Maxine. For all she knew this could be her cunning way of conning money out of people. The first time is free but then she would be expected to keep coming back and the bills would mount up. Why was Maxine so keen to be her friend? But the fresh sea air ruffled her hair and she decided to take a chance. Living with Gary had made her suspicious of people. If she wanted a truly fresh start she needed to look at her own behaviour as well. Gary did not like her to have friends; they threatened him. But she could start again.

As she approached the front door of the apartments it opened and the bronze god appeared. There was an awkward moment, like actors trying to remember their lines, until Nell mumbled hello, acutely aware that she was blushing an unattractive shade of purple.

"Hi. You've just moved in upstairs, right? I'm Leon."

He had an Australian accent which evoked images of hot desert sand stirred by a fragrant breeze. Unable to speak at first, Nell took the hand that was offered and flinched at the strength of his shake.

"I'm Nell," she managed to squeak.

"Hi, Nell. Look, you staying long only there's a party at the Ship on Saturday night? You know, the pub in the village? If you're around you should come. It's gonna be awesome."

"Wow. Thank you."

"Make sure you're there. I'll be looking out for you," and with a grin he extracted his hand and ambled towards his car. Nell stood by the door and watched him slip behind the wheel. She was suddenly aware that she had stopped breathing and with a conscious effort to pull herself together closed the door behind her. The foyer was filled with the musky scent of his aftershave and as she ascended the stairs she brought her hands to her still scorched cheeks. As the apartment door closed behind her she was suddenly aware that it felt like home and, she congratulated herself, she had made another friend.

"Awesome."

But an hour later the heavy mantle of isolation bound itself around her as she lay reading in bed. She now realised that the cheer the evening had given her was only temporary, and wearing off by the minute. Even the encounter with Leon began to worry her and she felt foolish. The apartment beyond her bedroom door lay like virgin snow, repelling her footsteps. How could somewhere which had felt like such a sanctuary hours before now feel so cold? She was alone, and loneliness filled her like chloroform, stiffening her limbs and face. This was what she had dreaded, why she had stayed in the war zone with Gary for so long. The fear of being absolutely by herself. But it was too late, her mind was already shifting from everyday normality to a daydream of surreal nightmare proportions. The walls around her seemed to pulse.

"Put the telly on, Nell." She wanted to fill the apartment with the outside world to drown out the voices which were beginning in her head. Her imagination was rising, the dreams she created of a different Nell in a very different world. A world where she never moved in with Gary. Or jumped ahead to living in a different world with a loving husband and maybe a baby on the way. The scene when she told him she was pregnant, waited on pause for her to press play. But part of the dream had been the home she lived in and what was really worrying her now was that it resembled the very real apartment that she was standing in. Had her imaginary life created this, or had she had a premonition of what was to come? Could the bliss for life, the besotting husband, the baby, her artwork selling, really happen just by her imagining it and believing it could be true?

Did normal people do this? she wondered; blot out the life they were living by constantly imagining another. A film of their other self constantly ready to be played to ease the pain. When you are on the wrong track and unable to get off surely it was normal to sink into daydreams of being in a different life. That was why films and books were so addictive. People watched the same DVD or box sets again and again, so absorbed and addicted were they in the stories and characters. Falling in love with a character so much that you missed them with a genuine ache when the book or film ended, so that you mourned their passing over the next few days or weeks. Then the next book, film or series came out and there they were again, back in your life.

But Nell had sometimes worried that she relied on her daydreams too much, that they stopped her facing the simple fact that real life was toxic and however hard or scary, she had to get out.

"You are not alone, Nell," she told her reflection in the glass windows. "Out there are thousands, no millions of people just like you. Battle weary and shaken, bruised and fearful, alone. The world belongs to people like you. It is for you that all the stories of the world were written, to give comfort and hope, courage and strength. Now snap out of it, focus on the good stuff."

Nell thought back over the evening and Maxine's last words to her. Don't have nightmares.

Her first dream had been innocent, filled with scenes played back from her eventful evening. Then everything shifted. She was sitting in semi-darkness on a cold wooden step. Around her damp air moved sluggishly. In the distance, way above, she could hear the rattle and thunder of a large lorry passing overherad. She was in a cellar and deadly afraid. Suddenly she heard it, the telltale sound of footsteps. Holding her knees tight to her thin chest she turned her neck to look at the cellar door above. With a sharp crack the key blotted out the thin scrap of light coming from the keyhole. Spurred into action she scuttled down the steps, feeling her way in the dark with a small hand on the wall. Hide, she must hide. The light bulb above the stairs suddenly glowed, the dusty glass bare on its thin cord. And there he was. Jeans and dark boots coming down the stairs towards her hiding place, his upper half hidden from her sight from the alcove she cowered in. He walked past, filling the air with choking smoke from his cigarette. Then he stopped by the bed.

"Oh, clever little girl. Get here now. Don't play stupid fucking games with me, or I'll play some of my own."

This was her chance. She sprang from her hiding place and bolted up the stairs. But she was too slow and large arms gripped round her waist and pulled her down again.

"Why do you always make it so hard?"

In response she struggled and let out a scream.

"Now I'll have to go over the rules again, won't I?"

Her heels scraped and caught on the rough slabs as he dragged her back to the narrow iron bed. She screamed once more, then his rough hand pressed into her mouth making her teeth ache and her lip split again.

"Lesson number one. Little girls who wear sexy clothes get what's coming to them."

She couldn't breathe; his hand was over her nose and she could taste blood.

"Lesson number two. Little girls who don't do as they're told are punished."

The dust motes spiralling in the yellow light seemed to dim for a second as they were joined by dark spots. Her chest heaved to bring in air but instead flooded with panic and pain. As her ears began to ring she heard the sly noise of his belt being unfastened followed by the zip of his jeans.

"And you know what your punishment is by now, don't you, Emily?"

18

Friday

Can a head injury cause hallucinations? After scrolling through the ads for personal injury claims Nell found some new things to worry about. Traumatic brain injury more affectionately known as TBI. Psychosis, aneurism and dementia. She sipped her coffee and contemplated the horizon. Scary words but this had all started after the funeral and got worse after she hit her head. Surely she just needed an MRI scan, not a séance. She read somewhere that the mental health institutes of the world were filled with those who had dabbled in the occult and here she was putting her fragile mental state in the hands of a complete stranger. The ghost tour last night had been fun, but to take it any further was dangerous. What about Emily? 'Probably just the landlord's kid'. She had caught an update on the story last night and the girl did look very much like Emily Blake but then so did hundreds of teenage girls out there who were in class right now not being kept captive in a cellar. Reality check; she needed fresh air and to get among real people again.

As she left the safety of the penthouse, Nell felt her face freeze in nervousness. Alone, single, without a companion. The world was designed to receive and accept only people in pairs or groups. Those who stood alone invited attention, suspicion. She remembered the days before Gary, when she had still had friends, how nervous she had made people feel. Any invitation out was invariably accompanied with the words 'feel free to bring a friend'. Eventually everyone made it their job to pair her off. 'Who do we know who would do for Nell?' and she went along with it, knowing they meant well. And after all, no one wanted to trek the burning desert of life without a partner, someone to share it all with, to make it real and make it all matter. It took a brave person to take on the trials of life alone, thought Nell. Surely no one did it truly by choice. But it was strange how alive she felt now she was alone. Was that just the post-apocalyptic shock of escaping him?

Today she was not feeling quite so brave. She was aiming for a point of land at the end of the beach which the map in the apartment told her led to the coastal path. Dimly, she remembered walking it as a child. Then it had seemed many miles long and impossibly high with just a narrow strip of pathway stopping her from falling onto the rocks below. She had pretended she was riding a pony when she was little, cantering at one point ahead of her parents which had made them shout in alarm. She had wanted to feel alone, to be the only person on that precarious path, no one visible in front or behind; just her, the sea and the odd seagull. Closing her car door, she felt safe again for a moment and her face lost some of its rigidity. Last night's nightmare clung like an emotional hangover and she needed fresh air and exercise to chase it away.

Her car felt like a tiny piece of home. There was a Twix wrapper on the floor, left over from a much needed sugar fix when she had been leaving the hospital after visiting Nana. There was also the abandoned route planner from Tuesday's trip. It already seemed a lifetime ago. She really had to clean this car up, but not today.

Negotiating the constricted road, boarded by the now all too familiar stone walls and high earth banks, Nell drove to the car park which was used by beach goers and walkers alike. She was waiting for it to seem familiar but no such feeling came. Walkers with Nordic poles and backpacks strode off in front of her as she took her place on the path. Past a tea shop and a surfers lodge. She looked across the beach and could see the sun glinting off the railing of her own building. Below the surf pounded, and surfers appeared, trotting back to their car. Obviously another shortcut down to the beach.

The wind made her eyes weep, and turned strands of wispy hair into needles. How easy it would be to slip on the narrow path and then roll out of control onto the rocks and into the sea below? She imagined that split second of horror as realisation slammed in that this was not going to be an embarrassing trip, but a bowel loosening, uncontrolled plummet to the rocks below. Grabbing grass, ripping your hands on rocks, to try to stop your fall. Your life over because of a clumsy stumble on a narrow dirt track. How like her life that sounded.

The seagulls cried, the wind roared and the surf crashed, yet still she could hear the voices in her head. Emily's cries, the man's grunts, the mewling of the crying doll and Ruby's petulant lisp. She could walk as many cliff tops as she liked but her head was truly mangled and it was time to accept she needed help. And surely that was either the séance tonight or a GP. But if it was psychosis would they put her away? The path behind her was empty and as she looked forward again she realised that she had been peering behind every few steps, like a Tourette sufferer ticking. But the webcam did not point this way so if Ruby was following her again she would have to stay hidden. Shame she did not do the same in the nightmares. Shame Emily did not do the same. But as Nell plodded forward towards the horizon she acknowledged that she may be the only chance Emily had of surviving. So she would go to Maxine's séance and face the fact that for some reason Emily had made contact and however insane it sounded, she would try to help. And if it did not work she would see a doctor.

The path ended and Nell was faced with the choice of walking on to the next bay, or sitting with the sheep and looking out to sea before returning to the car. The wind was battering her fragile face so she scooted beside a rock which gave her some shelter. Out of the wind the warm sun made her drowsy. The earth smelled sweet and strong, and the sheep bleated in a song taken up by the gulls above. A man's voice drifted by in the wind, a head appeared then another. What Nell had taken for the end of the cliff was actually hiding a pathway down to the sea. The two men caught their breath, nodded in acknowledgment to Nell, and then trudged past. Intrigued Nell heaved herself out of the grass and ventured to the end. The path was narrow and steep. Rough steps appeared to disappear off the side of the cliff. Taking a deep breath, Nell began to descend.

It was too steep but gravity pulled her downwards and the rocky beach at the end was worth every step. Totally hidden from the cliff above, Nell wondered if this had been one of the smugglers' beaches that Rory had spoken of. Secret. If she had not seen the men she would not have known it existed. The waves were rougher down here. Spray showered the rocks and Nell moved back to the path as an especially large wave flooded the beach. As it dragged back, the shingle hissed and grated. She was just about to climb back up the steps when she spotted the cave. Definitely a smugglers' beach. The tide was coming in so she needed to be quick if she was not going to be cut off from the steps, but the cave was too tempting. The sharp stench of urine betrayed the fact that someone had been caught short and taken advantage of the privacy. About fifteen metres across it appeared to get narrower as it stretched into the rock. How far did it go and was there another entrance at the back, maybe from above? The thought of a long tunnel of rock slowly filling with sea water made Nell's eyes fill with dark shapes so she quickly walked back to the safety of the steps. As her first foot descended on the rough stone she heard the cry. Probably a seagull she reasoned. The second cry was not so easy to dismiss. Muffled and weak, it reminded her of Emily last night as she fought to scream through the harsh hand that gagged her.

The rectangular lobster pot lay just inside the cave. A weathered rope tethering it to the cave side. As another large wave flooded the beach Nell heard the cry again. She was back in the hospital dream again when her feet moved forward on their own. Something lay curled up inside the cage, something young and terrified. The toddler's hand reached through the rough rope towards her as another wave crashed toward the cave. Tiny fingers, swollen and bloody as no child just out of babyhood should be. Frozen, Nell saw the scene unfold on fast forward. Wave after wave, getting closer and closer, until the cave was flooded. The shrieks and whimpers getting fainter and fainter as the water rose until only the rope was left in the air. The child drowned, unable to escape the cage it was put in. Left to die a slow agonizing death.

A voice above announced that more walkers had found the path down to the secret beach. A dog pushed its soft muffle into Nell's hands as she slowly uncovered her face. The dog roared into the cave, sniffing the urine, and Nell joined the living again. Another hallucination then. Toddlers drowned in lobster pots. Had she seen it in a horror film once, or did Rory the ghost hunter talk of people being drowned down here? Drowned, yes, but by wrecking their ships, not by being stuffed in cages. What if something had happened here years ago and she was tapping in on it? Devon was supposed to have hundreds of ghosts so if the knock to her head had reprogrammed her brain into receiving these grisly images she was in for a terrifying time.

Despite her shoes being soaked in seawater her walk back to the car resembled more of a route march. She was only aware of how tightly her fingers were clenched when she tried to unlock the car.

Back at the apartment she sipped coffee, watched a black and white musical, and kept her hands away from her laptop.

Austin glanced at the elegant timepiece on his wrist and swallowed his irritation with a slug of espresso. Late. Very late. It showed contempt for him and his work. But then the bar door opened and DI Carter landed in a cloud of stale tobacco smoke and extra strong mints.

"They will kill you."

"What?" Alex shook the hand that was offered, slightly out of kilter by the remark.

"Cigarettes."

"Oh, well if they don't I expect the fast food and red wine will."

"You do not change." Against his will there was a note of affection in his voice. It had been nearly eight years since they had worked on the same team but the bonds of mutual respect were still firm; despite her being five minutes late. Email was a wonderful thing, he mused.

"So," she pulled a face at the coffee menu then glancing at the optics above the bar got straight to business, "what makes you think our abductor is your man?"

"I would have preferred we talk at the station."

"The boss would have loved that. Your maverick manner doesn't endear you to the hierarchy."

Austin nodded sagely and steepled his hands together.

"Have you spoken to him?"

"What, the boss? Everyday." Her dark eyes sparkled teasingly then she held her hands up. "I need a single malt, then we'll talk."

Austin settled down on the worn leather sofa and waited for her to return. He was so used to working alone these days; he had to admit it was nice to meet up with an old friend.

"Right. Back to the case. We spoke to all the area's paedos when she first went missing. Standard procedure, you know that. Your bloke isn't on the register."

A couple were making their way across the bar towards a table by Austin and Carter. At this time in the evening there were still plenty of other tables free and Austin glared territorially at their progress. He wondered if he should put his foot down and demand Alex and he move somewhere more appropriate, but he knew Alex wanted their meeting to appear casual.

"I know he is not on the register."

"I thought you said he'd molested a child."

"Pages from a teenage girl's diary. Probably pure fantasy."

"But this is the guy who abandoned his family and changed his name. I see why you think he was guilty of something."

"Montague planned to leave at the end of term but escaped

abroad suddenly after an altercation. Dieter Morgan's daughter disappeared at the same time and was in his class."

"It was her diary?"

"Indeed"

"Ouch."

"The diary has only just come to light."

"The police?"

"Morgan does not need the police to ensure justice is done and he feels they failed him last time."

"Right. I checked that name you gave me – his false name – and there is someone who might fit. He is a partner in a building firm round here – actually I think those snazzy apartments over there might be his – but he spends most of his time in France. Mind you the firm is in financial shit, so he might be back over here. I can check."

"If he is back it might be because his daughter has just come into money. She has not seen him since she was a child and is unaware if he is alive or dead."

Alex shook her head. "You can't help feeling for Morgan, but if his daughter is still alive she'd be in her thirties."

"He always assumed she had been killed, but then finding the diary opened up a new plane of pain. Since then Morgan has looked everywhere. And the places he did not search, I searched. He contacted me three months ago and as you know, I cannot resist the lure of a missing child. Now he wonders if Montague's daughter might inadvertently hold a missing clue."

"Why? What about his wife? Montague's wife, I mean."

For a moment Austin faltered, unsure of how much to confide.

"Dead. I'm sure she knew nothing. Montague's mother died recently and we hoped he might make an appearance at the funeral. We still hope he might make contact with his daughter again."

"And of course you owe Morgan a mighty big favour."

"That is not the reason I took this case."

Her dark eyes held his for a moment in disbelief. However, now was not the time to bring up ancient history.

"So, you are convinced that he's back and is responsible for Emily."

"Possibly."

"That's one hell of a jump. There are a lot of scumbags out there fiddling with young girls and boys. What makes you think these cases are connected?"

Austin opened his weathered briefcase and extracted an envelope. He slid it towards Alex who held out a small brown hand to take it. It was then he noticed her ring was missing.

"I see you are wearing less jewellery than when we last met."

One glance from Alex told him to leave well alone.

"Very well. I will leave your demons alone, if you leave mine. There is a photograph of Ruby Morgan in that envelope."

Still ruffled, Carter slid out the photograph and turned it over.

"Well, will you look at that. They could be twins – apart from the hair colour."

"Now you see why I'm so interested in your case. Apart from the obvious reasons."

"I'll have to tell the boss. But he won't be happy when he knows who you're doing this job for."

"I am doing this for me. What her father has done is a separate matter, he needs to know what happened to his daughter."

She tore her eyes from the photo and caught his eye.

"Austin, what happened to Lily was not your fault. You were a good copper."

"And I make an excellent private investigator. Let me help you find Emily and we might just find Ruby too."

"Well, I hope you're right because at the moment we have nothing on this case but a viper's nest of angry, frightened parents, and the press circling like vultures. Let's find this bloke and give him a shake."

"DI Carter you astonish me. What would your superiors say?"

"Oh, I know exactly what they're going to say to me. I pray we get a live child and a locked up paedo at the end of all of this. I just hope we're not pissing in the wind."

Austin left the pub and walked to his Mercedes. Despite himself he was smiling, and this made him smile even more. He had missed Carter more than he realised. Did he also miss working in a team? Maybe, but he had always struggled with obeying rules and regulations and it had been this which had ultimately been his undoing. Surely the result justified the method? He had never killed anyone – well, no one that would be missed or that mattered. The world was a very dangerous place where the real criminals and gangs – people who tortured and raped, and stole eighteen-year-old girls to use in brothels – people who destroyed lives, these people did not follow any rule book but their own perverse lust and greed. So surely it was understood that to catch one of these deviants required following a different set of rules? Austin's rules. But it made sense to keep in with the police when it would benefit him. Morgan had helped him find Lily. Had known people who knew people. It had been too late, she had been destroyed by her experience and all the rehabilitation in the world had been unable to reach her. She had finally taken her own life just after her eighteenth birthday.

But at least he had a grave; somewhere to visit. He would never get over her senseless death but he could at least mourn her. Morgan had nothing. Ruby had been his precious angel, his princess. Lily had been taken to punish Austin for being instrumental in closing down a very lucrative business. Morgan had upset far more people in his life but the diary had convinced him Montague was to blame, that he and Ruby were living abroad somewhere or that he had violated then killed her.

Austin slipped behind the wheel, turned the key and listened to the purr of his engine. Why was it always the innocents that suffered? But Ruby had not disappeared alone. Something of immense value had also vanished that night and common sense alluded to Ruby having it on her person.

19

Friday evening

Nell nursed her coffee and peered at the ever shifting mass of water beyond her balcony. The wind lifted her fringe and cooled her swollen eyes. She looked again over the heavy sea towards the low-lying island. She should get her paints out, see if she still had the power to bring life to a blank page. She should also ring work and her solicitor. But most of all she needed to stop the nightmares and hallucinations.

After picking at a microwave meal, she had finally succumbed and spent the last hour on the internet looking up everything she could on the Emily Blake case. The girl had been waiting for her mum to pick her up from a ballet class. The mother was running late so assumed one of the other mums had given her a lift home. But when she had not shown and numerous phone calls had drawn a blank she had called the police.

Nell swept her hair out of her eyes and felt the exhaustion settle once more on her shoulders. And she had to leave for the séance soon, or ring and cancel. What if her mother or Nana came forward? More likely Maxine was a fake and nothing would happen. How much had she told her about her past? Not much really, so if Maxine was faking it should be easy to spot.

At that moment her mobile rang. She grabbed it, saw who was ringing and then answered it.

"Hello, Jane. How's work?"

"Never mind work. How are you?"

This was the call Nell knew was coming but despite her nerves it was good to speak to her supervisor.

"Not too bad. Got my hair cut."

"Oh, good girl. Look I need to tell you this."

Nell steeled herself for what might be coming next.

"Gary's been plaguing us. Where are you? When are you coming back? We are all liars. He's worried about your mental health. You know the sort of thing."

"Unfortunately, I do..."

"And we're all worried about you."

"I know and I'm sorry. Could I maybe just have another week? I'm owed the leave or I could take it as unpaid."

Why was she lying to her? Had she not run away, or was she really just taking a holiday from her life? But somehow telling Jane she was not coming back seemed too permanent. Although acutely aware that it was this fear of moving forward that had partly contributed to her problems, she was unable to destroy the link just yet.

"Unpaid? Not a chance. You're entitled to it. Just take care. Oh, and another thing—" There was a sparkle in Jane's voice.

"Yes?"

"Now, I shouldn't be telling you this really—"

Now she was interested. "What? Tell me."

"Mr Page is rethinking the whole expansion so there isn't a promotion going at the moment for anyone. So rest yourself and get better."

After the call Nell hugged her phone and let the glow of Jane's soft voice gradually fade from the room. So familiar; it felt like a letter from home. But this was her home now, wasn't it? For a beautiful moment she imagined the warmth of her work colleagues again, but this time without the ever-present black cloud of Gary in the background. The loneliness hit her again like a cold wave. Everything was new, sharp and metallic tasting. Colours seemed brighter, clearer; sounds were louder. Even walking amongst people felt like breaking through sheets of glass, making her skin sting, her jaw ache. New apartment, new friends, new haircut. New Nell?

Unable to help herself she rang Mr Elliot her solicitor, hoping he would still be there.

"Yes, Ms Montague. Everything is in order. The money has been transferred to your account, though I must say we are a little worried about our recent break in. The police are involved."

"So, the intruder knows about this place and what else I've been left?"

"Well, yes. It was in the file, but I'm sure you have nothing to worry about."

"Mr Elliot. I think I know who might be responsible." And she gave him Austin's name and mobile number.

The fear returned and with it anger. She had escaped Gary to be safe. She had met Austin against her better judgement but when he had brought up ghosts from her past she had run from him too.

'You are in danger.' Austin had said that others were looking for her, hoping to find her dad. The thought that someone would break into an office, break the law, just to find an address was terrifying. Was she just being paranoid? It could just as easily been Gary. Her nights were haunted by dreams of Ruby and Emily and it seemed she was not safe in the day either. But now it seemed that real people might be out to harm her. Suddenly she wanted to be amongst people and just as she was leaving the apartment she grabbed her scrapbook. Maybe it would help lure some ghosts of her past out in the open. Laughing uneasily at the thought she tucked it under her arm and headed downstairs.

Whatever picture Nell had conjured in her head when she thought of Maxine's home was quickly erased when she was welcomed into a stylish living room which held a faint aroma of basil and garlic.

"Sorry about the clutter. This furniture fitted nicely into my warehouse in London but when I moved here I didn't have the heart to sell it. It's far too big of course."

Nell's eyes drifted over the huge leather sofa, wide screen TV and large prints on the wall as she was led to a dining area beyond. A large round table dominated the room, surrounded by eight straight backed chairs. The room was lit by a standard lamp in the corner and the light was restful and calming. The warming scent of vanilla soaked into the modern furniture and pale walls. Two large framed photos hung on the wall, depicting surfers on monstrous, tsunami sized waves.

"Do you surf?" asked Nell innocently. Maxine's long lean body was made for a wetsuit, pondered Nell, then considered that if she donned one she would look more like a marooned seal or an overstuffed sausage.

"Me? Hell, I don't swim too well. Big waves, scary. Now, I find this light works best, but we can put the main light on if you prefer. You've got to feel comfortable."

Any hint of Victorian melodrama was quickly dispersed by Maxine's rich voice. "You look terrified."

Which made Nell laugh despite the accuracy. "Oh shit, yes. I've never done anything like this before. But it can't be any worse than the nightmare last night or what happened earlier today."

Maxine beamed. "Now this is what I hoped you'd say. I mean it's horrible for you to be haunted like this but it means something is bound to happen tonight."

"Be careful what you wish for, you might not be squealing in such glee at the end of the night. It's not much fun watching a little girl be raped in a cellar." Cellar. Nell felt the word charge into the atmosphere.

"What just happened there?" Maxine had stopped squealing but still looked excited. "Come on, let's kick this off."

Hesitantly, Nell pulled back one of the heavy dining chairs.

"Do we have to touch fingers?"

Maxine's eyes crinkled as she smiled.

"Well, I don't generally unless we go into a full séance, but if you want to touch my fingers you can."

"Sorry. I don't know what I'm doing." Then in panic, "It won't make things even worse, will it?"

"Could it get worse? Now, sit back and relax. Close your eyes if it helps. When we're finished I have a nice bottle of red breathing in the kitchen or juice if you'd rather, but for now just concentrate on Ruby and Emily."

"Right. OK. I'm concentrating."

"Actually, I think you might be hyperventilating, so if you don't want me to get you a paper bag I suggest you take some slow, deep breaths."

It was rather unnerving, thought Nell, to see Maxine's beautiful features in a state of calm concentration. She really did have amazing cheekbones.

"You OK?"

Startled, Nell closed her eyes again and listened to the traffic outside. They were sat at the table – hands not touching – but with Nell's scrapbook in the middle. Maxine had said it was an excellent idea to bring it.

Nell's stomach rumbled and she felt nervous laughter bubble up.

"I've got snacks in the kitchen for afterwards if you're hungry." Hungry. The room pulsed again in response to the word. "Hold tight, Nell."

Nell heard her own shallow breaths fill the room and she made a conscious effort to relax. She thought about the rape of Emily she had been made to witness and Ruby's arrogance as she brushed out her hair. But strangely all that came to mind was a small knitted rabbit with button eyes and a bow round its neck.

Maxine snorted. "Well this is vexing. Apart from the reaction to 'cellar' and 'hungry' I can't feel a damn thing."

Nell opened one eye. "Give them time, they are usually queuing up to torment me."

"Try telling me again what you know about Emily or Ruby."

So in stilted sentences Nell went through it all again. Ruby, the original nightmare, and then Ruby's bedroom. Emily and her dash for freedom which had gone so wrong. Even the red haired figure following her on the webcam whom she supposed was Ruby and the obscenity she had been made to witness with the lobster pot in the sea cave.

"Nothing. No wait, what was that over there?"

"What do you mean?" Nell's head spun round to see.

"It is like someone is in the other room, listening to us and watching." Silence.

A cold prickling started on Nell's neck and she rigidly resisted the urge to turn around again. A movement caught her eye as if something just flashed past the mirror on the wall above but then looking again she noticed a crane fly.

"Is there anyone here who would like to talk to Nell Montague?"

Silence

"Come forth in peace."

Nothing.

"Maybe it's me, Nell. Nobody wants to talk to us. May I look at your book? I might pick up something from that."

Relief that nothing had happened, or disappointment? Nell smiled and opened the book.

Watching Maxine slowly turn the pages, Nell felt her shoulders unknot a little as she shyly explained what this or that was. More pages turned and Nell felt her childhood unravel in front of Maxine. She should feel vulnerable that a stranger was looking at her most private possessions but somehow watching those elegant fingers handling the pages so respectfully she felt safe.

"Oh, and that's a scrap of wallpaper from my bedroom at Lark House. Sorry, I was a bit of a strange kid." Nell joked.

Maxine's smile faltered.

"Now that's got some power in it."

She turned a page and Nell's key lay taped to the page.

"Oh my God." Maxine pushed the book away. Her face ashen.

Alarmed, Nell grabbed Maxine's trembling hands.

163

"What is it?"

Maxine shook her head and closed her eyes.

"That was intense. I had a sudden rush of such panic and fear. Someone was very scared and alone."

"Who? Who are you talking about?"

Maxine opened her eyes which were bright with anger.

"That key. If you unlock the door you'll find her. She couldn't get out. She waited and waited but no one came. Nell, where did that key come from?"

Nell opened the page and touched the old door key on its ribbon.

"I found it."

"Where? Nell, this could be the root of it all."

"In the grass. Outside Butlers Yard."

A car hooted in the street outside and its thread of normality seemed to give Maxine strength. Taking a deep breath she rubbed Nell's shaking shoulders and gave a wobbly smile.

"Well, I hope you are feeling brave, girl. Because if you want to find out why you're being haunted we're going to have to go where this all started. We're going to find the door this key fits."

"But I don't know, I just found it outside." Nell stammered.

Maxine gave the key one more hesitant look.

"Oh, don't worry. Once we get in this Butlers Yard we'll find the door. She'll let you know where she is."

"Who will?"

Maxine stood and reached for the wine bottle.

"Ruby. She's trapped somewhere in the damn house where she died all those years ago."

20

"I'm not going back there." Nell's jaw protruded in petulance, unable to hide her alarm.

"Well," Maxine's grin narrowed an inch at Nell's reaction, "not tomorrow anyway, I've got a late shift at the hospital. But I'm free on Sunday." The grin was back to its full width.

"But you think there's a body there."

"Probably a skeleton now."

"Maxine that's not helping. Look, I escaped from Wiltbury. The idea is not to go back. I might run into Gary." Not to mention a million memories she was trying to forget.

"Good. It will show you've moved on, in more ways than one."

"Yeah, but—"

"Yeah but what? Seriously, I think Ruby is haunting you because she wants to be found and given a decent burial. Well, you would, wouldn't you?"

Nell couldn't deny that this made sense. But what about the other haunting? "Then Emily's dead too?"

Maxine's smile dulled at the mention of Emily. "I don't think so. But I bet you can find her."

"How?"

"She's made contact with you, hasn't she? Let's see if we can say hello back."

"Oh, you soon recovered from the key in my scrapbook incident."

Maxine shrugged. "Occupational hazard. Hang out with the spirit world and sometimes you're going to get spooked."

"I don't want to go back." For a moment she remembered the phone call with Jane that afternoon. Why had she made out this was just a holiday, that she was seriously considering going back to work next week? Was that the agreed time limit for getting over a battering from a boyfriend, running away, and the death of the last member of her family? Stunned, she realised she had not counted her dad, but then did she really think he was still alive? The dad that she had known – who had told her stories and made her feel safe – had died a long time ago. The man that Austin was looking for had been out of life for twenty-three years.

"I'm trying to start a new life, Maxine," Nell said softly.

The smile was gone and sympathy glowed from Maxine's eyes.

"I know you are, my love, but somehow I don't think this is just a body in a house. She's haunting you for a reason. Something to do with your past and that key."

Nell looked away but Maxine had not finished.

"Have you asked yourself why you kept it? I mean you found it when you were a kid but why did you put it in your scrapbook? And there was a faded luggage label tied to it."

Nell blushed. "Oh, just kids' stuff."

But she wasn't fooling Maxine.

"What did it say? And don't pretend you can't remember."

Nell's blush darkened. "Ruby's room. But, it's not what you think. My dad used to tell me stories – when I was little – about a girl called Ruby. I told you that, didn't I? That's all. I wanted to believe she was real, that I was like her."

She hated seeing the conclusion jump into Maxine's eyes. "Well, she was real, wasn't she. Seems to be a bit of coincidence. Don't you want to know?"

"I think she was the daughter of someone Dad knew, that's all. Or maybe one of his pupils. I don't remember."

Nell didn't like the way the conversation was going.

"More reason, Nell, to go back and put this behind you permanently."

Nell sighed and rubbed her neck.

"I'll think about it. I'm just not sure I'm up to it."

Disappointment flashed across Maxine's face and Nell felt guilty.

"But if I do change my mind I want us to have a plan. I feel safer with a plan."

Maxine offered to top up Nell's glass but she shook her head. Maxine took a gulp before replying.

"We go to Butlers Yard, find Ruby and call the police. Then with her out of your head, we concentrate on Emily. I don't think we will find Emily until Ruby is at peace. I know someone in the police here, she might be only too happy for a fresh approach."

"And if I see Gary?"

"Why would you? He doesn't live next door does he? We can leave here first thing on Sunday morning. Oh and maybe bring an overnight bag. It might take a while. Have you anywhere we can crash, if you do decide on this course of action?"

"If you bring a sleeping bag." Nell sighed and resigned herself for the ordeal ahead. Yet something felt right. Maybe she needed this to put her demons to rest.

Maxine held up her glass to toast Nell's decision. "OK, Sunday morning then. I'll meet you in the café. I'll drive if you like, oh and can I keep the scrapbook?"

They both glanced down at the innocent scrapbook with its faded flowery cover.

"You sure?"

But Maxine just shrugged. "Something might come crawling out when I'm alone tonight, like a map of where she's buried."

"Oh Jesus."

"Joking! Lighten up and get your game face on. Sunday, we're going to find ourselves a body."

Nell reached for the wine bottle.

"Bloody hell."

Whatever she dreamed that night dissolved within seconds of waking. All that remained was the faint memory of a man and woman shouting.

'You brought this filth into our family.'

'How dare you? It was one drunken night and you'd know all about those.'

All through the day, she kept hearing it in her mind, like a stuck record. The man reminded her of Gary but she knew they had never had a conversation like that, firstly because 'family' was not a word they used for their relationship, and secondly she had never cheated on him.

21

Saturday night

One week after Cindy's party and she was dressing for another. What the hell did you wear to a surfing party? Then, as the evening approached the air shifted and became heavy. Clouds spread like ink dots on blotting paper until the sky looked too heavy to remain airborne. Then the first crack of thunder ripped through the sky.

Nell was in the kitchen when she heard a knock at the door. Panic flushed through her and for a moment she did not move.

"Hey, Nell. It's Leon from downstairs."

Smoothing her fringe in an unconscious habit that she'd had since she was a teenager, Nell approached the door.

Leon was dressed in faded cut off jeans that showcased his muscular legs to perfection, and a sleeveless vest, which did the same for his arms and chest.

"Hello," she managed.

His shy grin made the breath catch in her chest.

"Look, they say we're gonna have a mega storm tonight so I'm having the party here. The lightening will look awesome over the sea."

"Wow." Wow? She really had to do better than this.

"We can do a barbie on the terrace."

"Brilliant. What do you want me to bring?"

He raised one arm to lean on her doorframe then rested his head on it.

"No, you'll be 'right. Just make sure you come. Katie and Jez are going back to Brissy for the summer – well a few will be leaving soon to go back to Uni or whatever – so we're going to watch the storm, drink some beer and fill our faces."

"Marvellous."

Then there was one of those pauses in conversation, which should have been awkward, but Nell was too preoccupied trying to decide if Leon's eyes were grey or blue. She became aware that she was softly stroking the side of her neck and stopped immediately. Leon opened his mouth to say something but then apparently changed his mind and said instead,

"Well, I'd better get going. Come on down when you're ready. Anytime after seven will be cool."

"Excellent. See you later."

Nell softly closed the door and listened as Leon sprinted down the stairs. She rested her forehead on the smooth wood of the door and closed her eyes. For a second she just enjoyed the feeling of breathing in and out, every nerve ending in her body hummed like a tuning fork. What had he considered saying before changing his mind? The view would be better from her apartment. She indulged in a daydream, which involved Leon's arm around her shoulder, watching the lightening, but then quickly progressed to more energetic activity.

"Oh God." She was acutely aware that she had not felt like this for a very long time. The last thing she needed was a new relationship, she chastised herself, but a little voice somewhere south of her belly button was muttering about a harmless one-night stand.

'It was one drunken night and you'd know all about those.'

"Oh hell." Nell took a deep breath and headed back to the kitchen.

Thunder resonated through the apartments and lightening shocked the sky. Dressed in her plum silk dress and a light touch of make-up, Nell gave herself the once over in the bathroom mirror. There were still bruises on her face and arms and new pink skin from the scrapes, but otherwise she looked tanned and healthy. She had considered a long sleeved shirt but then remembered her resolution not to be ashamed of her scars.

"Battle wounds," she reasoned, and evidence that she had fought and survived. For a second her stomach lurched at the thought of returning to Lark House the next day but steadied when she remembered she would not be alone. A touch of perfume, a coat of lipstick and she was ready to head downstairs with a bottle in her hand and industrial booted butterflies in her stomach.

The ground floor apartment looked larger than hers and boasted a generous terrace surrounding it on three sides. A barbeque was smoking happily and a tall dreadlocked man with weathered skin was nursing it with one hand while cradling a beer with the other. The rest of the party were watching the storm from the front. They seemed much younger than her – early twenties Nell guessed – and were all casually dressed. Leon had changed into jeans and a Rip Curl T-shirt and Nell felt old and frumpy in her silk dress.

"Come on, Leon. You're missing it." A tall girl with long dark hair grabbed Leon by the hand and pulled him to the rail as another whiplash of lightning slashed the sky. Leon laughed and turning reached for Nell's hand to pull her forward for a better view. His hand felt warm and dry in hers, and as she stepped towards the rail, she felt his thumb graze over the back of her hand sending shivering sparks over her body.

One, two, three, she waited for him to drop her hand but he held it firmly. The other people faded away and the storm was muted. All that Nell felt was the warmth of Leon's hand, the firm pulse of her own blood and the mantle of peace settling over her. When had she last felt like this? The simple act of holding another's hand was powerful and beautiful. Her silk dress rippled in the breeze, fluttering against her leg like a nervous hand. She closed her eyes and drank in the moment: the storm, her new life, Leon holding her hand and her loving it.

A car pulled up. The rain was coming down in torrents and the driver ran to the safety of the front door. Nell felt Leon stir.

"Aw shit." He pulled away to look over the rail. "Sorry, Nell. It's Tash. She wasn't invited." Puzzled, Nell felt the sudden cold air hit her naked hand as Leon disappeared inside. Who the hell was Tash? But from Leon's reaction she had a very good idea.

All that was left of the storm was the driving rain so they drifted to get food and return indoors. Nell had suddenly lost her appetite but followed them and made an effort to talk to the other guests. Leon sat awkwardly beside an ethereal girl with long blond curls who sucked her drink through a straw. Her doll like eyes were fixed on Nell.

"That's Tash. Leon's ex. She's a right madam." The girl with the long dark hair whispered in Nell's ear and gratefully Nell turned to speak to her.

"I didn't realise…"

"Yeah, well that's Leon for you. He loves the ladies. But he's also a really nice bloke. Just be careful."

Tash, obviously aware that she was being spoken about, continued to glare at Nell like a spoilt child. For a moment Nell thought of Cindy from just a week ago. Seeing Nell, Leon rose from the sofa and headed for her. The pouting lips parted and in a public school accent, Tash spoke.

"You must be Nell. From the penthouse." She made it sound like a brothel. "Leon's new chum. How is it up there?"

"Tash. Leave it out."

Puzzled Nell looked between Leon and Tash. "Yes, I live in the penthouse, and thank you it's very nice."

"Seen the ghost yet?"

"TASH, shut it!" Leon was clearly not amused. "Look, you can't just turn up here and start causing shit. This is Katie and Jez's party."

So the apartment had been haunted already. Stifling her fear, Nell allowed the fight in her to surface.

"Yeah, Tash. Chill out." This was from the dreadlocked chef. This little brat obviously had not been popular with Leon's friends.

It would have been so easy to ignore her. To treat her with contempt, but if Nell had learned anything in the last week it was that doing nothing, ignoring things, just encouraged more of the same behaviour.

"Have I seen the ghost yet? Well, let me think. I see many things, Tash, and hear even more. Some of them don't belong to the living world but then I don't spook easily." Well, strictly speaking this was a lie, but it sounded good and a slightly paler Tash returned to pouting.

"It's just a stupid story." Leon smiled ruefully at Nell.

"No, it's not. I've seen her. The little red haired girl. That's why the owner moved out. He was supposed to live on in the penthouse when they were finished building, but she drove him out."

The little red haired girl. Nell felt the blood drain from her body.

"Tash. You're trashed. It's just a story. My parents said he moved back to France."

So Ruby had been here before her. Why here? Not for the first time Nell wondered how long Nana had owned the apartment and why she had bought it in the first place. However, the fight was still in her.

"I know a medium," she interrupted. "I'll ask her to check it out." And suddenly the thought of Maxine's wide lazy smile filled her with comfort.

Leon brightened at the change of subject. "Ah, you've met Max? I invited her but she was busy tonight." A woman, who had been sitting quietly, enjoying the argument, suddenly sat up and took more interest.

"You invited Max? Did she know I was coming?"

"Yeah, Alex, but I don't think she was bullshitting."

Puzzled, Nell felt the need to defend Maxine.

"She told me she was working tonight." Alex seemed to accept this and conversations began to bloom around them again. Tash was ignored. Touching Nell's arm gently Leon guided her to the kitchen.

"Look, I'm sorry about Tash. We had a thing a few months ago, nothing serious but she's not happy."

I don't blame her, thought Nell. But then Leon winked, placed his hand over hers and Nell suddenly felt like she was standing on an air mattress. Time slowed down so that when Leon lifted his hand and placed it behind her neck, and then slowly, slowly drew her towards his parted lips, Nell felt her whole life had been in preparation for this moment. Their lips grazed, then a movement at the door caused Leon to turn his head.

Tash stood in the doorway; hand on hip, with a face that would have made Medusa proud.

"So you know Maxine?" she spat.

Aware she was blushing Nell turned to face Tash.

"Yeah," she nodded slowly, "she's great."

"Yeah, she's great, if you're into lesbians."

"Tash. Look, I'm sorry but we're over. Go home." For a moment Nell's head went into a spin, fuelled by the kiss, shock at finding out Maxine was gay, and obscurely worry and sympathy for Tash who slammed out of the house and was clearly too drunk to be driving. In the turmoil, Alex came into the kitchen and stubbed out her cigarette.

"Give me a hand, Leon. She shouldn't be driving in that condition. I'll take her home before one of my colleagues picks her up."

Leon nodded, "Cheers Alex. Sorry guys – won't be long."

He gave Nell's hand a quick squeeze.

"See you when I get back?" Then he headed into the rain.

22

Three years ago

Rain streamed down the window, droplets madly crashing into each other, blending and separating again. Maxine sighed, misting the pane, making everything blurred. A red London bus rattled by, illuminating the torrent coming down. Harsh neon lights outside bored into her aching eyes. Closing them, she tipped the large wine glass back in one snapping motion.

One eye opened and she stared into the red stained bottom of the glass. Empty again. Damn it. Just how much had she drunk?

Not enough whispered a small voice. She padded to the kitchen area of her warehouse apartment on bare, sore feet. Holding up the bottle to the light confirmed it was empty and she knew there was no more alcohol. How did she know? Because she had been steadily drinking everything over the past few days – even the three year old bottle of Tia Maria she found at the back of the cupboard under the sink, left from an ex who had liked it. She wasn't a naturally tidy person; none the less the apartment was littered with clothes, pizza boxes, empty bottles and cigarette butts. This was what heartbreak looked like, she thought ruefully. In her case anyway.

She tapped the bottom of her cigarette packet only to find she was also out of smokes. There was nothing for it, she was going to have to venture out for the first time in seventy-two hours.

Snatching her leather jacket and keys she headed for the door, stabbing at the remote on her way. Silence blossomed in the room which had been subjected to eighties punk, thirties blues, and Beethoven in varying decibels since she had got the text.

Max threw the door open to reveal Sam coming up the stairs.

"Max, no wait, we need to talk."

Max's first instinct was to head back into the apartment and slam the door in Sam's face. But she was angry and needed alcohol and nicotine.

"Out of my way." She attempted to push past, but Sam blocked the way. She had been crying, her eyes swollen and bloodshot.

"Max, I need to explain. Please, let me. I have to."

Her lip quivered and for one moment Max felt her fist ball and she imagined Sam crumpled at the bottom of the stairs. Then she spotted the Threshers bag Sam was carrying. Grabbing it she headed back into the flat, careless of whether Sam was following her or not.

Slamming the wine on the counter she thrust in the corkscrew like a bayonet.

"I thought we could have a drink and talk." Sam tried again softly.

Max threw her a black look and gulped angrily from the open bottle.

"Max, look I really care about you but…Max, speak to me please."

"Shut the fuck up, Sam, and close the door as you leave. I only want the wine. Not you."

A small hand fluttered hesitantly on Max's sleeve. "But let me explain. It was Ray, you see, he…"

Crashing the bottle down, Max turned on Sam and grabbed her roughly by the shoulders. She was using her height to intimidate and took satisfaction in seeing Sam flinch.

"You don't need to explain anything, sweetheart. I've seen it all before. Hubby and you had a bust up so you decided to try a bit of soft. All the men want you, don't they, so you decided to see if you could work the same magic on women."

Sam's eyes met hers mutely and Max could smell the shampoo in her hair. A memory stirred, once sweet but now cancerous, of Sam laying her head on Max's shoulder, her arms wrapped around her waist. Only last week, before she had decided her curiosity was satisfied.

"I was confused."

Max laughed in her face and spun her around to face the door.

"I don't think so. I think you're just a tease, so fuck off before we find out just how angry I really am." And thrusting the door open with one hand she grabbed the protesting Sam with the other and threw her out.

She slammed the door, punched the remote to drown out the sound of Sam's pleas, and tipped the wine bottle back. Leaning against the window again she watched the rain etch its pattern against the glass and let the anger seep from her eyes in scolding tears. Inhaling, she smelt the sweet cloying scent of Sam's perfume. Fury and hurt chased each other around her bloodstream, making her face tense and limbs twitch. Finally, a figure appeared on the glistening road below. Sam stopped and looked up.

"Run away, little girl. Back to your husband." Max spat contemptuously. How had she been taken in? All the signs had been there. Their relationship had been very one-sided with Max doing all the corrupting. They had never slept together in any connotation of the phrase and now Max could not decide if she was glad or not.

Suddenly the Sex Pistols were interrupted by the Buzzcocks asking if she had ever found herself in love with someone inappropriate. Despite herself, Max felt one side of her mouth twitch.

Maybe she had had a lucky escape. Sam had turned out to be quite insecure and needy. It had been endearing to start with but was already growing tiresome.

"Snap out of it. Enough of the hurting already."

So for the second time she grabbed her bag and made for the door.

The night air was soft and cool to her aching head. Thrusting her hands in her pockets she tried to inhale confidence, the strength she had been so used to for so long and had now evaporated within a few weeks. The corner shop was just a few streets away. As she waited for the lights to change at the busy crossroads she considered turning and heading instead for the local bar. But then her mobile buzzed. For a second she wondered whether it was Sam and considered ignoring it. But curiosity won.

"Dad? God it's good to hear from you."

Max tucked in a shop door so she could hear properly.

"Maxine, you sound sad."

"Sad? No I'm OK."

The pause on the other end reminded her that her dad always knew.

"Have you eaten? You could come over."

"Actually, I'm a bit pissed…"

"I know."

"That woman I was seeing…"

"Where are you, Maxine? I'm just leaving the station now, we could get a curry and bitch about bi-curious women."

Despite herself Maxine felt one corner of her mouth twitch. She had inherited her sixth sense supposedly from her mother, but sometimes she had to wonder about her dad.

"OK, but I'm really cranky."

By the time her dad arrived she realised she was about as sober as she was going to get. The chair in the curry house was slippery and she had to keep adjusting her position. At a table across from her were a group of women she was on nodding acquaintance with. She made a conscious effort not to catch the eye of one fussy blonde who had been trying it on for the last few months.

Painfully aware of the empty seat opposite her she glanced at her watch and prayed for green lights from the police station to this part of town.

At last the door opened. Someone once said that you could always tell a nurse. She had thought it was bull until she heard the same said about the constabulary. Even in plain clothes his every movement shouted detective.

"My darling girl, tell daddy all about that stupid bitch who you are so better off without."

23

Sunday morning

Birthdays. Never a good day with Gary. And Valentine's Day had always been a bad one too, mused Nell. Jostling with others to find the perfect card had been difficult for other reasons. Nell was not just trying to say 'I love you' in the best way, she was guessing how Gary would take each card to see if it would set him off, as once a card with 'Forever' had done.

'Forever, what the fuck is that supposed to mean. Card shops are brimming full of "I love you" and "be mine", but you choose the only one with "Forever" on.' The card had been ripped up, as had the one he had given her, then the red roses beheaded and the chocolates stamped on. Nell had endured the coy comments the next day at work about other people's romantic evenings with bruised ribs and a tender scalp where her hair had been ripped. She had also lived in dread that someone would send her a joke card at work and Gary would find out. It was always the first question he asked, how many cards had she had? What about emails? Now she wouldn't be lying to him, would she? How could he be sure. Perhaps he would ring up her work mates, yeah, they'd tell him.

So Valentine's Day was always fraught with danger, then there was Mother's Day which wasn't much better, and Father's Day hard on its heels. All of Nell's memories were cloudy. Sometimes she caught herself doing something innocuous, usually in the kitchen, and wondered where she had learned it from. Any memories of her mum cooking were mixed up with visions of Nana in her blue and white striped apron whipping or sampling, basting and seasoning.

What was it about Nana which had always made her feel so safe? Even when she had been dying, just being in the same room as her had made her feel secure. Had she ever felt like that with her mum? Did it matter? Nana was all the mother she had ever needed and now she was gone.

She remembered the first time Nana's dementia had really made an appearance. Nana had been diagnosed with cancer but she had still been Nana. Then one day Nell had picked her up at the home to take her to a hospital appointment and Nana had sworn at her for being a few minutes late. Shocked, Nell had turned to defend herself and looked straight into the eyes of a stranger. Whoever the woman sitting next to her was, she was certainly not Nana.

'In fact why don't you just drop me off here and I'll get a cab home. Don't bother coming in with me.' And through her tears Nell watched Nana make her slow painful way into the hospital reception without a backwards glance. Nell had to park the car, find money for the meter and then make her own way to the Oncology suite. Nana was flicking through a magazine and ignored Nell even when she sat next to her.

'What time's your appointment?' asked Nell pointlessly.

'I thought I told you to go? I don't need you here snivelling next to me.'

And so ignoring the pitying embarrassed looks from the other patients Nell had been forced to leave. Unable to hold back the misery she had howled all the way back to the car, but then this was a hospital, people were used to seeing tears in the corridors.

When someone is diagnosed with cancer it unfortunately does not stop them also getting dementia. Mislaying things, forgetting appointments, being unable to find the right word for something. It could be explained away by the fact that Nana was eighty and undergoing one of the greatest stresses anyone had to put up with. But the shock of seeing Nana become a game of misfits, with one third an adult, another third a confused child, and the third an agitated, angry twin, was destroying. Sometimes Nana was her old self with her sharp wit and amazing intuition. Other times she seemed unaware of who Nell was. Sometimes she remembered she was ill and other times accused Nell of lying to her, of making it all up.

Was it selfish of Nell to be grateful that the dreadful cancer had claimed Nana before she became totally lost in her other reality, unable to find her way back? The last time Nell had seen her, before the hospital side room where she passed away, Nana had been back to her old self. She had seemed younger somehow, the pain irrelevant. They had talked about Nell's childhood and shared good times. They had even laughed. Had some instinct told Nell that this would be their last time together before their world became filled with machines and bedside manners?

Now Nell's birthday had arrived. The first without Nana, but also the first without Gary. It was her day, she mused, as she ate pancakes in bed, and she could damn well do what she wanted with it. There would be a text from Jane but no one else had her new number. Though no one else from work had had her old number either. Thirty. End of her twenties and beginning of middle age. No, thought Nell fiercely, the beginning of her new life.

Maxine waited for the traffic to clear before jogging heroically to her front door. Minutes earlier – and out of her neighbours' view – it had bordered on a Sunday stroll, but then a five-mile jog was not always the best hangover cure. Indoors she stripped out of her running gear, leaving a trail behind her. The shower was hot, hard and needled between her shoulder blades. She let the gushing water torrent over her skull in an effort to clear the last wine dregs.

Her shift yesterday evening had been in the emergency department of the local hospital where the sister in charge had remarked sagely that most of their patients were more in need of a drunk tank than experienced medical staff. But then the red phone announced a road traffic accident coming in by air ambulance. When she finally got home she was wide awake and the wine was more medicinal than anything else.

Curled up under the duvet one thought raced around her head. What on earth was she trying to do with Nell and her nightmares. If she had not sensed the terror from the scrapbook, she might have been able to dismiss Nell's problems as stress. But there was more to her than that and Emily's fetch had totally unnerved Maxine, not that she was going to admit it. The more she exposed herself to this unwanted gift, then surely the more confident she would get. But she would never be really comfortable with the insidious emotions and insight. Life was surely difficult enough without sensing and seeing things that did not belong in the world of the living.

When her father had suggested she move to Launton after her burnout in London three years earlier, she had hesitated. Could she get enough agency work as a nurse in a sleepy surfing town? But she had got a bank contract at the large general hospital twenty miles away, and found her outgoings were much less than London's. Probably because she did not have a life or any friends. What social life she had came from the hospital, Erin, and the migratory surfing crowd, the latter being far too young for her to hang out with but in this tiny town people were far less cliquey. And not working full-time had given her a chance to explore her psychic side and see if she could learn to control it. If she wanted to. Stretching her lean limbs in the water, she thought through her next move. Caffeine, croissant and two paracetamol.

Leaning on her kitchen counter she gulped scalding black coffee and gazed at the distant sea view. Leon had texted last night with the change of venue. But would she really have gone had she not been working? To see Nell perhaps, but Alex might have been there. A heavy object shifted in Maxine's throat, reminding her that it was still early days with Alex. Before she could stop them, her eyes drifted to the photo she still kept on her mantelpiece. Last summer and a police retirement party. Definitely a good night and one that Maxine held on to as proof of the few good times in their relationship.

Ancient history and she was not moving again. Maxine switched her mind from wallowing to the job in hand. Nell's ghost. She switched on her laptop and then quickly dressed while it woke up. Could she really do this? Maybe she should not meddle but someone had to do something. The magnitude of what she was attempting doused her. She was trying to find a skeleton, a murder scene. This could all go very wrong and she could end up getting nicked and lose her job. There were times she wished she still smoked. She hit Google, typed in 'Wiltbury' and 'Ruby', then reached for her phone.

There was a long squeak of brakes as a large van stopped outside the coffee house. The vast windows had a mirror-like quality and Maxine checked her hair. Satisfied, she returned to her coffee.

"I'm here, sorry I'm late."

Startled she looked up to Nell. "Hello. You look like shit. Are you alright?"

Nodding, Nell sank in a cloud of nervous energy and loud scraping of chair on stone floor.

"Storm keep you awake?"

There was an awkward silence as Nell flushed purple.

"Umm. Yeah. A bit."

Nell eyed Maxine's coffee and ordered her own. Maxine watched on in amusement as the normally bright Nell folded in on herself like an origami bird, one wrong move away from turning into a frog.

"Are you hanging?"

"What?" Nell now looked like a wounded baby bird, which had nothing to do with her bruises.

"Do we have a hangover this morning?" Maxine said louder and laughed as Nell winced. "Oh, we do, don't we? Well snap, only I'm ahead of you with the caffeine and I find a seven mile run helps." Liar, said a small voice.

But it was not just a hangover, thought Maxine. Nell was having trouble looking her in the eye and her usually expressive face was devoid of all movement.

Suddenly a possible truth dawned on her. Nell had either got laid last night or she had found out Maxine was gay. Mentally shrugging Maxine let it go. If Nell could not handle it then that was her problem. But she would be disappointed not to see the project through. Still, other people's prejudice was just that, their prejudice. Coming out had been hard enough without feeling responsible for the fragile feelings of everyone else.

For a moment she searched for something to say, while Nell nuzzled at her cappuccino, inhaling the steam. Finally, Maxine caught her eye and coaxed a wonky smile from her. Nell had one of those faces that displayed every emotion and thought that was going on in her head. At first, Maxine had found the unconscious face pulling rather distracting but now saw it as one of Nell's charms.

"Don't ever play poker, Nell."

"Uh?"

Not for the first time Maxine felt her protective nature come out in full force for this brave, beaten brunette. It must be the nurse in her, it certainly was not anything else, she told herself fiercely. Falling for a straight woman was not something she was ever going to do again; the burnout in London had taught her that.

"Nell, your face is like subtitles of what you're thinking. Now, I'm guessing you were at a party last night."

"Yes, at Leon's. He's on the ground floor of where I live." Nell confirmed. "But you probably knew that."

"Ah, yes, Leon. His rich mummy and daddy bought the place so Leon could play at being surfer dude."

"What?"

"He arrives in the spring each year, opens the surf shack, breaks some hearts and then flies back home in the autumn. Nice guy but not really into relationships."

The guilt she felt at her disloyalty to a friend was overtaken by the cause of it. What was it to her if Nell and Leon hooked up? Still, she finally had Nell's full attention.

Suddenly, the van moved and the man himself appeared from the shop opposite with company. For a second time Nell's face flushed. Leon's face had spread into the lazy lopsided smile Maxine recognised, as a slim blonde with tiny shorts and long legs stopped in the street and embraced him. They spoke for a moment then walked up the road together.

"Leon is everyone's friend. Bit of a soap bubble, you know? Nice to look at but one touch and he disappears into nothing."

Nell's hand drifted to the scab on her temple and Maxine could have kicked herself for being so insensitive. She obviously had one hell of a crush. Probably understandable after what she had gone through. Poor kid was probably desperate for some affection.

"But who knows, maybe he is just waiting for the right woman to come along, with wavy brown hair and dark brown eyes, so that he can fall in love and settle down."

She realised she had been trying to get Nell to smile. It came now, albeit a rather watery version, but it still lit sparks in her eyes which reminded Maxine of smoky quartz.

"We sort of…you know…last night."

"You don't need to tell me. It's your own personal business. A kiss or something more? No, no you don't need to answer."

Now she had Nell laughing. An infectious deep rumble of a laugh.

"Just a sort of kiss. Which was really stupid and childish of me."

"Where's the harm? Live a bit, just don't get hurt."

Nell's eyes locked on her. "There's always harm in letting your guard down when you're feeling vulnerable. That's how Gary got in." All that was left in Nell's cup was froth, which she absent-mindedly scooped up with her spoon and ate. "Anyway, he left early. He and Alex had to take Tash home and I don't think he came back home 'til this morning."

Maxine felt her stomach tighten at the casual mention of Alex's name.

"Alex was there?"

"Yeah, and before you ask, she mentioned you. We reassured her that you were working else you would have come to the party."

A heavy silence again which only Maxine could break.

"So, I guess you know about me then?"

Despite herself, Maxine was shocked to hear the uncertainty in her voice. When would it ever get easier? Straight woman did not have to sit in coffee shops and say, 'So, I guess you know I like men?'

But she was worrying unnecessarily. "Maxine. Chill."

Another silence, but Maxine decided to take Nell's comment at face value.

"OK then. Ready to hit the road or are you hungry?"

A shiver attacked her body so suddenly she had to sit back down.

Hungry. A cold dusty floor in pitch black, waiting for him to come back. Then a familiar voice and the café came back into view.

"Max? What's wrong?" Nell's face was puckered into a frown and her bottom lip quivered. Maxine took a deep breath to steady her breakfast.

"Come on, let's go find a little redhead. I think I know where she might be."

24

Nell felt like a child in the huge front seat of Maxine's four-by-four. Maxine had finally stopped channel flicking and settled down to eighties rock. This time last week she had been packing. Now she was heading back to finally put her past behind her. But would it? It might stop the nightmares but what about her dad and Austin? Something else was worrying her too. Before the party had finally dissolved and Nell returned to the penthouse, she had had a strange sensation, almost as if she expected to see someone there. She had looked round but nothing, only a feeling that some of her boxes had been touched, that they were not quite in the same angle she had left them. But then it was probably just Tash and her stupid talk about ghosts, like that could scare her after what she had seen.

For a while she thought over what had happened with Leon and could have slapped herself. Was she really that desperate for attention? She did not know Leon and had acted like a silly teenager. Stupid and dangerous. She had got in too deep with Gary before she realised what he was capable of. And squabbling with Tash like that, like a schoolgirl. She felt ashamed. Learn your lesson girl and be more careful of your heart. She had barely escaped the last relationship and was certainly not ready for another. Embarrassment and shame kept her awake until nearly two by which time the computer was back on and she was looking up stories of drowned children in cages. She had nearly not turned up for Maxine this morning. Music had been coming out of Leon's apartment and his car had been back in the car park. She had had to stop herself from knocking on his door to apologise. It had not been until she had seen Maxine's sleek blonde crop seated in the café that she had remembered Tash's words. For a moment she had felt herself withdraw slightly but then remembered the odd looks she received when people saw her battered face. A token look of concern covering the fear on their faces. They had looked embarrassed almost but Nell knew what they were thinking. I don't want to know. Don't get me involved with your mess. I'll just pretend not to realise what is happening. So deciding not to be a hypocrite, she had put Maxine out of her misery.

"Wake up, Sleeping Beauty."

"Urr...ouch!" Nell stretched and knocked her knee.

"Wiltbury is ten miles and I need my navigator."

Nell rubbed her eyes and looked around. They were just approaching the Abbey Park Hotel and the sight of its stone walls brought back mixed memories.

"I'm so sorry. I've been boring company."

"Nah, forget it. You didn't snore much. Now, which way am I heading?"

Approaching Wiltbury felt like returning to school after a summer break. It felt smaller, scary but at the same time so familiar. After a week when everything had been new and strange, it was dangerously easy coming back. Guiding Maxine through the streets to Lark House increased her panic by the moment. Like stepping innocently, only to find too late the trap is sprung. Then they turned a corner and there it stood; solid if a bit ugly with its galvanised scabs. A bit like me, thought Nell. But it was good to see her old home again. Just over a week since she had last been here. What a week. Suddenly, she was thinking about the penthouse and realised for the first time it felt like home. Her bed, her toiletries in

189

the bathroom, her clothes in the wardrobe. Safe again.

She looked across to Maxine who was whistling appreciatively at the house. Her new friend. Her gay friend. God, how Gary would have hated that.

'Dykes? They just want a dick inside them. Then they'd know what it was for.'

Good old Gary. Always an open mind and a pleasant turn of phrase.

They wandered around the house; Nell kept peeping at Maxine to see if she was sensing anything but nothing disturbed her composure.

"And this is the garden; bit of a wilderness. And that," she pointed over the garden wall, "is Butlers Yard."

Maxine's nose twitched.

"I hope you don't mind but I've contacted a local who chairs the real crime society here. Yeah, I know, it's all a bit Miss Marple, but I found her on the web and she seems to know about old mysteries in Wiltbury. But only if you agree?"

For a moment Nell felt giddy.

"You really think we're going to find her, don't you?"

Maxine turned to stare at the grey façade of Butlers Yard again.

"Oh, I'm sure of it."

The wind picked up, causing the grass to hiss and sway, and the trees to creak. Butlers Yard stood like a gravestone beyond the wall. It had always scared Nell, now she was terrified.

"Maybe backup would be good."

"Excellent, now I had thought we'd camp in the garden but…" she looked around uncertainly.

"No, I've already decided. If we do stay the night, and I think we might need to, I'm going to shout you a night at a rather lovely hotel. Actually, we passed it on the way here. Abbey Park? Remember the big gates?"

"The posh place? That's very kind but…"

But Nell had made up her mind. She had never had a penny before but she had been overwhelmed by Maxine's generosity of time and help. It felt good to be lady bountiful for a change.

"You will love it and I won't be argued with. Anyway, it's the least I can do after all the help you've given me."

"Well, that's very kind. Let's give this woman a ring and get to it. Ready?"

The wind rose again, lashing the grass into Nell's legs. She took a deep breath and faced the inevitable.

"Let's do it. I don't fancy waiting for nightfall."

Footsteps fell on the stone steps outside Lark House. Nell and Maxine roosting on the staircase inside, exchanged looks, then rose to their feet. Three heavy knocks at the front door. The sound of them echoing in the hallway brought back childhood memories for Nell. She was first to the door and the shock was like a trap opening up under her.

"Celeste?"

Equally surprised Celeste grabbed her hand.

"Well, I didn't see this coming."

"I thought you were a taxi driver."

Nell felt a calm descend as introductions were made.

"You're looking a prettier sight than last Sunday," Celeste commented with a smile.

"Got my hair cut too." Nell tugged at a stray lock. Warm arms enveloped her and for a moment she fought back tears.

"You're all healed up."

"Physically getting there. Just my head now. Oh, what's that lovely smell?"

Laughing Celeste pointed to a basket on the porch. "My own chicken curry. I thought you could eat while I tell you what I know about the Ruby Morgan case."

They sat in the conservatory, the only room still to have furniture, albeit fragile looking. Maxine took out a notebook, "crap memory," she apologised, and Celeste told them what she knew.

"Now I've been interested in this case since it happened. Ruby Morgan was thirteen years old, the only daughter of Dieter and Susan Morgan. Yes, Maxine, the same Dieter Morgan."

Nell looked at them both in bewilderment and held up her hand. "I don't know who that is."

"Dieter Morgan is a very successful business man. Some say he is part of this county's answer to the firm, but other than a bit of trouble at his clubs, nothing else has ever stuck. Now Ruby ran off at the annual Halloween festival and was never seen again. Initially put down as a runaway, the police got more interested when they heard one of her teacher's had taken quite a shine to her and this same teacher disappeared around the same time."

Celeste took a breath and met Nell's glare.

"My dad had nothing to do with her disappearance. He just wouldn't have done that." A scene flickered in her mind of Ruby being given a lift, *'They still see you as a kid; they haven't noticed you're all grown up now.'*

"Nell's dad?" Maxine finally caught up.

"Yeah, but he actually came forward and had an alibi for that night, so it was another dead end. But not for Dieter Morgan and not for the town, you know how mud sticks, so he moved abroad and started again. Do you remember any of this, Nell?"

The cane chair bit painfully into her back and legs as she shifted in an attempt to get comfortable. "Bits. Mum and him had been fighting for ages before he left, and Mum was sick too so I guess he had just had enough of it all."

"Still, it's a hell of a coincidence him leaving on the night she disappeared and what was that about taking an interest in Ruby?" Maxine's eyes were glowing. "I mean he doesn't sound completely innocent, does he?"

"Not helping," warned Celeste. "Anyway, the police cleared him so that was considered a dead end. But then a story started going around about something else that went missing that night. Weeks before Ruby's class had been doing projects on family history, you know bringing history to life and making it personal. Well, Ruby apparently based hers on a necklace which had belonged to her great-grandmother. This same necklace apparently escaped the Nazi's greed in the Second World War and managed to get smuggled out along with the Morgan family when they escaped to Paris, and then on to London. The necklace is supposed to be a huge ruby and I'm sure the Morgans would not have wanted Ruby bragging about it at school where all the excited little girls then went home to tell their parents about the priceless stone the Morgans owned. Susan Morgan wore it to banquets and the like but after Ruby's disappearance it was never seen again."

"So, everyone thinks Ruby ran off with it?" Nell struggled to keep the disbelief from her voice.

Huge shoulders shrugged. "Maybe, but for a while after the police put the file in storage, amateur sleuths and treasure hunters swarmed over the story, trying to solve the mystery. My little group even had a go, but there was nothing to go on."

Something Austin had said pricked Nell's memory but she dismissed it as being too fanciful.

"Well, as I explained on the phone last night, Nell has been having nightmares about a little girl called Ruby and the house over that wall. And I got a really nasty sensation from a key she's got in her scrapbook from that time so," Maxine's eyes shone, "we thought we'd have a poke about."

As they descended the garden steps, Nell had the unpleasant sensation that she had just fallen into a badly scripted television murder mystery and had been given the worst role. How the hell was she in this situation with people she did not even know, meddling into one of the most painful and private areas of her life? But somehow her life had fallen into this fast flowing river, and if it stopped the nightmares it had to be worth it. Better this than having to explain to a doctor about her hallucinations and being medicated or sectioned.

It was three o'clock when they opened the garden gate and approached Butlers Yard. Boarding over the front door still held firm but at the back and out of sight the back door stood ajar. Stepping through the leaves and dirt they made their way through the kitchen and into the hall. The stench of sin and decay clung to their shoes as they were forced to step over a stash of porn magazines scattered and torn on the floor. Nell remembered watching people come and go from her tree house when she was a child; teenagers mostly, kids up to no good or couples looking for privacy. Suddenly an old memory raised its head like a cobra, preparing to strike. She grabbed at it but it turned to dust. Couples looked for privacy. She tried again but there was nothing but the faint scent that this was important and it would return when the time was right.

"This place has a bad feel." Celeste shivered by her side. Maxine wandered ahead, whistling again through her teeth. Nell shuffled along, her feet clumsy and heavy, into a living room where empty beer cans and fast-food containers made a low barricade in one corner.

Maxine frowned. "Weird. But I can't find the door to the cellar and that's where we need to go. I'm not getting anything up here."

Cellar. Nell felt a wave of misery flood her stomach. No time for explanations, she fled outside and threw up. The late summer sun was warm after the damp chill of the house. Nell spat in an effort to rid her mouth of the bitter taste and took a steadying breath. Maxine's head appeared through the open doorway.

"You OK?" Nell nodded and scuffed dirt over her pile of vomit in an attempt to hide it. She was in no hurry to return indoors. Across the wall, she saw her old tree house. Whenever she thought of childhood summers, she remembered the garden, Nana, and her beloved tree house. And it was then that she remembered what was important. The kids she had watched had not used the front door, but a hole in the ground that led to the cellar steps.

"Maxine, Celeste?" She yelled, disturbing the birds and attracting the attention of someone parking nearby. Austin stopped to listen and smiled.

"What impeccable timing."

25

October, twenty-three years ago

The leaves of the horse chestnut tree were beginning to crinkle in the autumn air. Spiked orbs, hanging heavy on burdened branches, gazed at those already fallen on the sodden ground below. Nell squished one under her trainer and felt the satisfying pleasure of flesh splitting to reveal a shining brown conker. She wasn't allowed to use the tree house on her own, it wasn't safe, but as she clambered up the wonky wooden ladder, grimacing at the green slime under her small hands, she decided it was safe enough. Anyway, that had been in the summer when she was only six. She was now seven years old and not a baby any more.

Pulling herself up into the crude wooden box, she felt a moment of memory, which left her giddy. Last year's leaves carpeted the tree house floor and a dusty harvest of conkers and fur cones huddled in one corner. So much had happened in the last year, even in the last few months. Mum was strange. She slept a lot – which was good – because when she was asleep she was not crying or hugging Nell so hard that it hurt.

They were staying with Nana now because Mum was so poorly,

and in the big house and garden, Nell could finally be alone so her head could catch up with everything. Mum was at the hospital a lot, but when she was home she was either in bed or on the sofa. Dad sometimes did not come home at night and Mum did not like it when Nell asked where he was. She got cross and her hands would flutter to her face as if to ward off invisible bees. He was strange too but still very nice to Nell. Nicer than normal almost and Dad was always nice.

Now, sitting on the cold wooden floor, looking through the slats at the ground below, Nell could forget the sounds of crying which came from her mum's room and the strange marks on Mum's arms which she thought Nell did not know about. They were part of the illness, she concluded. Nell could not touch cut grass without her skin itching and going all bubbly. She needed medicine and lotion to soothe it. Maybe Mum's marks were because she was allergic to something. Nell hoped there was lotion for her too because the marks were now on her legs too and looked more like cuts.

But Mum was feeling a little better and had gone out for the afternoon, so Nell had some peace. Here, in her private hideaway she had left all her worries behind her and could just listen to the wind stirring the leaves around her. The cold seeped through her jeans and drifted up the sleeves of her anorak. Shivering, she pulled up the fur-lined hood, but it pressed her ponytail uncomfortably into her head. Pinching at the elastic band, she found the silver bobble and pushed it to release her hair, which spilled warmly around her neck and made her scalp tingle.

Now, Nell turned her attention to her real reason for climbing the tree. From the tree house you could see over the tall garden wall and into the grounds of the derelict house next door: Butlers Yard. Nell never tired of watching it and the teenagers that came and went. There had once been steps leading down to the cellar but over the years, they had been partially filled in with debris and soil. Now only a small part was exposed and the kids kept this carefully hidden with plywood. No one used the doors, which were heavily boarded up, as were all the windows on the ground floor. Nell loved to imagine what was going on inside. If she was honest it scared her a bit, but it was a nice scare. Nothing could hurt her because no one could see her peeping through the wooden slats of her tree house through the branches of the conker tree. Weren't the teenagers scared? Butlers Yard was haunted, she was sure of it.

Suddenly, from around the corner came a teenage girl with pink boots and rusty coloured hair. She stopped in front of the house and searched the ground. Finally, she found the plywood board which covered the entrance to the cellar, and quickly glancing around to see if she was being watched, kicked it aside with her foot. For a moment she just looked down at the dark hole. Nell could sympathise; that was all she had ever done. It was OK for the older kids to venture down that old ladder which led to the steps, but they didn't believe in ghosts like Nell. Maybe the girl with the pink boots was scared of ghosts too. Although much older than Nell she was still younger than most of the visitors to the haunted mansion. The girl looked at her watch, glanced round once more, and with a deep frown that even Nell could clearly see, she lowered her foot onto the first rung. Slowly, inch by inch, she disappeared from sight.

Now Nell realised who the girl was. She was one from Dad's class. When Mum had picked him up from school once, Nell had been in the car and asked who the girls were who waved and giggled. *'Some of my airheaded class who are too silly for words,'* had been the reply, but Nell had thought they looked very grown up. The wind found the cracks in the wooden walls and Nell shivered. Time to see if tea was ready. But as she clambered down the ladder she felt drawn to the garden gate. It creaked open and she peered through the gap.

"Who are you looking at? Little spy."

The red haired girl in the pink boots was emerging from below ground and staring straight at Nell. Shocked, Nell backed away and heaved the gate shut.

26

Sunday afternoon

"Oh, yuk, there's woodlice." Maxine's face crumpled in disgust as she kicked at the plywood. Nell took over when the wood shifted an inch and a fresh wave of scuttling insects made their escape. Suddenly the cavity was revealed along with the first metal rung of the ladder.

"Down there? Jesus, Nell, do you think it's safe?"

Nell hugged herself, shivering in a chill of memory despite the warm afternoon sun.

"Safe enough."

Safe enough. The ghost of her seven-year-old self stirred within. So this was what facing your demons felt like. Her stomach churned again as she fought back nausea.

Maxine's foot was on the first rung; she smiled and opened her mouth as if to say something funny, then caught Nell's eye and snapped it shut.

There were four rungs down and then they hit the steps. It was murky and smelt of damp, dust, and secrets.

"We should have brought a torch, Max. I can't see anything."

But Maxine was one step ahead of her.

"Ta da!" She flourished a thin torch, which produced a surprisingly strong beam. Its neon shaft revealed a door which stood wedged half open by years of debris. Stepping carefully, they entered the cellar and left the summer afternoon behind them.

Immediately, the atmosphere changed. Gloomy and cold; the cellar kept its secrets close. Maxine went ahead, whistling through her teeth. She aimed the torch's ray into each corner, uncovering a pile of plastic crates which lurked furtively against the wall, and some empty bottles tossed in a corner. Porn magazines and old newspapers; their pages littered like the discarded wrappings of a black and white matinee mummy. Then Maxine stopped whistling.

"I know this is right, but something doesn't feel right."

Silence billowed like smoke around her.

"Wrong room or wrong house?" offered Celeste in an attempt to bring clarity.

Maxine shook her head, "No, it's right, but not quite there yet."

"I don't think it goes any deeper." Contributed Nell, then in an attempt to lighten the mood. "Maybe there is a secret room."

As soon as the words were clanging in the air she knew she was right and so it seemed did Maxine and Celeste.

How did they do it in the film? Tap walls, push a bit of skirting board. That did not really happen though, not in real life, thought Nell desperately.

"We have a key, so let's find the door it fits. Exciting." Nell stared at Maxine incredulously but was met with a barely apologetic shrug of shoulders and a badly concealed grin.

Nell, unaware she had been reversing, hit the side of the cellar door. She needed air or she would be sick. But seemingly unperturbed, Maxine carried on.

"God, I feel wobbly. Can you two feel this?"

In the silence which followed Nell thought she heard footsteps close by.

"Feeling something, something bad, but it feels old. I mean really old, like it was here before."

Maxine and Celeste were slowly surveying the room. One corner got them both excited and in horror Nell saw them begin moving a dusty, stained sofa from the wall.

"Nell," Maxine held out her hand, speaking slowly and calmly, as if taking a gun from a lunatic, "I'll need the key and some help to find the door. You OK?"

"No."

Nell had not meant to sound so pathetic but the only thing stopping her from heading back above ground was the physical need to be close to someone living. She did not want to be alone.

Maxine was scouring the wall in front. There was a dusty bookshelf and as she shifted it to one side, she let out a chirp of excitement. In the gloom it was just possible to make out the small key hole. Maxine held out her hand again and Nell fumbled in her pockets. She extracted the key, dropped it and had to grope on the dark, gritty floor to find it again. Again, she thought she heard footsteps. Maxine slipped the key in the lock and for one moment Nell imagined what would happen if it did not fit. All this for nothing? Would Maxine insist they kick the door down? But the key turned with a soft click and Nell met her demon.

27

Halloween night, twenty-three years ago
The rain had stopped but the wind stripped the remaining leaves from the plane trees and sent them swarming like enraged bats. Vampire bats. It was Halloween after all. And Nathan felt like a total dick. As he stomped down the pavement, crunching on fallen conkers, he muttered under his breath. They were supposed to get dressed up at his house but his mum had wanted to leave early to take his little sister so he had to meet his friends down town. If he was the only one in costume he was going to kill them.

He was not even sure what he was dressed as. A goblin maybe; his mask had a hooked nose that practically met up with the chin, and the outfit came with a stupid hat with a bell on it. Fuck this he was going home.

"Nathan." A group of kids on the other side of the road were waving. There was one zombie, one witch, a couple of ghosts and his friend Matt had just taken off his evil clown mask and was crossing the road.

"Man, you look awesome. We are going to scare the shit out of people." Nathan winced at the swear word and Matt shrugged, but his mum and sister were walking on.

"Don't be too late and behave yourselves." Then as an afterthought, "And if you see your older brother tell him he missed his physio appointment. His leg will never heal unless he keeps up his appointments."

So, his friends had come to meet him after all. They made their way to the main square where the bands would be starting shortly. Diablo were a home grown rock/punk band who were making it big but still remembered their roots. This freebie gig for the town's Halloween festival was typical of them, and they had attracted crowds from the cities nearby, so the car parks were full and the incoming road congested. Dress to scare the posters had said and amazingly it was not just the young crowd and kids who had decided to take part. Unemployment was high and the idea of a free party was appealing so that when Nathan and his friends turned the corner into the main square they were met with a sea of masks, witches hats and flashing devil horns.

The first act were aerial acrobats who were suspended from what looked like a crane. Nathan was here to see Diablo but as he bumped and pushed his way to the stage he was grateful for Matt's foresight in getting there early. Now with a can of cider in his hand he watched the acrobats spin and twist high above the square in hypnotic patterns. The PA system boomed the music against the old buildings and statues, and the trees shook off their final leaves like confetti on the partygoers below. Drinking in the square was illegal, as was drinking at fifteen but as a mystical quality began to drift over the throng, Nathan stopped hiding his can in his nylon black robe and swigged openly. Then the human mobile turned into a musical box as each acrobat produced a xylophone and eerie tinkling music dropped like burning embers below.

Something was happening, Nathan felt his body tremble with adrenalin as the acrobatics descended, bowed and disappeared into the dark. The rumble of the crowd rose and then fell as a single light appeared on the stage, and then the lead singer could be heard in the dark. Nathan scanned the stage but could not see him and then he rose from the back in the same mask as Nathan. His friends turned to Nathan in awe, and then with a crash of drums the gig exploded.

Was it the cider, the music, the sly whiff of spliff that floated by? Whatever, it was the best night ever. Diablo threw out T-shirts and their lead singer insisted that his twin in the audience must have one, so Nathan discarded his cape and thrust it over his head. The next song was *Punchinello* and Nathan then realised the significance of the masks he and the lead singer wore. Not some goblin, but the evil Mr Punch. He knew that, of course he did. Well it did not matter if he did not know; all his friends now thought he was in tune with the band.

The crowd dynamic changed as the younger kids were taken home and their parking spaces filled again. Clusters of police watched the press of people which flowed like an engorged river around the streets. The bass pulsed against Nathan's chest making him light-headed as he jumped and roared with his friends, but then too soon the last song was sung and the people began to trickle away. But Nathan did not want it to end. Blood roared through his body. He was strong, mystical, invincible.

"What next?" but his friends were talking about getting the bus home and what they were doing tomorrow. "You boring fucks." And with that Nathan drifted back into the throng. There was magic around tonight, he could feel it, he was part of it. The mask, his T-shirt, Diablo. How could this evening end? At the back of his mind he knew that something incredible was going to happen, and that he just had to find it.

He had spotted her earlier; short skirt over fishnet tights, pink Doc Marten boots and flashing devil horns in her flowing red hair. Even through the Halloween make-up he could see she was pretty. Her cat like eyes flashed at Nathan. She seemed to be having a row with her parents.

"No, it's still early. Don't be so boring."

"Ruby, don't start."

But then a siren ripped through the night and all eyes turned to the police car edging through the crowd. It was perfect, meant to be; in the confusion her parents went one way and Nathan grabbing Ruby's hand, yanked her the other.

"Princess." He turned to see her parents frantically scan the heaving crowd for their daughter then the police car blocked their view and Nathan and Ruby slipped like eels into the throng.

Her hand was small and warm in his and he could hear her laughter as they weaved away from her parents. Out of the square and down an alley. Nathan cursed as sly icicles of rain began to fall, but Ruby turned a beaming face up to his. "I know somewhere we can go." And they joined another stream of people heading out of the city centre.

The shadow puppets flickered for a moment on the rough wooden planks and then disappeared as Nell dropped the torch again. It was Halloween and there was supposed to be an orange moon as big as a dinner plate with witches on broomsticks passing in front of it. But Nell could not even see the moon. She tapped the torch against the floor until the light came on again and picked up her book, *The Witch Family*, all about how Halloween should be with witches on brooms and magic. Then there was a giggle outside. Nell snapped off the torch and crept to the wall of her tree house. Somewhere nearby she could hear voices.

A ghostly flame was making its way along the path to Butlers Yard. Nell held her breath, for surely this was the Halloween magic she had waited for. Then another flame joined it and illuminated two masked figures. Nell took a gulp of air and held it again until her chest hurt.

"Your horns have gone out."

"Cheap market rubbish. Hold the candle still or I won't find the entrance."

Nell frowned in recognition at the second voice. The lisp made her sound more Nell's age. Someone she knew at school maybe, but who would be out on their own without their mum or dad? Then the girl turned and in the light of the boy's candle Nell saw the long red hair. It was pink boots again. But as she moved the planks away from the entrance and turned to the boy her candle lit up his face.

"Wow, your mask looks incredible in this light. Really evil."

Then they disappeared into the ground.

Carefully, Nell backed away from the wall. Had they really gone into Butlers Yard or were they creeping through her gate. She peered out of the doorway but the gate was still firmly shut and bolted from her side. A light flickered on in Nana's house and now she felt real panic for if they found her bed empty she would be for it. But no shout came from the back door and looking at her watch she confirmed that she had only been gone a very short time. This was a real adventure. Like in books.

For a long time there was nothing else to see and Nell got bored. She felt in her pocket and brought out a chocolate bar Nana had given her earlier. She had a ritual for eating these. First you nibbled at the chocolate around the outside and if there were any bubbles on the chocolate's surface these should be popped by pressing your thumb against them. The craters that were left were pleasing to Nell for some reason. She nibbled the chocolate all around until the biscuit was exposed.

Suddenly, a scream ripped through the air making Nell jump. She waited but there was nothing now, only the wind. Had she dreamed it? The minutes passed and a soft rain began to fall. Soon the tree house was filled with the comforting sounds of rain dripping and dropping onto crispy leaves and rough wooden planks. Nell felt sleepy. She closed her eyes and imagined she was aboard an old sailing ship with wood creaking and the endless slap of waves and rustle of canvas.

"Eleanor?"

Nell jolted out of her daydream; she was in trouble. As she shuffled over to the tree house opening there was a loud bang from Butlers Yard. In the yellowy glow of the street light Nell could just make out a dark figure emerging from the hole. Nell started. Was it the same boy as before? He ran off in a slow, odd way, like an old dog, head down and knees not bending. Nell waited for what seemed like a long time. No one else appeared from the hole and there was no sound except for the rain and the rustling leaves. Where was the girl? Maybe she had missed her while her eyes were closed.

"Eleanor? Where are you?" Nana sounded angry. Nell flew down the wooden ladder, jumping the last few rungs.

They had left the crowds behind and were heading down the posh streets. Nathan shivered as the misty rain soaked through his cheap nylon cloak.

"Hey, she-devil, where are you taking me?"

Turning she grabbed his hand again and smiled wickedly. "Nearly there, a secret place I know."

Butlers Yard: the letters engraved in the stone wall were dark with dirt and barely legible in the neon street light.

"Wait, girl. Do you live here?"

But she laughed and raising a thin finger to her lips delicately shushed him. In truth, she was surprised she had been able to find it again. Aaron had brought her here a few weeks ago. Aaron who was twenty and thought she was sixteen, or so he said. He worked in one of her dad's bars so she felt safe with him, but not too safe that it was boring. He had taken her to the underground den and they had hung out, smoked a little weed and drank some cider. She supposed she liked him but not as much as Mr Montague, her history teacher. Now he was something else and lately had seemed to take a special interest in her.

Every night she wrote in her diary about things that had happened, but mostly about how she was feeling. Lately, it had almost entirely been taken up with Mr Montague and Aaron. Well, some of it was made up a little, but that was fun too. Mr Montague had given a few of them a lift home after working late on a school project, but her imagination had worked over time when she had written it up in her diary. But then it was *her* diary. For her eyes only. Now, fumbling by the garden wall, she found the candles and lighter that Aaron had hidden. The rain had been replaced by a brisk cold wind and the candle took a few attempts but when it finally took the boy's mask could be appreciated in its full glory.

"Your horns have gone out."

"Cheap market rubbish. Hold that candle still or I won't find the entrance."

Later that night when Nathan thought back over the evening he could not remember when it had stopped being fun. Long before his brother Aaron had gate-crashed and things got out of hand. Perhaps when they had left everyone else and started down the posh streets. Either way he could honestly tell his mum that he had seen Aaron, his older brother and the one that was always in trouble. Things had been going alright, the cellar had stunk and he had not wanted any of the cans the girl had found stashed, but they were having a laugh. Then something had crashed down the steps and his brother bowled into the room.

"What the fuck are you doing here?"

He was looking at Nathan who had removed his mask in the hope of some lip action from the she-devil.

"And you." He turned on the girl. "Who said you could bring someone down here? That's my little brother."

And then it had all gone nasty. The girl had started flirting with his brother, they had history apparently, and they had both started taking the piss out of him.

"Have a drag."

"I don't want to."

"Then fuck off back home then and leave us grown-ups to enjoy ourselves." The girl had giggled at that so glaring at them both he headed for the steps. Chastened, she tried to stop him but he pushed her away. She flinched when he threw first his mask, then his stupid cape at her. His brother's mocking laugh made him throw one more item, his Diablo T-shirt; it was itching round the neck anyway. Then he was gone, up the bloody ladder and out of that stinking hole in the ground. Humiliated, he lifted his face to the soft rain falling to hide his tears and ran out into the street.

Ruby was feeling a little woozy from the joint and suddenly very tired. When Aaron's cold lips found hers she started for a moment and then gave herself to it. Her first proper kiss; she would have all sorts to write in her diary tonight. But as he pushed up her top and his icy hands met her warm skin she froze.

"Stop."

He grabbed at her again.

"I said stop." She pushed him away to show she meant it. Then he slapped her hard to show he meant it too.

"I'm going home. My parents will be looking for me."

"No one's looking for you, Red. Stop being a fucking tease." He found her mouth again while his hand sought warm soft flesh. She began to cry and tried to wriggle out of his hold.

"This is what you wanted, isn't it? Why did you bring my little brother here? If you want to play with the grown-ups then you have to play their games."

He ran his hand up her thigh.

"Remember who my father is?"

In answer he thrust his hand up her skirt while she squirmed and hit.

"Your boss, Dieter Morgan." She tried again.

That stopped him. She made a dash for the ladder but slipped on some wet papers and crashed to the ground. Every instinct told him to stop, that this was suicide, but the sight of her on the ground, vulnerable and in terror, awakened something deep in him. Something else was awake too and unbuttoning his jeans he strode over to her. She tried to stand. He pushed her back down. Reaching high he found the waistband of her tights and yanked hard. Soft, so soft, like a baby. Smooth as silk, he stroked her, then thrust. Ruby screamed so he slammed his hand back over her mouth. She had wanted it, he acknowledged, why else was she down here. Some of them like a bit of role play and he was more than happy to play. But the little bitch had scratched his face and he had blood on his shirt. Grinning, he grabbed his brother's discarded rag and dragged it over his head.

Ruby stirred at his feet and in the intimate silence of the cellar, Aaron stirred again too, then hesitated when he saw the blood gushing from her nose. He reached into his pocket and brought out the key. Ruby began to whimper, then cry, loudly, her eyes wide. So he slammed his boot into the side of her head. Frightened for a moment that he had killed her he checked she was breathing and then the full horror of what he had just done washed over him. She would say it was rape, though he knew better. Girls always cried rape and then Mr Morgan would be after him. Now he was scared. If he could explain to her, get her to calm down, then he had a chance.

He picked her up tenderly in his arms, loving the way her head slumped against his chest, and took her to the room. In the dim candlelight he stepped over last night's takeaway container and laid her on his sleeping bag. She groaned slightly and began to open her eyes. Such beautiful eyes, glistening with tears and enormous in her terror. He wanted her again. And, he reasoned, what harm would it do? He would take off, be miles away when she went screaming home to Daddy.

Her eyes were open wider now. She looked so much younger when she cried, maybe eleven or twelve. He let his hands run through her silky hair, loving the way she whimpered, then moved his hands under her jumper. He had to hit her again when she started screaming, but that was satisfying too. After, kicking the door closed he leaned against it pondering what to do. He needed a few days head start. Decision made he locked the door and headed out into fresh air. He'd let her calm down overnight. It was his word against hers anyway. The secret room was known by only a few people but someone was bound to use it in the next few days and would let her out.

"Eleanor," a voice ripped through the air close by. Too close. He grabbed Nathan's cape, pulled on his stupid mask and crept up the ladder listening. Soft footsteps running; had someone heard him? Frantically he thrust the key in the gap between two bricks and fled. Silence but for the wind in the trees and the soft thud of the key falling out of its place and onto the ground below.

28

Sunday afternoon

"Oh, sweet Jesus. OK, I see something." Maxine's voice faltered as she took a deep juddering breath. The torch splashed into the narrow room and Nell could only imagine what Maxine was seeing. Fixed to the floor in terror, she knew she should look but couldn't move. Suddenly, there was a creak behind her and turning Nell saw the faint summer light blocked by a tall figure at the door.

"Miss Montague. So you have returned home."

Maxine spun round, shining the torch into the eyes of the intruder.

"Hello, can I help you?"

Nell let out a strangled laugh at the absurdity of this. They had just found a twenty-three-year-old corpse and the exit was blocked by a familiarly solid shape.

"My name is Austin. I am a private investigator – Miss Montague and I have already met. I have been engaged to find the present whereabouts of Ruby Morgan." His eyes flicked to the back of the cellar. "Perhaps you might help me with this?"

A dawning of recognition stirred between them and to Nell's surprise Maxine smiled.

210

"My God, you're Alex's ex-copper friend. Am I glad to see you."
And incredulously they shook hands.

How could they be so normal?

"There's a fucking body over there. How can you both be so normal? Am I the only sane one here?" Nell was embarrassed to hear that tears were close to the surface. Maxine motioned Austin over to the room and together they looked. Nell shuffled closer. There was silence, heavy with grief and studded with misery. Austin moved away and Nell saw a calculating look on his stony face.

"Well, this does look hopeful, but I need to be sure. It could be anyone. Her father is convinced she is alive somewhere. How on earth would she come to be down here?"

Maxine and Celeste quickly brought him up to date with their knowledge so far. His eyebrows arched slightly when she described her ability and Celeste's interest. Reaching into his jacket pocket he extracted an expensive looking ultra slim mobile. "I have a phone call to make, then I expect the local constabulary will need informing. Perhaps you should all wait outside."

Maxine let out a snort of fury. "Your phone call can wait, mate. I'm calling the police now, so don't you start ordering me around." Maxine's hands were on her hips, her chin jutting out. Austin glared back and as he took a step towards Maxine, Nell found herself at the door of the room. Inside she could just make out a slither of pale pink fabric emerging from something bulky lying on the floor. The room tilted to the left, then the right, as the horror of what she was seeing hit. Then an elusive memory crowded in and she remembered with perfect clarity what she had seen from her tree house all those years ago, and recalled the noise she'd heard the next morning. She had seen Ruby enter, had heard her cry out. Something horrific had happened to her down here. Was she murdered? But then her dream came back to her; the little girl on the stairs with blood between her legs. She'd been violated then trapped down here, and Nell had heard her that morning and done nothing. Nothing.

She had killed her. She should have told Nana what she'd heard.

They should have got the police down here. Ruby died because Nell forgot about it. Forgot about her.

"It's my fault. I should have done something, but I forgot." She turned to the others to explain. "Halloween night, I was in my tree house and saw a boy and girl come down here, then there was a scream and the boy left. Nana found out I wasn't in bed and called me back in but the next morning I was looking through the garden gate and saw the key and when I picked it up I heard a shout from below." So this was the memory that had been flickering in her peripheral vision all day. She looked at their faces, trying to explain, seeking forgiveness, "I heard a girl cry out. She said 'please'. But then Nana called because we had to go to hospital and Mum was so ill. But I should have told them what I'd seen and what I'd heard. What did I let happen to her?"

Nell crumpled onto the threshold of the tiny cell, her sobs echoing eerily. She imagined she was shut in that tiny room. Dark, alone, hungry. It was too much and despite Celeste's soothing voice in her ear, she couldn't control the anguish and misery which flowed out of her. She was wheezing, wheezing badly but she couldn't stop crying.

"Nell, Nell...it's not your fault. And it wasn't your dad's fault either."

"No...it wasn't. I remember seeing a boy leave, but I can't remember if it was the same one I saw arrive." Nell raised her tear washed face, vaguely aware of Austin looking on in acute interest.

"What did he look like, Miss Montague? Try to recall." Austin's voice was soft but there was no disguising the hard edge.

"Yes, I saw him." She stuttered as she tried to give voice to the vision she was seeing. "I think he had a mask over his face." The hospital dream slammed in. "Mr Punch I think, and he wore a T-shirt. Oh, God, which band was it?"

Impossibly patient, they let her revisit it in her mind. But the vision was clear now.

"Diablo. That was it. Diablo Rocks."

It was nothing; a mask and a T-shirt on a night when most kids would have been wearing a mask.

"I will just pop above ground and make that phone call."

Nell heard Austin leave and was grateful that she was alone with Maxine and Celeste for a moment. Too many thoughts and memories were crashing about in her mind.

Nell lay her head against the rough bricks and gazed at the dark shape on the floor, thankful that Maxine's torch beam was elsewhere.

"Sorry, Ruby. I'm so sorry."

Celeste knelt down and rubbed her shoulder.

"You weren't to blame. You were a little kid."

"But the key outside; I found it the next morning. Maybe he came back to let her out, but he couldn't find the key. She starved to death down here and all the time I had it. How long does it take to starve? It is my fault."

"No, no," whispered Celeste again. "Not your fault. Let it go."

"Where's Austin? He's taking a mighty long time, isn't he?" pondered Maxine.

"Maybe the police are asking lots of questions," suggested Nell.

"Or maybe he hasn't got around to calling them yet. I bet he's called Morgan first. If he turns up here, I swear I'll wet myself. Ghosts I can do, even poor Ruby over there, but a real live hard man like Morgan? No fear. I'm going to find out what's happening."

But Austin's heavy footsteps could be heard negotiating the steps again.

"The police are on their way. They suggest we wait outside. We are trespassing after all."

Relieved to leave the crypt, Nell headed for the fresh air and reality. She was shaken by the past which clung onto her like a cloying perfume. Desperate to shake it she thought of normal things. But what was normal anymore? Ten days ago it would have been her job, Gary and Nana. The possibility of her promotion, how to keep Gary happy and therefore herself safe from harm. Nana's illness and visits to the nursing home and later the hospital. Now normal was the penthouse. But it was too new.

Suddenly, Maxine winked reassuringly and Nell remembered that she only had to do one day at a time and if that was too hard then one hour at a time. All she could think about for now was what to say to the police when they arrived. Austin patted his pocket suddenly as if he had mislaid something and saying as much, disappeared back underground.

"Did you say that Alex knows him?" whispered Nell.

Maxine nodded, her eyes fixed on the hole. "What's he doing down there?"

But just as she was about to go after him he reappeared.

"What did you go back for?" Maxine challenged.

Austin held up his torch in answer, but his eyes flashed anger.

"Your hands are very dusty," Maxine prodded again.

He smiled, a tight smile, that looked painful. "Heavens, Alex said you were overly suspicious."

Maxine flinched at the low hit but carried on. "What were you really doing down there?"

"I have already told you, Ms Georgeham."

"Who did you ring first? The police or Morgan?"

"I have a job to do. Now, I will stay to help you with the police. You might want to prepare yourselves."

But Nell was already thinking about that.

"Maybe Morgan will stop the witch-hunt on Nell's dad now," said Maxine, obviously not finished yet.

"He will certainly be pleased that this business is over."

"You certainly look mighty pleased with yourself."

"So suspicious – my client can now bury his daughter. My job here is done."

"I thought you were looking for my father?" ventured Nell.

"Because we thought he could tell us what happened to Ruby. Now we know, if you are to be believed, he was not involved."

The police arrived and Nell's mind was a vortex of images and emotions, past and present. But one image from the present stayed with her. There was dirt on Austin's immaculate linen jacket, as if he had put something in his inner pocket.

29

Twenty-three years ago

Dark, so dark. Ruby listens carefully. Her eyes begin to make out the sides of the room. She can't hear him so maybe he's gone. Sitting up, she struggles to her knees and begins to crawl across the gritty floor. When she moves it feels like there is broken glass inside her jaw and skull. She feels sick again. Something warm and sticky runs down her neck. He's hurt her badly, her jaw and nose are throbbing but it's the other violence which dominates her thoughts. She hurts. Down there. A raw, scraping pain, in contrast to the dull ache in her jaw where he hit her. She knows what has happened, she heard him ripping off her clothes; the sudden cold air on her warm skin, the suffocating weight of him, and then the sharp, stinging pain, like a knife being scraped in and out of her.

Ruby reaches up to the door handle. She knows it is locked – she heard him do it – but still she tries, pulling it, pushing it. Something is trickling down between her legs now and shamed and sickened she lays her cheek against the door, making it damp with her tears. He'll come back and then he'll do it again. She feels dizzy. A sickly stench is rising up from her and suddenly she vomits onto her hands.

Why had she run away from her parents? Why didn't she leave with Nathan. He would be home now, in bed. Asleep and safe. Stupid, so stupid. She wants to go home. Mum will be worried. She wants water to swill her mouth out, but there is nothing. Then the horror of being imprisoned in this underground cell, violated and abused, erupts in her, as if she has been pushed into a dark, never ending pit. Oh God, please don't let this really be happening. Her vomit is acidic in the small room, which already smells of sweat and urine...and him. She trembles and waits. Hungry and cold.

Nell was playing in the garden the next morning when she thought she heard a sound. Feeling very brave, she followed the sound, which seemed to be coming from the hole that went into the haunted mansion. Opening the garden gate Nell crept towards the house. Every step she stopped and peered around her but no one was watching.

"Please."

She stopped in her tracks. Was her mind playing tricks or was someone down there? Something grey lay in the mud. A long old-fashioned key lay half hidden in a booted tread mark. She was standing at the hole now. Taking a deep breath, she stretched one foot out to plant on the first rung down.

"Eleanor? Quickly. It's your mum."

Nana's voice had a nervous quality Nell had never heard before. Nell turned and ran back to her garden, up the lawn, and into Nana's warm arms.

"Oh darling. I've called an ambulance. Your mummy's very, very poorly."

Behind the locked door Ruby shouted again. She banged on the door, she scratched, she kicked. But silence filled the room again like water, leaving her gasping for breath.

30

Present day, Sunday late afternoon

Nell fidgeted on an uncomfortable plastic chair in the reception of Wiltbury Police Station. Opposite, a young lad slumped so low in his chair only his back seemed to be making contact. He stared at Nell with a lopsided smirk on his face. Every thirty seconds he sniffed; a thick, wet sound, and his eyes closed briefly. Then he went back to staring, and smirking.

"Tyler, sit up." The woman next to him batted his arm with the out of date *Heat* magazine she had been flicking through. "Stop making a show of us."

Without taking his eyes off Nell, he slowly inched his way back up the seat. Then his gaze shifted as Maxine emerged from one of the interview rooms. The police constable who had taken her statement looked no older than twelve. Didn't they say that was a sign of getting old, pondered Nell, when the police started looking too young to have left school? Next to Maxine, she looked even younger. Wasn't there supposed to be a height restriction? Maxine was five-tenish, Nell nearly five-five and this pint sized plod seemed to barely scrape five. How tall was Tyler's mother? Anything to keep her mind off what she was about to do.

"Cheers, and thank you again." Maxine sounded almost jovial but as she walked towards Nell, she pulled a face as if to ease some of the tension from it.

"You're next. I'll wait in the car."

It was like waiting outside the headmistress's office. Not that Nell ever had. She had been a good student; a bit quiet, unsociable sometimes, and a habitual daydreamer, but never in trouble. Only when Mum had died, did she sit in the headmistress's office, being told how everyone was there to help her and to not hesitate to let someone know if the other children gave her a hard time. The door was always open. Nell remembered squirming on the edge of her chair, folding the hem of her grey skirt into concertina pleats, nodding and whispering 'Yes'. Nervous in the spotlight, like now.

"Miss Montague?" Pint size was smiling frostily at her, holding open a door. This was it. What did you do on your thirtieth birthday, Nell? Oh, I was wobbly from a day when I helped uncover the twenty-three-year-old corpse of a little girl, so I just spent what was left of it at a police station, giving my statement. Great. But then it could have been worse. Gary had wanted to throw her a party, full of his friends. Hideous, and would have ended with a very drunk Gary kicking off. There would have been cakes at work; that would have been nice. When one of the secretaries turned forty last year they had tied a balloon to her desk and there had been flowers, presents and pastries.

But instead she had a drab room and a copper with hair scraped so severely back from her hard features that all she needed was a nose clip and a swimming pool of water. The false smile of a synchronised swimmer was already there. Slowly sinking, but still smiling; Nell knew how that felt.

When she met up with Maxine later and was greeted with, "And, how did it go?" she could remember very little. Someone nearby had been shouting and there had been door slamming. Despite the smoking ban, there had been a definite lingering odour of cigarettes and Nell cradled her inhaler for comfort, flicking the lid off and on. She had tried to be objective; giving the plain facts but quickly realised that they didn't give the reason for why she found herself in the cellar in the first place.

"So, you asked Mr Austin and Ms Georgeham for their assistance in this matter?"

"No, only Maxine. Well, actually she offered. Austin has been just following me around. He's hoping to track my father down through me."

Then randomly.

"What happened to your face?"

"My ex-boyfriend happened." Nell heard the tone of her voice and wondered what had made her respond with such sarcasm. Perhaps because it was part of her old life, the life she was trying to forget. Perhaps because she was tired, nervous, and sitting in a police interview room.

"Nasty. Do you want to press charges?"

"No, I left him."

"You can still press charges."

Nell considered it for a second, just long enough to imagine standing in court recounting all the bad times "No thanks. I just want to forget him."

Back to Ruby. She recalled what she had seen all those years ago. The little redhead in the pink boots. The boy in the Diablo T-shirt. The call for help the next morning.

"You were very young and worried about your mum. Could you have imagined hearing her cry out?"

Nell had been expecting this; she had asked herself the same thing like a stuck record ever since regaining the memory earlier. Like a stuck record. Would anyone who grew up in the post-vinyl years understand that simile in a few years' time? Singles, twelve-inch extended remixes, double A sides, B sides. Turntables were reserved now for those with DJ aspirations or the retired. Like Nana, who had treasured her old suitcase style record player and her LPs as thick as tablemats. Only Nana wasn't retired, she was RIP.

"No. I didn't imagine it. It's been lying in my subconscious all these years, haunting me."

Damn, she hadn't wanted to say that. She had been desperately trying to keep any link with the supernatural out of it. Facts, the police just wanted pure facts, and there was the Emily factor to be considered. Because like it or not Emily was still missing and whatever the connection was between Ruby, Emily and Nell, if there was a connection, it just didn't feel over yet. So should she just blurt out, 'I'm seeing Emily Blake too. Maxine was going to help with that.'?

Now that would really get their attention. A twenty-three-year-old missing person case was good to finally close; good for statistics and even better for the powerful local godfather of a dad, Morgan. But Emily, the missing teenager, had everyone's attention, especially as the days went by and the hope of her turning up alive grew dusty and cold. Or worse still, she became another Madeleine or Ben; missing but presumably growing up somewhere in the world, while parents suffered the birthdays which came and went. She'd be a teenager now; sixteen, eighteen, an adult. Lurking beneath this thought was the grudging acceptance that this is how it had been for Morgan. Ruby had disappeared. Nell's dad, Will, had disappeared, and Morgan had just carried on. How many other private detectives had there been over the years and what had happened to them when they failed their task? And what happened to Ruby's mum, Nell wondered?

"Did you touch anything at the scene?"

Nell was abruptly brought back to the present as an image of dirt on an otherwise spotless linen jacket floated into her mind.

"No, I didn't." That wasn't a lie, she hadn't.

"Did anyone else?" Nell's eyes flicked to the detective's steady gaze. Too late, she realised she had given herself away.

"Ms Georgeham, perhaps. Or Mr Austin?" Yes, the detective had seen.

Nell licked her lips, suddenly dry.

"Who was it, Miss Montague? Someone touched something, didn't they?"

Easier to tell all. Nell felt a momentary prickle of disloyalty but swallowed it down.

"I think Austin may have. I don't know for sure. We were outside and he went back underground. There was dirt on his jacket pocket. You need to ask him."

The detective nodded.

"Thank you, we will."

And that was all Nell could remember. She'd given her new address.

"I've no idea what the postcode is. I only moved there last week." And she was free to escape into the fresh air. For now.

"It's your birthday? Why the hell didn't you say?" Maxine was waiting for an inexperienced driver who was trying to back a 'keeping up with the school run mums' size vehicle into a narrow parking space, before she could exit the Police car park.

"Not really into birthdays." Nell glowered.

"Well I'm with you there. I've got a really scary number coming up next year."

Nell started to speak then hesitated. Maxine was over thirty but surely not forty yet. The large vehicle had finally wedged itself in and a child erupted from the back, banging the neighbouring car's door.

"Ouch. I'm glad that wasn't mine. They just don't care do they?"

"Thirty-five?" Nell offered.

With the slickness of an eel, Maxine's car oozed out of the car park and into the road.

"Oh, I do like you. I'll be thirty-nine and that almost seems older than forty."

Nell turned navigator again as she guided Maxine to the hotel. Suddenly the roads became horribly familiar.

"Hang on, Max. Can you pull over?"

"Are you feeling sick?"

Although said in jest, Nell felt dangerously close. "No, but I used to live over there. Gary still does."

"You left in a hurry, didn't you?"

"Yeah. If he isn't around I could grab the last of my stuff."

The key turned with the familiar click she had grown to hate when she heard it from the inside. But as she walked into the hallway, the silence was heavy around her. She stopped and listened intently but there was no sound and Gary was incapable of being home without noise. The radio would be on, or the TV. He couldn't even make a coffee without rattling the spoon around the mug as if he was whipping eggs.

The place was a tip. Over flowing ashtrays in the lounge. Newspapers everywhere. CDs, DVDs, once so familiar yet now so alien. Then Nell noticed something else. Kicked under the sofa was a pair of neon pink stiletto heels. A quick inspection identified them to be size seven from Faith. Cindy. Amid the dog ends was a splash of pink lipgloss and as Nell walked further into the lounge she could just detect Cindy's sickly sweet perfume. For a moment she felt injustice click into place and a sickening thought surfaced; how long had it been going on? A fair question as Cindy was pregnant. Would Gary have treated her any better if she had been pregnant, pondered Nell, but then an image of the sofa and her own face being pressed into it brought her back to life. If Gary was seeing Cindy then good luck to them both. Back to the job in hand.

Over the last week she had suddenly been remembering things she had left behind. Stupid things some of them; a mug Nana had given her with 'Eleanor' on it. But also when she had gone through her things from her childhood she had noticed a few items missing. Mostly some old postcards and letters from Mum and Dad, which hadn't made it into the scrapbook.

While Maxine kept watch, she scuttled upstairs and to the spare room. On the landing, she hesitated then quickly detoured to the bedroom. Cindy's underwear littered the floor and as Nell stepped over them on her way to the wardrobe she shuddered; Gary wouldn't put up with this mess for long and when he'd tired of it he'd have his own special way of putting Cindy in her place. For a moment Nell thought of poor Cindy; naïve, brattish, spoilt. She wouldn't put up with being knocked around as Nell had. She'd leave him immediately.

But Gary was none of her business anymore. She quickly found the items she'd missed, careful to hide all trace of her presence, disappeared into the study and withdrew the box of memorabilia.

This would be her very last time here. She popped into the kitchen quickly and noticed the pile of post addressed to her. Must have just missed the redirection she'd requested. If she took it she'd blow all attempts of secrecy. Was it worth it for a few bills and junk mail but then she noticed the thick cream stationery that Nana had favoured. Nell imagined Gary attempting to open it without being detected then getting impatient and ripping the thick paper. But there were no traces on any attempt. Puzzled that she hadn't received it before the funeral, Nell began to open it.

"Nell, my lovely. You might want to hurry it up." Maxine on lookout duty was getting restless.

Shoving it into the carrier bag she'd found, she turned to go.

As she closed the front door and heard the echo resonate through the terraced house, she considered posting the keys back through the letterbox. Thought about it and then thought, nah. He'd know she'd been here. Let him think she could come back anytime she wanted.

Dumping her bag and the precious box onto Maxine's back seat, she looked once more at the house and then closed her mind finally to her past.

"You done?" Maxine ventured.

"All done." Nell fixed her eyes and mind firmly to the future.

All the way to the hotel Nell kept touching the card, as if to check it was still safe in her bag. A soft pat, as she imagined Nana's hand on it, holding it steady as she wrote. Licking the flap. With an iron will she waited until she was in her hotel room before finally looking at it. Nana had put a second class stamp on the envelope. Why had she not got it before? She had been buried over a week. The postmark suggested it had been posted last Tuesday; perhaps it had been found in Nana's room when they were tidying, but Nell had cleared all of Nana's things herself. She could ring the nursing home but then shrugged and decided that it really didn't matter.

This was the last post she would ever get from Nana.

Lifting the flap she pulled out the contents. It was a card and with a sharp stab of pain Nell saw it was a thirtieth birthday card.

'For my granddaughter on her birthday,' it said, and Nana had written a large thirty on the front in the blue parker pen she used.

The tears flowed and threatened to hit the precious card. Putting it down she waited and wiped, and blew her nose before attempting to look at it again.

'To Eleanor, on your thirtieth birthday. Love always from Nana.' She had always used Nell's formal name in cards. Love always from Nana. Her loss hit again as fresh as the first time. This was one of those time bombs that she had known would come, and she could expect more. Time may be a healer but it was spiral, not linear, and would return close to the original pain, time and time again on its orbit to recovery.

Memories: memories of a week ago when battered and broken she had stayed here, contemplating her future. Memories of twenty-three years ago when a little girl made a mistake which would haunt her for the rest of her life.

There was a knock to her door.

"Nell, lovely. Are you ready?"

Maxine: calm, cool, able to talk to ghosts and the police with the same ease. Nell felt safe and smiling, opened the door.

"Hurry up, Nell, I'm starving." The word brought them both to a standstill, and Maxine met Nell's large brown eyes apologetically.

"Sorry, that was stupid."

But Nell just shrugged and raising her eyes towards the ornate ceiling in mock exasperation, she shooed Maxine into the corridor.

As she was halfway down the stairs, she spotted Austin in the foyer, mobile to his ear, waiting for them. He saw them and raised a hand. A large ornate mirror suddenly grabbed her attention and shyly she checked out her appearance. She looked tired but tanned, healthy, slim, even happy. Then she noticed the small, pale hand that hovered just above her shoulder. She froze. Slowly she leaned to the left to reveal a small figure directly behind her. There was the roar of a thousand waves, and she was just aware of Austin and Maxine rushing to her side as the plush carpet rose to meet her and the image of Emily faded to nothing.

31

Eight years ago

"Please take another look. Her hair is a little shorter now. Perhaps lighter." Austin pushed the photo back across the beer speckled bar hoping his coaxing smile displayed more encouragement than desperate pleading. Meeting the barman's eyes, he saw only pity reflected. But he looked at the photo once more before shaking his head.

"I'm sorry, mate. We get so many girls in here. Try some of the locals over there."

Austin was being dismissed but he thanked the barman for his time and advice. Being grateful, polite, went against every instinct in his body. He wanted to stand on the nearest table and shout, 'Lily is just sixteen years old. She's five-foot-two, stutters sometimes when she's nervous and I need to find her.'

Tantalizing aromas of strong beer and hearty food rose towards Austin as he approached the first tables. His stomach responded feebly but Austin ignored it, as he had ignored it since seven o'clock yesterday morning, when he found Lily's bed empty.

"I am sorry to disturb you, but I am looking for my daughter.

This is Lily. Could you take a look at her photo and see if you recognise her please."

Even to his own ears he sounded like an actor at the end of a long run. Only the words held any power now; his spirit had long since deserted him. All yesterday and today he had asked questions; messages left on mobiles of Lily's friends, acquaintances. Everyone, everywhere, then finally anyone and anywhere.

But amazingly he thought he saw a flicker in the eyes of one of the lads. There was a long pause; perhaps he was wondering if he was mistaken, or maybe weighing up whether to get involved. Austin resisted the urge to shake him.

"Please, if you even think you recognise her..." *Jesus Christ just give me something.* Telepathic pleading hadn't worked out so far but there was always a first time.

"I'm not sure...I might have spoken to her last night."

The flicker of hope was clad in sharp razors; Austin felt each cut as it whipped at his heart.

"Her name is Lily."

"Yeah, that's her. I remember I couldn't hear and she said 'like the flower'." His voice rose as he gained assurance. He locked eyes with Austin.

"She was with another girl." He glanced at his brother. "Anna."

The acne on his brother's face rippled in a grimace.

"She's trouble."

Austin opened his jacket and took out a notepad and pen.

"Where do I find Anna?"

Shivering, Lily tucked her hands into the sleeves of her cardigan, trying not to dislodge the sleeping bag around her shoulders. Anna would return soon, wanting an answer. The bare bulb held little power, but it still illuminated the grim scene around her. Walls pocked black with mildew; a window with a weeping cataract of condensation, an old mattress draped with faded covers. The dusty radiator she huddled against gurgled and hissed with tepid trickles of water. Closing her eyes she tried to rest; she'd had no sleep last night, trapped in a nightmare of cigarette smoke and bloated pupils. The night had started off badly; she had been so alone and angry, then she had met Anna who had offered her a bed for the night and things had picked up. But she had spent the witching hour fogbound on a sofa, pushing off unwelcome advances from a man twice her age. Anna said she could stay until she sorted herself out and had invited her to a party at the club where she worked. But that meant seeing the rat faced man from last night again.

'Be nice to him, Lil. He's my boss. He could be your boss too.' But Lily hadn't wanted to be nice. Mum used to say...but Lily stopped herself. Mum couldn't say anything anymore. Time to grow up.

She struggled to her feet on limbs stiff with cold. Plucking her bag from the stained carpet she scuffed across to a chipped sink, which hung off the bedsit wall like a crooked tooth. Using her sleeve she rubbed a clean patch in the spotted mirror. The face looking back was pale. There were new dark circles around her pale grey eyes like rings around a full moon. A hard ridge of spots had erupted over her broad forehead. Somehow the word 'dreadful' seemed ineffective. She looked dead; like Mum.

There was a shout from the hallway downstairs; angry voices. Already she was flinching less, getting used to her new environment. Somehow though it didn't quite penetrate. Months of trying not to show any feelings, of being brave and grown up, had frozen to a thick crust around her emotions.

'I'm fine, really. Don't worry about me,' had been her mantra for so long now that she had forgotten how to express herself. Apart from yesterday morning when she had woken from multiple nightmares to find that it wasn't all a dream. Mum had died the day before and however many times Lily had prepared herself for it, and the nurses had prepared her, and even Austin; nothing could prepare her for waking up in her bed with the white daisy duvet cover that Mum had chosen for her – which Lily hated – wearing pyjamas which Mum had given her for Christmas – which she loved – knowing that Mum had really gone and would never be back.

Lily cooled her forehead against the cold mirror. There would be no more operations, or 'in remissions', and there never would be an 'all clear' for them. She was dead; and that was as final as it could get. So, Lily had run. Anywhere. Away from Mum's coat hanging in the hallway, her pink 'best Mum in the world' mug on the mug tree, and her Kia still parked on the drive waiting for a day that would never now come.

She waited to stop coughing before she raised the mascara wand to her eye. Anna would be here soon.

The click, hiss and snap of the Zippo lighter sounded like an old friend. Austin dragged shakily, taking what comfort he could from the nicotine. Two years; he had given up smoking two years ago, but the first thing he had done when he left the hospital was buy cigarettes. He'd had one lit in his mouth before he remembered that he didn't smoke anymore. Too bad. Lily called him a hypocrite; he had flown at her once for being returned from a party too drunk to walk, then the next night he hit the single malt while her mother was overnight in hospital. After that she took no notice of his attempts to parent her, to keep the family normal for Mum. While she was in hospital the house divided; Austin in the living room, Lily in her bedroom. The kitchen was the only common ground; Lily entering only when she was sure Austin had already vacated.

Could there be a true union between father and daughter? The union between mother and daughter was forged through the heat of soul ripping pain and the baptism of blood. Whatever happened to the relationship, afterwards the fact remained that the child had once been a physical part of the mother; from the heart's primordial beat to the first independent gulp of air. The first flesh Lily had ever known had been that of her mother. Now that flesh was cold. How could Austin ever hope to fill that gaping hole in Lily's soul?

The Club Zero looked like every stereotype of a seedy club. Austin had been in a few of these in his time and as he approached the doorman he almost felt in his pocket for his warrant card.

"Hello, I'm looking for Anna."

He walked in slowly, letting his eyes stray to every corner, taking in the drinkers at the bar, the dancers on the floor, and those who just watched and waited as he watched and waited. The music vibrated in his chest and rage flavoured his blood. He would find Lily and bring her home if it took every last grain of sanity he possessed.

The drink was bitter and cold but Lily sipped as instructed.

"That will get you in a smiley mood." Anna winked.

The music thumped into her head making her breathing uneven behind ribs that felt too tight. After a few more sips the music seemed to fade but the lights brighten. Blue, green, pink, yellow: she watched them, mesmerised as they splashed puddles on the wooden dance floor. Then she was on her feet and the man from last night was dancing with her. Her feet didn't seem to move but he had his arms tight around her body. Without him she felt she might fall, then he pushed her dress strap down and she felt his rough chin graze her neck.

No.

The words echoed in her head but already the lights were fading. Hands were on her thighs and she felt a sensation of being lifted.

Lily.

Through the blur of faces Austin suddenly saw his daughter as she slumped against a man in his forties. Ignorant to the protests of writhing couples, Austin pushed through to reach her. Arms from behind grabbed his, and she was gone. With a roar he shook them off, spun round and punched the first face he saw. There was a satisfying crunch as fist met flesh. The man's lip split and a spurt of warm blood covered Austin's fist.

The wiry man who had been molesting Lily tried his hand. Austin resigned himself to the blow to his gut, too late to dodge, but then grabbing the man's shoulders he hammered his forehead into the rat-like nose. It collapsed and after that no one else tried.

"You want this slut? Then have her. We have." The man sneered through the blood that flowed down his face. A metallic stench mixed with the perfume, aftershave and sweat. Austin wiped his forehead.

He wanted to destroy the sneering man but something deep inside, perhaps his training, told him to grab Lily and get out of there before someone else felt like having a go. She slumped against the oversize chair like an abandoned soft toy. He lifted her, amazed that she could weigh no more than a child. But then a child was all she was. Her head flopped against his shoulder and he headed for the door and into the cold air.

Less than forty-eight hours after sitting by a similar hospital bed, Austin sat beside another member of his family. But Lily wouldn't die, he promised himself. He promised her mother. Finally she opened her eyes and stared at him incredulously.

"Dad?" Austin nearly glanced behind but then realised she was speaking to him.

"Yes. You are safe now."

"I'm sorry. I just..." but there were no words to describe the emptiness, the fear. The urge to lose herself so completely that it wouldn't hurt any more.

"I'm sorry too. But we will get through this. You and me together."

He touched her hand, small and pale against the white hospital sheet, his knuckles bruised and raw in bitter contrast. He had spilt blood tonight, his own and those who threatened his family. The only family he had left. And through the aching pain, the cold clamp biting into his chest in lieu of a heartbeat, he felt a new stirring. It was the first time his stepdaughter had ever called him Dad.

Looking back the old pain reared its head. That was the trouble with this case, it brought back too many memories; memories that he had buried deep and covered over with life, with purpose, with routine. They had found Ruby and were trying their luck with Emily. Austin let the single malt warm his mouth before swallowing. Actually Miss Montague and Miss Georgeham's juvenile meddling vexed him to his very core but they did seem to get results, so far anyway. But a real live case? Highly improbable. His mind flicked back to Lily.

He had thought recklessly that the gods had thrown everything at him but Lily running away had been the start of it. He found her that time, brought her back and for a while they had worked through their grief together, breaking down to become stronger again. But the self-destructive gene had been activated and the lure became too strong. Lily would disappear, and he would find her. It became a game of hide and seek. The therapist said Lily needed to feel secure, in control of her own pain. Like an adrenalin junkie she would throw herself into dangerous scenarios to prove that she was strong, but in reality required rescuing. And this finally put her on the radar of some delinquents Austin had closed down. Austin would never be sure what the tipping point had been; guilt that he had had to put his career on hold to look after her, or perhaps the drugs had unpicked the fragile seam of her reality. But although with Morgan's help he had found her, that final time she overdosed at the age of eighteen and vanished from his life.

'Look after Lily,' his wife had said. He only had to do one thing and he failed time and time again.

In a conscious effort to stop the negative drenching, Austin thought of something else. Ruby's mum. Morgan was fairly easy to read; he was in work mode, but Ruby's mum had fluttered on the doorstep, all social niceties forgotten.

'Is it her? I mean it could be anyone. Well it could, couldn't it?'

'Shall we go in and sit down, Mrs Morgan.'

'Oh God, oh God, it doesn't get any easier. How can you tell it is her?'

In the end Austin had pulled out the ruby pendant he had found. In the dirt and dark and half hidden, it had looked like cheap tat, but the sight of it curled up in the evidence bag buckled Mrs Morgan's knees.

'Bastard. I want the police to fingerprint it. I'm going to find that piece of filth who killed my daughter.'

After that there had been profuse gratitude which sat uneasily on Austin's shoulder, explanations, and a glass of single malt. The lounge walls were accessorised with professional portraits; Ruby's younger brother in graduation cap and gown followed by his wedding and then baby shots, the Morgan's anniversary on their elegant lawns, and finally Ruby as a bridesmaid, just before her disappearance. The sweet face showed all the innocence of prepubescence, but in her eyes Austin could detect a smoldering self-awareness of her budding allure.

These silly little girls, he pondered, not unkindly, they suddenly discovered the power they held over men and boys alike and had no idea what a responsibility it was. They flirted and played and teased, and it should all have been part of their growing up. But if they attracted the wrong moth it could have truly devastating consequences. They were just little girls; how could anyone take their out of control hormones as anything more than that? How could people harm them or put them in harm's way?

He had done his job and the Morgans had a body to bury. It might not be the happy ending they deserved but it was an ending, though he knew the pain and loss would be just as fresh today as it had been twenty-three years ago.

32

Monday

Nell was heading down to breakfast when her mobile chirped. It was a message from Austin.

'I have checked out. Will endeavour to keep my grateful client from speaking to you. Should you need my help with the liberation of E then please contact me. I think we make quite a team, a detective triad.'

Despite herself Nell smiled. She had found Ruby and now wanted to move on with her life. At some point she was aware that she would have to uncover the truth about her parents, if it could be uncovered, but for now there was Emily to think of.

Suddenly, there was the sound of electronic bleeping and as she turned a corner she saw a familiar figure sitting on a low wall outside, her long limbs angled like a praying mantis. Heading into the courtyard, late summer sunshine warmed her.

"Hello, Max." And Nell was pleased to see her jump before she quickly regained her composure.

"Did you just get a text from Austin?"

"I did." Nell confirmed, lowering herself onto the wall beside

Maxine. "You know, I still can't quite work him out. Yesterday he admitted to following me like there was nothing creepy about it."

Maxine smirked. "That's the police in him. Or ex-police anyway. They are all sneaky by nature. Have to be."

Maxine was clearly talking about Alex again, thought Nell.

It was peaceful in the garden. The roses were past their best and everything was looking a little dry and tired but Nell felt she could have curled up on the warm soil like a cat and watched the wispy white clouds sailing the blue sky for hours.

"Nell!" Maxine was grinning in a worryingly familiar way. "I have a plan to find Emily. In fact, I feel a little spot of séancing coming on. And she seems to like mirrors so we could try something with that. What do you think?"

Nell groaned.

"Oh, come on spoilsport, we're checking out in a minute. We found Ruby, so let's have a go tonight and try to find Emily and restore my reputation with the Devonshire police."

"You mean with Alex."

"That too."

Suddenly a thought rose unbidden into Nell's mind, but Maxine hadn't finished speaking yet.

"And just think Nell. As it was your birthday yesterday maybe your mum with get in touch."

Nell shuddered. Sometimes it really seemed like Maxine could read her mind.

"What was your mum like?" Maxine asked, probably to divert her.

A pale face with dark blonde hair drifted into Nell's memory like a helium balloon in a strong wind. It wavered for a second and then was gone.

"I'm not really sure I remember anymore. I mean, I suppose she was nice, I can remember her hugging me when I fell over once, but it's all mixed up with her being ill. I do have one memory though." She smiled. "She had a sewing box and if I ever tore something she would say to leave it on her box. I had a knitted rabbit as a kid, I think

Nana made it, and whenever it lost an eye or an ear I would leave it on her box. But soon whenever anything broke, even smashed or something, it would end up on the sewing box waiting to be fixed." It was a lovely memory and having its first airing, Nell felt the need to put a pink ribbon round it, like her knitted rabbit, and put it somewhere safe.

"What did she die of, if you don't mind me asking?"

"Cancer."

"Cancer of what?"

Shocked, Nell turned to look Maxine in the face. No one asked that. In all her experience whenever you said the word cancer people just looked fearful and then fell quiet.

"Umm. I'm not sure. Cervical I suppose. Or breast. I don't know."

"Nell," ventured Maxine kindly. "For your own health, you need to find out. Didn't your Nana ever say?"

"No. We didn't talk about it. She was in hospital a lot and had marks on her arms and legs."

"Like dialysis?" Maxine offered.

"How would I know? I'm not a nurse. No, no they were like cuts."

"Like self-harm?"

"No, I mean. I don't know." Suddenly Nell felt the floor tilt again. Fragments of overheard conversations from her childhood. Someone, Dad, telling Mum she was taking too many pills. It was like opening a Pandora's box; the box of her childhood where she had carefully stashed information she had been too young to understand and never thought to examine as she got older. Was it an addiction to something? Now to her adult eyes she realised things didn't add up.

"Maxine. I just don't know. I thought I did but, it doesn't make sense, does it?"

Maxine's strong arms helped her to her feet.

"Don't feel too bad, Nell. We get told things as kids and we just believe them. I'm only guessing but I wonder if your mum was depressed. It's really frustrating because we'll never know now."

Nell felt the last strands of comfort from her childhood memories unravelling before her. Who the hell were her parents really?

"Despite everything, Dad should have come back when he heard Mum had died. And something else is bothering me. What was Ruby doing at Butlers Yard? Bit of a coincidence, right next to Nana's house. I thought Ruby was a story Dad told me. I wanted to be like her, and all the time she was real, and he knew her, spent time with her. Celeste said that he'd been taking more interest in her lately. I was right all along. He preferred her to me. I was too quiet, too...like Mum. Maybe he wasn't my dad. My whole past is a pile of bullshit that I believed without questioning. Now I'm dreaming things, and seeing Emily. Is that just the stress of Nana dying and Gary beating the shit out of me? Maybe it's a gift, a bit like yours? Maybe I could always do it. Maybe Mum was the same and that's why she did stuff...to block it out?"

"Umm, Nell. Are you going to draw breath anytime soon?" Maxine was smiling her joker smile, but then it faded. "I wouldn't call what I do a gift. Most of the time I just get flashes and strong emotions, totally out of context with where I am and what I'm doing." She paused, but maybe it was time for full disclosure. "I've been trying to expose myself to more triggers to see if I can learn to control it. That's why I was so keen to do the ghost tour again and one of the reasons I wanted to help you. But I'm not convinced it really is getting any better." Then she flicked her smile on again. "Still, ever the optimist, let's see if we can find Emily and put all your demons to rest."

33

Monday

It was dark. But then it was always dark. Emily tucked her bare knees under her dirty T-shirt, trying to find some warmth against her small ribcage. She was hungry but resented her body for betraying her like this. He would bring food which she wanted to throw back in his face, but gobbled down like a dog. In her fist she clutched her broken necklace with the small silver Emily, which she had found under her camp bed only this morning. She had cried then, cradling it in her palm, remembering when Mummy had given it to her – her birthday, when she had worn a new dress at her party with friends from school and ballet.

Only eighteen months ago, but she hardly recognised the girl she had been. Ballet lessons, pink tights, black leotard and trying to outstretch Harriet Johnson – her arch-enemy – at the barre. Daddy telling her off for wearing lipgloss which her best friend Phoebe had lent her. He said it made her look too old.

Her heart ached at this; Daddy would stop loving her now she was dirty. He would look at her like he had then, with disgust and sadness in his eyes. Her body began to shake. She mustn't think about it. Mummy and Daddy would understand that it wasn't her fault. She'd make them understand and forgive her. Was it because she'd been wearing lipgloss again, that she'd been taken? Had she looked older than she was? He said she was a tease. That she had asked for it. Even, that she enjoyed it. That secretly all sluts did. And that was what she was now; a slut.

Shakily she got to her feet and grabbing the metal bedhead placed her feet into first position. She arched her bare foot into a point and then moved into second position. It wasn't perfect, the floor was too rough and dirty, and the chain around her ankle was heavy, but practicing her ballet steps stilled her mind for a short time. He would be back soon, stomping down the stairs with hopefully some food in his hand for her. The stairs were steep and dark, easy to trip down.

The chain was getting in the way, it had slipped down her heel. Sitting on the edge of the bed Emily examined it. Probably the cuff was designed for a grown-up and therefore too large for her ankle; and she had lost a lot of weight.

And then her mind cleared. Forcing her foot into the perfect point, she pushed the cuff downwards, ignoring the grating pain as harsh metal scraped her raw skin, slippery with fresh blood. If she could get the chain off, she could get to the top of the stairs. He would be back later and this might be her only chance to get out.

A sudden cold chill wrapped around her bare legs. There it was again. Peering into the gloom she tried to detect its origin. Cold but fresh and not unpleasant, the draft came and went during the day, and sometimes there was a rumbling sound but very different from the traffic above. This seemed to be coming from below somehow. Could there be another way out? In this bottomless crevasse she was locked in there was nothing else to think about but hunger, thirst, pain, fear, family and inevitably shame. Now she concentrated on the layout of her cell, the rough floor below her that seemed at odds with the walls and ceiling, the sounds around her – below her – and always listening for the sound of the front door's sly opening and then ominous slam shut above her which sent her heart pounding in panic as she waited for the sickening footsteps that would lead to her door.

34

Monday afternoon

The air felt light and whipped, like a mousse. Full of salt and strong earthy scents. Nell climbed out of Maxine's four-by-four and took in a deep lungful. The sea sparkled in the late afternoon light and walkers dotted the beach below. Home: and it did feel like home. She'd been here a whole week now.

"And don't forget our curry later," shouted Maxine.

"Looking forward to it." Nell answered as she grabbed her bag from the back seat. "See you later, and Maxine…" Were there really words to express her extreme gratitude? "Thanks for helping me to find Ruby."

Their eyes locked for a second; the last few days had been a shared experience they would never forget.

"My pleasure, Nell. Just Emily now."

Nell winced.

Maxine caught the look, slid the gearstick into first, and pressing a button began to close the passenger seat's window.

"Have a little faith, Nell. We'll find her. I'm psychic remember. I know these things."

And with a broad smile she oozed out of the car park and disappeared down the road. Nell felt her own smile, and a wave of delirious pleasure filled each dark corner and crevice inside her mind. Sure, there were still questions concerning her past, and poor Emily was still out there. But they had found Ruby so they could do anything. Maybe even find Nell's dad.

She trudged over the scrunching gravel towards the front door, just as it swung open to reveal Leon.

"Hello, beautiful. Did you enjoy your trip?"

Nell felt her face flush with what was probably a dreadful shade of deep plum. They hadn't spoken since he had disappeared into the night with Tash. Now he beamed down at her, and Nell felt as if invisible threads, fired from his eyes and lips, had embedded themselves in her skin. One tug and her body would jerk within kissing distance. Her skin erupted in goose bumps and she felt her lips part. Hello beautiful indeed. She should be angry, say something cutting about Tash. Nevertheless, at the end of the day, she had just escaped one relationship and although there was no denying her body's response to him, she really didn't need any more emotional drama. They'd kissed, that was all. That was enough.

"Yeah, I exorcised some ghosts." She finally answered his question, smiling at her own joke.

His eyebrows rose. "Literally, if I know Max. Look, about the other night..."

There was an awkward pause. Nell examined the stone chippings around her feet.

"Tash is a pain. We are totally over. Maybe you'd let me take you out for a drink sometime, so I can apologise." He was smiling again but more hesitatingly. The sun was hot and the sound of surf and seagulls filled the air.

Nell had not the fight in her to play the coquette.

"Yeah, that would be good. But not tonight, I'm busy." She had nearly said she was seeing Maxine.

"Tomorrow?"

"Perfect."

As she lumbered up the stairs with her bag, a thought kept bumping around her head. By the time she opened the penthouse door it had reached her mouth.

"I have a date," she told her cream coloured walls, and the walnut flooring.

Now back in her own space, Nell found herself drifting from room to room, reacquainting herself with everything. Her bed – she smoothed the cool cotton – in her own sanctuary. Her wardrobe where only her clothes hung. Her bathroom where the toilet seat remained permanently down. Her space; where she was safe from harm, and safe to be herself. Where she had a future.

Later that evening Nell entered the Indian restaurant in Launton to collect her takeaway. This was no curry house, she thought, taking in the elegantly dressed waiters, the thick linen napkins on the tables, and the smart clientele who sat there. She was invited to wait in the bar area where a tray of drinks was being prepared. On the bar was a clip containing the takeaway orders for that night; hers lay on the top.

"Just one moment, please." Her friendly waiter took the top slip and disappeared out to the kitchen. With nothing else to do, Nell let her eyes wander over the takeaway slip that had been below hers. A Fletcher, 12 Island View, he had ordered a lamb madras and beef burger with chips. Obviously, the wife didn't like curries, or maybe it was for a child. Nell let her eyes drift once more, this time to the walls above the bar. A framed picture had pride of place, showing the beaming restaurant manager handing what looked like a trophy of some sort to a middle-aged man. The caption below explained that a delighted Aaron Fletcher had received 'Volunteer of the Year' for his work with the local youth arts programme. Nell inhaled the fragrant spices and waited.

A growing unease was beginning to build in the bottom of her stomach. The smiling duo in the picture looked down at her obliviously. Leaning on the bar, Nell caught her reflection in the mirror behind the optics. She smoothed a stray lock of hair from her face and as she lowered her arm, she met the now all too familiar eyes of Emily. Nell gasped in shock and the bartender flicked her eyes in Nell's direction. Emily's eyes also flicked, but this time upwards, towards the picture. Nell looked into the face of Aaron Fletcher, lover of lamb madras, and felt her face flush. The floor also tilted at an alarming angle before righting itself.

"Miss Montague?" Her curry was ready. She looked once more at the picture, grabbed the curry, smiled politely as the door was held open for her, then disappeared into the street.

Ten minutes later Nell sat nervously in her car outside 12 Island View, with all thoughts of curry far from her mind. Her stomach gave a growl; clearly not every part of her body was committed to the current course of action. The sun was setting, fiery red over the rooftops: red for danger. Island View was probably a bit over hopeful, Nell thought, as she struggled to see the sea beyond. Maxine, sitting in the passenger seat next to her, glanced at her watch and swore.

"She's not coming Nell, we might as well do this without her."

"We need Alex. What if I am right and Emily is there? Anyway, the slip said he was collecting so he's either already gone or about to leave any minute."

But Nell knew her instinct was right. Somewhere, behind the normal looking front door of the turn of the century house, was a teenage girl. Imprisoned, fearful, violated. She could smell it as clearly as the prawn dhansak, which had enjoyed a brief journey to Maxine's kitchen counter via her Ford KA.

"Shall I just knock on the door?" Nell whispered hesitantly, hoping for back up.

Then a car pulled up behind them.

"Late as usual. Just like the cavalry," mused Maxine. Nell jumped to the same conclusion – expecting Alex – but then saw Maxine's badly disguised smile implode.

"He must have been right behind you."

A thin man stepped out of the car. Nell held her breath for the sign she was waiting for and wasn't disappointed. The man with the takeaway bag was limping. A memory of him from twenty-three years ago shuttered before her eyes. Diablo; the horrific figure from her nightmares. He cast a glance at Nell's car then opened his front door and disappeared inside.

"She's in the cellar," whispered Nell. Then in explanation. "When I've had nightmares, when I see through her eyes, she is always in a cellar. Just like Ruby. He'll be unlocking the door now to take her burger to her."

"No, wait, Nell." But Nell was already out of the car.

"Nell," Maxine hissed through the open passenger window. "Don't be stupid. You'll get hurt." But Nell was at the door. Then she hesitated, unsure of what to do. She couldn't just knock, could she? And say what? She peered back at her car to see Maxine gesturing for her to get back in.

Suddenly, from behind the front door there was a bellow of rage and a second later a high-pitched scream. Nell's breath caught in her chest where it beat angry wings against her ribcage. Then with its liberation, she realised what she was hearing.

"Emily," Nell howled, then slammed both hands against the front door. Suddenly rough hands seized her shoulders and thrust her aside. There was the crash of something solid hitting the door, and with a groan of splintering wood, it fell open.

"Apologies, Miss Montague," Austin muttered as he vanished into the hallway. Startled, Nell rushed after him.

The sight that met her would have done justice to the final scene of a horror film. Aaron Fletcher – Diablo – was hissing curses from the end of the hall, with a flailing teenage girl in his arms. Her small naked legs kicked like a devil held marionette, while her terrified whimpers were muffled by Diablo's strong hand. He was struggling to edge her back to the cellar doorway but stopped in the shocking spotlight of Austin and Nell's entrance. He dropped her to the floor, but before she could move he grabbed her matted long blonde hair, yanked back her head and placed a blade against her small throat. Emily's eyes closed, squeezing tears to mix with the mucus on her face. Her heavy breathing brought her throat too close to the knife for a moment and a small bead of blood formed.

"Do not make it worse for yourself. The police will be here soon. Why not let her go?" Austin stopped halfway down the hallway and held out his hand.

Nell watched from behind. Emily was dressed in the pink T-shirt she had seen so many times and yellow pants with white flowers on. Nothing else. Blood trickled from a wound around her ankle, and pale legs and arms were bruised and scratched. Her nakedness appalled Nell and she ached to take the small body into her arms. Diablo was looking from one face to the other, licking his lips nervously. Then he began to laugh.

"Police on their way, you say? I've nothing to lose, then."

Nell winced as Emily's head was dragged further back and the knife dug in again. Suddenly, the hallway was filled with the bitter stench of ammonia as Emily's fear loosened her bladder.

"You filthy whore." Diablo roared, stepping backwards from the expanding puddle, dragging Emily with him.

"Is that what you called Ruby?" Horrified, Nell recognised her own voice.

Startled, Diablo loosened his grip on the knife.

"Well did you? You remember Ruby, surely. Red hair, pink Doc Martens."

Diablo's grey eyes flicked to the right.

"You're seeing her now, aren't you?" continued Nell. "We saw her a few days ago."

For a moment there was a flicker of relief in the cold eyes then Nell snuffed it out. "You left her to starve to death, you bastard. We saw her dried up little corpse."

Incredulously his head shook from side to side.

"No. I didn't kill her."

"Actually, yes you did. Now kindly give us the knife and let Emily go." Austin had taken advantage of Diablo's distraction and was now within feet of them.

"I didn't..." he began again.

"You don't want to kill Emily too, do you?" continued Nell. Suddenly a siren split the evening air in two, and the scene went

245

on fast forward. Everything happened at once. Diablo thrust Emily away from him and dashed to the cellar door. Austin shot after him and Nell took a trembling Emily into her arms. Her own tears fell as Emily's body juddered with violent sobs. Her greasy hair smelled musty against Nell's cheek. The hallway filled with people and Nell nearly shouted at them to mind the puddle of pee. But it didn't matter anymore, nothing mattered, only the small body in her arms. And as she rocked her gently, absorbing her pain and shock, she felt a little of her own pain begin to dilute.

"You're safe now, baby. You're found."

Austin tore down the cellar steps after Aaron. Floored for a second by the apparently empty room, he listened acutely and then felt the fresh sea air coming from the corner. The stone steps were treacherously smooth from centuries of feet and led sharply down into the gloom but Austin gave chase, his torch bouncing of the rough walls. Footsteps ahead reassured him it was safe to follow; no danger of an ambush in this cold subterranean passage. The air was colder now and in the distance a blob of grey light appeared. Behind him came the pounding of more feet; back up was always good.

He had assumed the roaring was just his breath and footsteps echoing but as the passage walls became clearer and gave way to a large cave he saw the white foam of waves crashing ahead. Icy sea water filled his shoes and fury his body. Time to end this. Waist-deep in inky water, Aaron turned to face Austin's torch. The monstrous wave sent him flailing and then it was easy to grab him out of the water and thrust him into the waiting hands of the uniform. Italian leather shoes and Savile Row suit ruined, mused Austin, but another little girl found and the perpetrator for both caught. And this time the little girl was alive.

35

The lighthouse flashed. Once, twice, three times into the night. The air held a warning of the autumn to come but Nell relished its scent as her freshly washed hair stirred in the sea breeze.

The curry abandoned, Maxine and Nell had spent most of the night at the police station, two nights in a row Maxine had observed wryly, before returning to the Penthouse. But they weren't alone; in the kitchen Austin and Leon unwrapped fish and chips, arguing gently.

"But you're 'spose to eat them out the paper, mate," laughed Leon, as Austin placed four dinner plates on the counter, having wiped them first. Then he placed four knives and forks next to them."And, you're 'spose to eat them with your fingers." Leon shook his head, smiling.

"Humour me, please, Mr Ford."

Nell returned to watching the lighthouse, shivering in the cold air. She could still feel the weight of Emily's body in her arms. Suddenly, a warm hand rested on her shoulder.

"You know, we make quite a team." Maxine's perfume drifted softly in the wake of her soothing voice.

"Yeah?" Nell felt the tears close again, and couldn't trust herself with a sentence.

"You see the living that are in trouble. I see the dead. Along with Austin's door breaking abilities we could make a fortune."

Nell could hear the smile in Maxine's voice.

"Yeah." She tried again.

"Leon, give this woman a hug and then let's eat." But Nell felt the warmth of Maxine's own arms wrap briefly around her shoulders before she stepped away for Leon. Strong arms filled the sudden space left by Maxine. Nell felt the energy drain from her limbs and she folded into Leon's embrace. She listened to the sounds behind her; Maxine was answering a call from Alex and failing to sound casual. Austin was uncorking a bottle of white and Leon was breathing gently in and out.

"You going to be OK?" he asked.

Nodding, she turned to face her friends. One day at a time, and if that was too hard, one hour at a time. But the healing had already begun.

In the car park below, the red glow of a cigarette end flared for a moment. Its owner drew deeply, before ejecting it onto the gravel in disgust. Will started the engine and drove away.

Epilogue

Twenty-three years ago

"Yes, I know you have a daughter. She's upstairs asleep."

"I have a daughter. From before."

"No, get your hand off me. From before? What the hell are you telling me?"

"Look. I didn't know. You have to believe me."

"I don't think I'm ever going to believe a word you say again."

"Look, don't walk away. I'm trying to explain. I didn't know. Her mother saw me at school and I suppose I panicked."

"What, she's at your school. How old is she? No, it's no good shaking your head, Will. I want to know. You owe me that."

"Thirteen. They just transferred her from the grammar school."

"Oh my God."

"Look, you and I, we weren't that serious at the time. It was just one drunken night. I didn't know she was pregnant."

"We were engaged, Will."

"No, it was before that, and it was just one of those things, not serious. Not even a fling. Something that happened before I committed to you."

"Oh, so that's alright then."

"No, of course it's not alright. I just had to tell you."

"Why bother? You didn't care enough to tell me before."

"Because I can't work there anymore. Maybe she senses something, I don't know but Ruby, yes, her name's Ruby."

"Your daughter. Your other daughter?"

"Yes, and she's started hanging around after class. I need to move schools, maybe move town. You always said you wanted to live abroad well maybe we can."

"Why don't you get back with her mother? You never want to be around Nell and I anymore. Oh my God, all those phone calls, the times you said you were with your mum, were you seeing this woman?"

"No, absolutely not. Look. She's married. She always was and he doesn't know, but you can see she's mine, she has my eyes."

"You bastard. Well, Nell and I don't need you. Fuck off to your married mistress and your precious daughter. Ruby; well it won't take long to work out her surname. If you don't go now, I will be telling some home truths myself. Go on, get out of here. I never want to see you again."

"Don't start threatening me. What about you and those pills. What about you and the filth you brought into our family."

"How dare you? It was one drunken night and you'd know all about those."

"Look, it's been a shock. I'll go and stay with Mum for a while and then we can talk. Ruby's father, the one she thinks is her father is not someone you want to play games with. Trust me."

"I'm not the one who's been playing games. How could you do this to me, to us? You have a little girl sleeping upstairs who adores you. I know I get wobbles sometimes but I am getting better, or I was until this happened. Half my problem was you ignoring me, never wanting to do anything with Nell and I. Now I know, don't I? We were second best. Well I suggest you run off to your mum's before I do something I regret. Does Elizabeth know?"

"No. I didn't know until this week. God what a mess."

"Well, it's your mess, not ours so go sort it out."

So, that had gone well. More drama and tears, more accusations and blame. Will pulled over and lay his forehead on the steering wheel. She would be reaching for her pills now, or the bottle. Doubt chased the guilt in his already cluttered head. Maybe he should have kept quiet, tried to keep it under wraps; but Ruby – now he smiled – Ruby was following him around like a puppy at work and people were beginning to notice, get the wrong idea. Actually, the smile faded, it was a little unnerving. He had assumed it was just a crush, but then had found himself looking at her cheeky smile and something in his gut had begun to respond. Now that had been scary; he had been teaching for years and perhaps he had looked appreciatively at some of the older girls but never one this young. Then, after giving her a lift home he had seen her mother in the garden. Shock, fear, anger, from them both, and then a phone call to the school where he had had to listen to her hisses while trying to look unconcerned in the staff room.

"I am not moving Ruby again, so you will have to move."

"Is that really necessary, Mrs Morgan?"

"Have you looked at her? Well look again and do the maths. You cannot teach *our* daughter. If Dieter finds out…"

Will started the car again and headed for Lark House and another confession.

251